THE LOST BONES

BOOKS BY RUHI CHOUDHARY

THE DETECTIVE MACKENZIE PRICE SERIES

Our Daughter's Bones

Their Frozen Graves

Little Boy Lost

The Taken Ones

THE LOST BONES

Ruhi Choudhary

bookouture

Published by Bookouture in 2022

An imprint of Storyfire Ltd.
Carmelite House
50 Victoria Embankment
London EC4Y 0DZ

www.bookouture.com

ISBN: 978-1-80019-890-6
eBook ISBN: 978-1-80019-889-0

To Aarav and Veer

PROLOGUE

The first thing Mackenzie felt was the heavy weight of her eyelids. She struggled to peel them open. Then she felt drops of water fall on her shredded lips.

Drip.

Drip.

Drip.

Her tongue poked out to taste it. A groan escaped her parched throat. Slowly the rest of her sensations returned. The harsh grooves of the rope cutting into her wrists. Her shoulders on the verge of popping out of their sockets. Her bare feet dangling. A sheet of sweat plastering her shirt to her skin. Wisps of hair falling in her eyes. Her labored breaths, which made her chest ache.

She swiveled her stiff neck to take in her surroundings through hooded eyes. It was dark. Pitch black. But it smelled wet and stale. The dripping water echoed. Was she in a basement?

Her foggy mind hunted for answers, but only questions were posed. Where was she? What had happened to her?

Her training kicked in. She wriggled her arms and yanked on the ropes, but they were too tightly tied.

"Damn it. Hello? Is anybody there?" Her voice bounced back to her.

A faint throbbing in the back of her head grew stronger. There was a patch of dried blood there. She could feel how sticky it was. Wondering how the hell she was going to get out of this situation, she felt a strange prickle.

Like she wasn't alone.

She whispered. "Who's there?"

She felt someone's breath at the back of her neck. Goosebumps spread like wildfire on her skin.

"You will bleed, Mackenzie." The voice spoke calmly.

To Mackenzie's horror, she knew exactly who the voice belonged to; she knew the person holding her captive. Everything came back to her, slamming into her with a mighty force. She should have seen this coming. After all, the writing was on the wall.

ONE

APRIL 10, LAKEMORE, WA

"Why the hell are we busting a drunk Darth Vader?" Detective Mackenzie Price muttered, dragging another old man reeking of alcohol and wearing a bedraggled *Star Wars* costume by the collar. "It isn't even Halloween. What's wrong with you?"

"The force doesn't wait for Halloween," the man slurred, and Mackenzie rolled her eyes.

"Haven't done this since I was on patrol." Her partner, Nick Blackwood, walked next to her with his hands in his pockets and wearing a cheeky grin. "Reminds me of the good old days..."

"When your head didn't have so many white hairs?" she quipped.

Even though Nick only had graying hair along his temples, his hand still shot to his head as he checked his reflection in the window.

"Gotcha," Mackenzie sang.

"Marry me, Detective," Darth Vader slurred.

"No chance, Derry."

"Then *you* marry me." He turned to Nick.

Nick snorted. "Flattering, but you aren't my type."

Derry groaned in displeasure when Mackenzie opened the

holding cell and gently pushed him inside. "I was just trying to share the force!"

"You were peeing on the ice statue at the mayor's party," Mackenzie reminded him, and gestured to a deputy to lock the door and keep an eye on him.

"Ready to head back?" Nick fixed his bow tie.

The two of them stood out in the throng of uniformed cops at the Lakemore PD. Nick was dressed in a tuxedo, while Mackenzie wore a floor-length gown that made her feel like an alien inside her own body. She caught her reflection in the window.

It stared back at her. Her blazing red hair was in a high bun with a few stray strands falling to her pointy chin. She had high cheekbones and a sharp nose with a hook. She didn't have a soft face or even a pretty one. There was a sharpness to it. Like someone had angrily etched it on a canvas. A combination of fierceness and steely guardedness that was a part of her personality.

"Ready," she answered.

When Mackenzie arrived back at the party, she took another steadying breath. The mayor's mansion in Lakemore was situated in Forrest Hill, the only plush neighborhood, a beauty spot in the otherwise grim and struggling town. As she observed the trays of champagne, elaborate fountains, and sweeping staircases, she stifled her discomfort.

"Drop that frown, Mack." Sergeant Sully sauntered over to her, the buttons of his crisp shirt threatening to pop off. "It's a party."

"Mad Mack doesn't know how to relax." Nick took a leisurely sip next to her.

Mad Mack. It was the nickname she had earned over the last nine years with the Lakemore PD. She had cemented a reputation for being tough, cagey, and brutally honest. Someone who immersed herself in her cases and often pulled all-nighters slogging at her desk until the morning without getting tired. She worked and acted like a machine. Never a hair out of place. Never a crinkle in her clothes. Never an emotion on her face.

"Don't listen to them." Pam, Sully's wife, waved her hand. "You look great, Mack. Blue is your color. I never thought we'd see you at a party like this."

Mackenzie nodded, taking in the mingling crowd and the floating photographer. Everyone important in Lakemore, and even some VIPs from Seattle. From judges and politicians to businessmen and football players. The ballroom was packed wall to wall with influential people and money. And every person who held the strings to this town had assembled here tonight.

Even Debbie Arnold was here. Lakemore's most notorious and most watched TV reporter who took sadistic pleasure in riling the audience up against the local law enforcement officials, especially Mackenzie. She kept throwing sour glances in Mackenzie's way, and Mackenzie made a point to avoid making eye contact.

It was very unlike Lakemore, a small town tucked next to Olympia and always drenched in rain and gloom. Poverty and a slow pace of life were its defining traits. But so was football. The fame the high school team, Lakemore Sharks, had garnered in local tournaments, and the future NFL players it had birthed, was drawing eyes and investments. And so Lakemore had surrendered its economy and future to the sport.

"I still don't get the purpose of this party," Mackenzie said. "And why are the Lakemore PD invited?"

"Not the Lakemore PD per se," Nick said. "Just the top brass and us. That documentary made for some good publicity for the town."

Six months ago, a documentary had come out featuring

women in law enforcement in Washington. Lakemore had chosen Mackenzie to represent its small town. Much to her dismay, she had garnered attention, with many people recognizing her.

"Still doesn't answer my question," she replied.

"Maybe *he* will." Nick looked past her. She followed his gaze to Mayor Rathbone, a short, skinny man, climbing up the sweeping staircase to face the room. He clinked his glass with a fork. Silence fell.

Rathbone cleared his throat. "Welcome, everyone. There are many reasons for us to gather here tonight. First and foremost, I would like to welcome our chief guest, Rafael Jennings, into the fold." He gestured at someone in the crowd. Mackenzie stood on her toes to peer over the heads in front of her. She could only see the back of a head covered in shiny black hair. "As most of you know, Rafael is the co-owner of our favorite NFL team." There was a big whoop. "He has started a sports entertainment company, which will see our Lakemore Sharks being featured and given much-deserved exposure at a national level." Another round of applause.

"Looks like things are going back to normal," Nick commented dryly. Over a year and a half ago, the Lakemore Sharks had been disgraced and Lakemore had been on the brink of economic and social collapse.

"This isn't normal..." Mackenzie said.

Rathbone fisted the handrail, puffing his chest. "There is another reason for this celebration. The last few months have been tumultuous in Lakemore. We saw loss and despair. We witnessed people lose their livelihood. There was chaos and a lot of uncertainty. As a community, we were on the cusp of losing what's most important—our identity. But we didn't let it break us. We *endured*. Our strength is defined by our ability to bounce back from adversity. And this town has proven its mettle. In the last six months, the crime rates have been record low, the Lakemore Sharks have once again brought the Olympic Championship home, and employment rates are surging. Lakemore has not just survived, it has *thrived.*" He raised his glass in a toast. "To peacetime."

"Salud!"

"What a speech!" Pam cried, finishing her champagne. "Right, honey?"

But the quirky sergeant was too focused on piling his plate with appetizers and hadn't paid attention at all.

"I guess we can finally relax." Nick smiled. "Derry is the worst guy I've busted in over two weeks. It's unheard of, isn't it?"

But Mackenzie couldn't share the sentiment. She gazed at the toothy grins around her; it was almost like Lakemore was in a trance. Palpable optimism had bewitched the town like black magic. She didn't feel like she was a part of it. She felt like a spectator. An outsider with a grim sensation swirling in her gut. Through the window, she saw a flock of birds flapping from left to right across the sky. Her grandmother used to say that was a sign of bad luck.

And she couldn't shake the feeling that this was the calm before the storm.

April 11

The next morning, Mackenzie ran through foggy woods coated in moss. It was a particularly chilly April, but the green was popping out, with thick bushes and shrubbery growing wildly. She threaded her way around the woods back to her street.

It was still early. The sun slowly climbed up, a rosy glow dribbling over the row of houses. The sky was still a chorus of gold and grays. She eyed the weeping willow in her front yard.

It was bending slightly lower than she'd like, but it was resilient. It wasn't the worst way to be.

Panting, she played with her keys as she jogged across to her house. She paused in front of the door and looked at her hands. Trails of blue veins ran down the backs. The street was deadly silent. The only sound was the silver plumes hissing out of her mouth. Even the hum of traffic and the chirping of birds were missing.

It was like she had stepped into a void. A little tear in the fabric of the normal world, where she was alone. The prickle came back to her. The one she hadn't felt in weeks. Like she was being watched.

She spun on her heel on a whim.

Nobody was within sight. So why did she feel like prey?

Shaking away the bad thoughts, she was about to unlock the front door when she realized that the trunk of her car parked in the driveway was slightly open. She frowned. Had she forgotten to shut it properly after taking out her gym bag yesterday?

She pushed it down with force, but something got in the way. She was mildly distracted, not really paying attention, but when she opened it, she went completely still, every muscle frozen and locked.

There was a dead woman lying inside the trunk of her car.

TWO

Mackenzie stumbled back, tripped, and fell on the concrete with a loud thud. The silence was punctured by her labored breathing. The woman's skin was clammy and almost transparent. Her light hair darkened at the tips. Her lips were blue and slightly parted. She lay on a brown blanket soaked in some liquid. But all Mackenzie could focus on were the eyes. Those arctic eyes that looked like glistening marbles. She could almost see her own reflection staring back at her.

The woman looked like a mannequin. A carefully crafted doll. Both beautiful and plastic.

Mackenzie was drawn to her. She stood up again and drifted closer. Recognition had finally dawned on her following the initial shock. Her fingers extended forward, almost trembling. The moment they brushed her cold cheek, a shudder ran through her. She gasped and stepped back, reality setting in.

"Fuck." She looked around the empty street. But now she heard the sounds. Sprinklers turning on. Birds chirping. The world was waking up. Quickly she pushed down the tailgate to hide the body and looked around.

She couldn't see anybody. But was somebody watching her?

Fear filled her, making the hair on her arms stand upright. A cold chill enveloped her that had nothing to do with the weather. She told herself she was out in the open in daylight. She was a trained police officer. But this feeling was something else. Something she couldn't put a finger on.

Dazed, she called a number.

"This better be an emergency. It's not even seven," Nick grumbled on the line.

"I..." Her tongue was heavy, like a chunk of iron. "I... There..."

"Mack?" Concern colored his tone.

She swallowed hard. "There's a body in the trunk of my car."

"*What?*"

"It's Sophie, Nick... Someone left her body for me."

"Stay there," he instructed, and hung up.

This was a crime scene now. Mackenzie scoped around. Someone had broken the lock of the tailgate, but the rest of the car looked untouched. The windows and doors sealed closed. No scratches or smudges. She pressed into the ground and looked under the car, then closely inspected the asphalt and gravel. Nothing was left behind. Whoever had put the body there hadn't dropped anything. Had anyone seen them? Were there any witnesses?

It wasn't long before the faint sound of sirens grew louder and louder. She hugged her chest, standing next to the car, finally registering the foul odor permeating the air nearby. Her neighbor, Mrs. McNeill, an old, stout woman who was sharp as a tack, came out into the yard to water her plants.

"Morning, Mackenzie!" she yelled in her cheerful voice.

Mackenzie's smile was watery. Timidly she raised a hand and gave a small wave. As Mrs. McNeill plodded forward, ready to make small talk, her face became marred with confusion. A string of cars came around the corner. A police squad escorting the coroner's van and the crime-scene unit. Behind them was a black SUV. They clogged the street, stopping in front of Mackenzie's house and drawing attention from the neighbors, who spilled out of their homes to see what the early-morning commotion was about.

Nick parked the car haphazardly and leapt out, still tying his tie. A young officer came to Mackenzie in uniform, clearing his throat. "Ma'am, I have to take your statement."

She saw his name. Jenkins. He was new, as was evident from the way he blinked nervously. Behind him she saw another uniform unroll the crime-scene tape and coordinate with Anthony from the crime lab to decide the perimeter. Becky Sullivan, the medical examiner, along with her team were all wearing protective gear.

"Detective Price?" Jenkins said. She blinked at him, struggling to find the words.

"I'll take it from here." Nick came up. "Go canvass the neighborhood."

Jenkins' shoulders sagged in relief, and he rushed away.

Nick's eyes trailed to the trunk of the car. Sophie's hand was poking out from the little space, hanging lifelessly. Her pale skin a stark contrast against the black of the car.

"What happened?" His eyebrows dipped low.

Mackenzie didn't respond. Her attention was glued to the crowd of people now encircling her car.

Nick gently pulled her away from the scene. "Mack?"

"Yeah." Her mouth was dry. "I... I came back from a run and noticed the tailgate wasn't shut. I tried closing it, but... then I saw..." Her knees gave way and she sank to the ground.

"Water! *Now!*" Nick shouted at one of the uniforms. He sat next to her with his elbows on his knees. "Are you sure that's Sophie? Sophie Fields?"

She nodded. Despite the slight discoloration of the skin, the body was fresh, with no major signs of decomposition. And it was a face Mackenzie knew very well. After all, she had spent last summer looking into her disappearance in an unofficial capacity.

"How long was your run?" Nick asked.

"Forty minutes max."

"Was the tailgate open when you left in the morning?"

"I didn't pay attention," she confessed.

"So the body could have been put there during the night. Did you notice anyone suspicious?"

"No."

"Anyone follow you?"

"No." She bit her tongue. That feeling of being watched returning with full force. She looked around in a frenzy. There were people everywhere. Too many faces. "I don't know..."

"You don't know?" He raised an eyebrow.

"I didn't see anyone."

"What's going on?" he demanded.

Mackenzie couldn't articulate it. There had been moments these past few weeks, even months, when she felt like she was being watched, when that peculiar instinct for self-preservation would start blaring like a siren. But her thoughts were too jumbled. "Nothing."

Nick's stare was hard. They both knew she was holding something back. He was the only one who was able to see through her steely demeanor. But he also knew not to push now. "We should check house cameras. See if your driveway is in view."

Becky ducked under the crime-scene tape and headed toward them, removing her goggles and skullcap. "Is that brown rug yours, Mack? The one on which the victim is lying?"

"No."

"Anthony will be towing the entire car for inspection. So you'll need a ride."

"Can you tell us anything, Becky?" Nick asked.

"Cause of death isn't obvious yet, though I noticed some marks around her neck. No bullet or knife wounds, so we can rule that out."

"She was cold," Mackenzie murmured. "When I touched her face..."

Nick's eyebrows shot up. "You touched her? That's against protocol."

"I know! I don't know what came over me. Just her cheek."

"Yes, she was stored in a freezer. It will make it a bit harder to discern time of death. I'll know more once I've cut her open," Becky said, watching Mackenzie warily.

"Is my house a crime scene too?" Mackenzie asked Nick.

"If you didn't notice anything out of place or a lock broken, then I don't see the need. But I'll have Peterson do a visual inspection with you inside in case you missed something."

They were discussing the details of how to tow the car and move the body when the first splat of rain fell on them, and then another. Suddenly the sky turned a shade darker, and a faint drizzle took over. Mackenzie felt the air thicken with gloom as the technicians rushed to put Sophie in a body bag.

The sound of light rain hitting the roofs was like a sad song. This rain didn't bring out any richness in the hues. It dulled everything, doused all colors in gray and black. Mackenzie felt it trace paths on her skin, almost leaving a cold burn. A harsh reminder that peace was a comforting lie. A sign that the page was turning. Thunder roared, almost shaking the ground, and then Nick said something Mackenzie had been too afraid to think about.

"Why was her body left for *you*?"

THREE

Mackenzie focused on the sound of her fingers tapping the wooden table at the Lakemore PD station. A cloudy morning had blown fully into a storm. It was only the afternoon, but the entire town was shrouded in darkness. She looked out the window and felt her chest tighten. Spring had been kind. Colors had been bright. Skies had been clear. There was a general fragrance of cheer in the air. Now monotony had been painted all over it. The spell was over and Lakemore was beginning to slowly slide back into normalcy.

"You satisfied with your statement?" Nick asked.

She nodded and signed the page. "I'm a person of interest now, aren't I?"

He shuffled his chair closer to hers. They were alone in the conference room, but the walls were made of glass. It was like being in a fishbowl. "Obviously nobody thinks you had anything to do with this."

"Then why is everyone staring at me?" She tilted her chin toward some officers in the lounge throwing her curious glances and gossiping.

Nick stood up, opened the door, and shouted, "Oi! Don't you all have something better to do?"

They scattered like rats fleeing a sinking ship. Mackenzie hid her face in her hands and took calming breaths.

"This is going to be a disaster. Does Austin know yet?"

"He's up in Seattle chasing some leads. He's on his way back now," Nick said. "Sully thought it'd be best to inform him in person."

Detective Austin Kennedy had arrived in Lakemore a year ago from Port Angeles. The tall man with golden curls and glacial blue eyes hadn't had the best start with Mackenzie, treating her like a suspect in a murder investigation. For weeks they had kept each other at arm's length, circling suspiciously, like each was trying to catch the other in a lie. It wasn't until much later that Mackenzie realized they both had secrets they were guarding.

Mackenzie had buried an innocent man when she was twelve years old, after being coerced by her mother, Melody, who had claimed she'd killed him in self-defense. Austin had come to Lakemore to look for his missing fiancée, Sophie Fields, not trusting the Lakemore PD, which had been under investigation for corruption.

The difference was that Mackenzie's secret was only shared with Nick. Austin's was out in the open, especially after Mackenzie had spent last summer helping him in her free time.

But Sophie had left no trace after last being spotted in Lakemore.

Until now.

"Speaking of which..." Nick tensed, looking past Mackenzie.

She followed his gaze. Austin was walking past the conference room to Sully's office. There was a puzzled look on his face, like he had noticed the whispers and stares, like he was wondering why Sully had given him an urgent call. His hands were stuffed in his pockets, his jacket draped over his arm. It was a last glimpse of him before his life would be turned upside down once more. He had no idea that something was going to break inside him forever.

"At least he knows now," Nick said after a minute. "That's got to count for something."

"It's always better to know." Mackenzie swallowed the lump in her throat. In her nine years as a police officer, she had been involved in a few cases where the person she was looking for was lost forever, found only on the Washington State Patrol website.

She looked up at the sound of heavy stomping. Austin barreled into the hallway, his hair disheveled, his face red. Sully was behind him, his expression one of grave concern. Austin swung open the door to the conference room hard enough for it to slam into the window behind.

"What the hell happened?" he demanded, coming so close to Mackenzie that she stood up and stepped back on instinct.

Nick was between them like a wall, raising his hands to shield her. "She knows nothing."

"You know everything we do," Sully said from behind Austin.

Tears shimmered in Austin's eyes. His nostrils flared. His wild eyes never left Mackenzie. "Why you? She's *my* fiancée. Why *you*?"

Mackenzie was never one to cower. She was tall, broad and intimidating. She had stared down dangerous criminals, wilted people larger than her with her piercing gaze. It came naturally to her. But this time she held back. Because underneath Austin's anger and confusion, there was the anguish of losing someone he loved.

"Mack was involved in the investigation," Nick pointed out.

"Her involvement was flimsy at best!" Austin argued. "There was never even an official investigation into Sophie's disappearance. For someone to leave her..." He squeezed his eyes shut and took a shuddering breath. "To leave her for *Mackenzie* to find makes no sense."

"We will obviously discuss this, but right now you need to go to Becky for the identification," Sully said.

The journey to the morgue in Olympia was eerily quiet. Nick offered to drive, since Austin was in no state to get behind the wheel. Mackenzie watched him in the rear-view mirror, fidgeting with his collar. No one spoke a word. Discomfort hung in the air. By the time they rolled into the parking lot, the rain had stopped.

The grim-looking building was tucked away in an industrial complex downtown, with woods in the back. The morgue was situated in the drafty basement. A stark contrast to the rest of the building, which had been otherwise renovated, the basement had dirty-looking gray limestone floors and yellow tiled walls. Bulbs hung loosely from the ceiling, casting shadows everywhere. Austin walked in a trance in front of Nick. Water dripped from the hem of his raincoat, leaving a wet trail behind.

Mackenzie followed, keeping her distance. As they reached the end of the hallway, Becky emerged from the examination room dressed in a lab coat with a solemn expression on her face. "Detective Kennedy, are you ready?"

He nodded silently, and Becky escorted him inside. At the sound of the door shutting, a harsh, cold feeling swirled inside Mackenzie's gut. She knew what was coming.

Seconds later, she heard a soft cry. And then a strangled sound.

She pinched her eyes closed, stifling the tingling in her chest. She had heard that sound so many times. The sound of hope being crushed. The sound of permanence. The sound of something tearing away from the soul.

After a few minutes, Becky came out alone. "He needs a few more moments with the body."

"He's not allowed..." Nick shook his head.

"My assistant is in there," Becky reassured him, and then looked at Mackenzie. "There's something more..."

She led them to her small office stuffed with thick books and framed certificates, where she produced her phone. She hesitated, pursing her lips, then slid it toward them and placed her hands on the table. "This note was found in Sophie's pocket. I haven't told Austin yet."

Mackenzie picked up the phone. Her breath became stuck in her throat.

"Jesus," Nick whispered.

Mackenzie felt Nick and Becky watching her. But her eyes didn't leave the screen. Her veins felt hot and scratchy under her skin. Like they were being chafed. On a small piece of paper were the words:

You're welcome, Mackenzie.

FOUR

By the time Mackenzie returned home, the sky was full of stars, looking like sugar sprinkled over black marble. She climbed out of the cab and paused in the empty driveway. Her car was still at the crime lab. Every inch of it was being scrutinized and inspected to find a hint as to who had put the body of Sophie Fields there. The prickle at the back of her neck had returned. A nagging, stinging feeling like she was being watched. It wasn't just paranoia, some residual trauma from her past.

She entered her house and turned on the lights. It was around a year ago when she had last felt unsafe in her home. When an enemy in the shadows had been leaving her threats before they revealed themselves, almost killing her. Now the feeling was back. She poured herself a glass of wine, the events of the day playing in her head on a loop.

You're welcome, Mackenzie.

What the hell was that supposed to mean? The body had been left in her car. Not only did they know where she lived, they also knew that she had been involved in looking for Sophie. But that had been last summer. Almost a year ago. Had someone been watching her since then?

Her heart rattled in her chest. Quickly she picked up the remote and switched on some random movie at loud volume. It was something she had started doing recently. Living alone in a spacious house had become claustrophobic. Even though she didn't really watch television, having it on made her feel like some activity was happening around her.

Gulping her wine, she opened her laptop and googled herself. She was on the internet now thanks to the documentary. But her address and phone number weren't available anywhere.

Someone had been following her.

But what did they want? Why did they kill Sophie? Where had she been all this time? There were many questions, but they would get some answers tomorrow morning when Becky completed the autopsy.

Mackenzie curled up on the couch and tried paying attention to the movie. There was a scene playing in which a young woman was sleeping and the door leading to a balcony outside her room was open. Curtains were blowing in the wind. A man in a trench coat and fedora climbed up to the balcony and gently padded inside the bedroom. An ominous tune swelled in the background as he got closer. The woman slept oblivious, lost in sweet dreams. By the time he reached out with his gloved hand to stroke her cheek, Mackenzie had begun dozing off.

But as she fell into a slumber, she felt the hand stroking her cheek instead. She felt that smooth texture of leather. That gentle pressure on her skin. And then she was out.

FIVE

APRIL 12

Coffees were poured. Coats were shed. Wet shoes squelched. Mops swept over the puddled water people had unwittingly brought inside the station. Mackenzie was in the restroom, tying her hair in a high ponytail and smoothing her ironed pantsuit. She powdered her eye bags to cover the dark circles from a disturbed sleep, then analyzed her face. All her pores and blemishes were covered by a layer of foundation. She felt safe, hidden behind her armor, not letting anyone know just how much she was affected. Mad Mack had a reputation to uphold.

"You'll be fine," she chanted to herself, and after steadying herself, she was ready to head to the meeting.

Everyone was already in the conference room. Lieutenant Atlee Rivera, who oversaw a few departments in the Lakemore PD, was a tough woman with olive-colored skin and thick dark hair. Her no-nonsense demeanor had gelled with Mackenzie. She stood next to a whiteboard, reading a file intently. Sully was snacking on donuts in a corner. Nick was sipping his coffee, listening to Jenna, a junior detective. Then there was Austin, who still wore the same clothes as yesterday, standing outside the room but peering in.

From afar, it looked like a regular briefing session.

But then Mackenzie noticed the little things. Rivera clenching and unclenching her fists. Sully swallowing without chewing properly. And the corners of Nick's eyes were tight.

"Detective Price," Rivera said in her strong voice, removing her glasses. "You're here. We can get started now."

Mackenzie sat next to Nick, throwing a glance at Austin outside.

"I don't know why he's so mad at me," she whispered. "It's not like I know more than he does."

Rivera cleared her throat and raised an eyebrow at Sully, who returned to the table. "All right. Let's begin. Since Detective Kennedy has a personal connection to the case, he is not to be included," she instructed sternly. "I had a chat with him this morning, but I expect him to be curious. His behavior is understandable, so the onus is on everyone in this room to be professional. Understood?"

A string of nods and grunts of agreement.

"Becky, can you hear us?" Rivera asked.

"Yep." Becky's voice came from the phone.

Rivera pinned pictures of Sophie and of Mackenzie's car to the whiteboard. "Sophie Fields was found in the trunk of Detective Mackenzie Price's car on the morning of April 11. CSU is still looking for any clues in the car, but the victim's body was left on a four-mil flat poly construction sheet, the brown rug, which Detective Price stated in her statement doesn't belong to her. Becky, what were the results of the autopsy? Do we have time of death?"

"The body was definitely frozen, as confirmed by measuring the activity of an enzyme called short-chain 3-hydroxyacyl-CoA dehydrogenase—an enzyme that plays a role in our bodies' thermal regulation. Also, her tissues under the microscope show formation of ice crystals and ruptured cell membranes. Unfortunately, time of death is typically inconclusive if the body has been frozen. It doesn't show any signs of decomposition, which suggests that the victim was frozen immediately after being killed. But based on levels of the enzyme found, I'd say she was frozen for approximately three months."

"But she'd been missing for almost two years," Jenna pointed out. "She was last seen in Lakemore in March 2018."

Mackenzie opened the case file on Sophie Fields that they had received from the Riverview PD. "She was wearing a white blouse and denim jeans. But the body was dressed in a yellow hoodie and black jeans."

"Any signs of her being held captive, Becky?" Nick asked.

"There are ligature marks around her wrists and ankles. I'm screening her blood and liver for drugs and toxins."

"And the cause of death?" Mackenzie asked.

"Strangulation with either a wire or a thin rope, based on the bruising on her neck."

"Signs of assault?" Sully asked.

"Few scrapes and bruises. A broken arm that wasn't healed properly. It's at least a year old. There was no assault antemortem. No signs of sexual assault either."

"Okay, thanks, Becky. Keep us posted on anything new." Rivera disconnected the line and sat back on her chair. "Suffice to say, Sophie was held at some point before being murdered. What's her background?"

"She was a graphic designer for a company in Port Angeles," Mackenzie recited without having to check the file. "Parents died many years ago in a plane crash. No siblings. Coworkers and fiancé said her behavior leading up to her disappearance was normal."

"We need to approach this case like it's brand new," Rivera declared. "Riverview PD was in charge last time, but I want *our* people to re-interrogate everyone and double-check everything." Her eyes drifted to Mackenzie and softened. "About that note found on her..."

Mackenzie pushed back her shoulders and sat straight, refusing to cower. "It's been sent to the crime lab to dust for prints."

An awkward silence brewed in the room.

"There should be a patrol car outside Mack's place at all times," Nick said with purpose.

"What?" She glared at him.

He sighed, frustrated. "Someone broke into your car and left a body."

"It said *You're welcome, Mackenzie*. I highly doubt this person wants to hurt her." Jenna rolled her eyes. She and Mackenzie had always clashed.

"Clearly this person is a psychopath and has access to Mack," Sully said. "I'll arrange for round-the-clock security."

"Why is everyone talking about me as if I'm not here?" Mackenzie grumbled. "I'm not consenting to this."

"Your boss's orders." Sully frowned, his unibrow dipping low like he meant business.

Mackenzie opened her mouth to argue, but Rivera spoke up warily. "Perhaps, Detective Price, you should sit this one out."

"*What?*"

"You are involved in the case."

"I have no personal involvement," Mackenzie argued, not believing what she was hearing. "I don't understand why I need to stay away from it."

"We need more information on why you were targeted," Rivera replied, not budging. "There are plenty other cases for you to work on while we make progress here. I mean, this is Lakemore. You can keep yourself busy."

Mackenzie fisted her hands next to her thighs. "But I can be helpful, and Nick—"

"Detective Blackwood can work this case without you. He can multitask. We all do." The steel in Rivera's voice was unmistakable.

Mackenzie looked around the room helplessly for backup. Jenna was inspecting her nails. Sully had his arms crossed and his eyes shut. She pinned Nick with a hard stare. When he didn't show any reaction, she felt anger bubble inside her.

"Thanks a lot," she muttered, and shot out of her chair, leaving the room in a huff.

She marched past Austin, who had been standing outside watching the proceedings intently. He didn't follow her. She went back to her office and fell onto her chair, her pulse racing. Ned and Dennis, the other detectives in the unit, eyed her curiously, but she ignored them and fiddled with her watch to calm herself.

Minutes later, Nick returned to the office, his tie askew and sleeves rolled to his elbows. "Do you want to go for a walk?"

"Oh, now you want to talk?" she snapped.

He ran a hand through his hair and sighed. "Please?"

Realizing that people around were beginning to take notice of the tension between them, she followed him out to the fire exit. The staircase in the back was rudimentary, with gray steps, off-white walls and high ceilings making sounds echo.

"Where the hell do you get off?" Mackenzie asked sharply. "First getting me a tail and then not saying anything when I'm cast out."

"I'm trying to protect you. Tell me that message didn't scare you. You would have done the same for me."

She hesitated, but clenched her jaw. "I didn't ask for protection. I'm also a trained officer, just like you. I'm not some damsel in distress who—"

He scowled. "Oh, come on, Mack. Last time you kept things to yourself, you almost got killed in your own home."

She felt that pressure on her chest again. The hands around her throat. The blood gushing out of her thigh. She blinked and composed herself. "I'm not keeping anything from you. We all know and saw what happened!"

Nick's coal-black eyes drilled into her brown ones. "You have a habit of being on your own. I get that. I respect your independence. But not when your pursuit of it puts you in harm's way."

"And how am I your business?"

Something clouded his face for a brief moment. Like Mackenzie's question had both surprised and hurt him. But he just scoffed. "There's a concept known as looking out for each other. We can go over it later."

She rolled her eyes. Before she could press further, the door to the stairwell opened and Peterson popped his head in. "Here you are. We got a missing woman."

SIX

Mackenzie watched as the middle-aged man with a receding hairline, saucer-like eyes, and a drum of a belly fidgeted and squirmed in the waiting area. Two young boys ran around in the parking lot. He kept looking over at them, biting his nails.

"Mr. Montenegro?" Mackenzie asked.

He stood up. "Yes. Brett."

"I'm Detective Price, and this is my partner Detective Blackwood. You reported your wife missing?"

"Yes, I gave my statement to one of the cops over there." He looked worried. "Courtney never returned home from work yesterday."

"And when was the last time you talked to her?" Nick asked.

"Yesterday around five. She said she was leaving work and to warm up some dinner." Tears glistened in his eyes. "She isn't picking up her cell. I even showed up to her work. Her car wasn't there and her co-workers said she'd left already. I was here last night too, but they told me to wait until the morning."

"And she hasn't done anything like this before?" Mackenzie asked.

Brett couldn't hide his anger. "Do you know how insulting that is? No. My wife doesn't just disappear."

"I'm sorry, but we have to cover our bases," Nick tried explaining.

"Do you see them?" Brett pleaded, pointing at the boys chasing each other outside. "She would never abandon them." He blinked away his tears. "I had to tell them she's visiting her mother. I don't know what to do..."

Mackenzie hadn't meant to be insensitive, but in their line of work they had seen many adults leaving voluntarily. She had lost count of how many times she'd had to crush hope in the eyes of frantic spouses and parents. She saw the young boys running with their arms outstretched, their light brown hair dancing in the wind, their mouths opening into toothy grins.

"All right, Mr. Montenegro. We'll track her cell phone and dispatch a team to begin canvassing her workplace," she said with resolve.

Brett looked dazed, like he had been expecting more, but then nodded.

"We'll keep you informed," Nick assured him. Brett dragged his feet out of the station and gathered his kids.

"I'll ask Peterson for the first incident report." Mackenzie sighed.

Nick checked his watch. "I have to head to Seattle to meet Anthony. See you later."

Mackenzie bit her tongue, knowing the meeting had to do with Sophie and her car. She felt frustration claw at her, but when Peterson handed her the report, she redirected her focus to Courtney. When she opened the file, breath spiraled out of her lungs.

She knew this woman.

"No guy will ever like you," sneered the tall, slender girl with dark skin and almond-shaped eyes. "You're fat, ugly, and you stink."

Mackenzie's lips quivered. She felt blood gush to her face, reddening under the stares of her classmates.

"Mack n Cheese! Mack n Cheese!" the girl chimed, and soon the rest of the class joined in. But all Mackenzie could see was the girl leading them. Her perfect face and angelic features hiding a bully who spent her days making Mackenzie cry. Courtney Goodman.

The face from Mackenzie's memory grew older, the skin thinning, stretching and sagging, until it morphed into the one in the picture in her hands. Courtney Goodman was now Courtney Montenegro. And she had gone missing yesterday evening.

Mackenzie grazed her fingers over the face she had forgotten over the years. She was twelve years old when she was shipped off to New York to live with her grandmother. It was only nine years ago that she'd returned with unfinished business to Lakemore. Back to her hometown, where years of witnessing Melody getting beaten had culminated in that fateful night when they'd buried a man. She'd always known she would return to Lakemore to right the wrongs of her past, to find closure, to get to the truth of what had really transpired that night, because her mother was not the innocent party she'd been led to believe.

And now a forgotten and inconsequential part of her past was in her hands. Courtney Goodman—the resident mean girl. She read over the report, gaining no new knowledge. She'd already dispatched a team to start looking around the area where Courtney was last seen.

She headed downstairs to the office of their IT guy, Clint—the tallest man in Lakemore PD. She found him sitting behind his spread of monitors, his mop of hair visible.

She knocked on the door. "Got a minute?"

"Barely." He sighed, typing at lightning speed, then rolled away and removed his glasses. "What can I do?"

She showed him the file. "Need to track this phone. Husband said it kept going straight to voicemail."

He skimmed through the details and raised an eyebrow. "Missing since last evening? Adult woman?"

Mackenzie suppressed a sigh. She knew what he was getting at. It was too early to label this a missing person case. "The woman's got two young kids. I knew her."

"You did?"

"I went to school with her."

Clint nodded, understanding, and turned back to the computer. "How's post-documentary life treating you?"

She paused. Clint was never one to make small talk. "You know."

"Sorry?"

"About the body in my car."

He shrugged. "People talk. How've you been doing?"

"Peachy," she muttered. Her mind wandered to what Nick and Anthony were talking about, whether there was some clue in her car.

"GPS is off. It was active last night at close to six in the evening. Triangulation gives the area, which I'm sending to you now."

"This is good. She left work just after five. This will give us something." She opened her email. "Thanks, Clint."

"It's strange, isn't it?" Clint said, tapping a pen against the table and narrowing his eyes at her.

"What is?"

"First the body in your car, and now your friend from school is missing. Two overlapping cases, and the only common element is you." He turned back to his computer, already losing interest in what he'd said.

But as Mackenzie walked away, goosebumps dotted her arms.

SEVEN

Mackenzie was never comforted by sunny days. She lowered the sun visor to shield herself from the blazing light intent on burning her corneas. The Lakemore PD had given her a squad car temporarily to get around. It was too conspicuous and something she wasn't used to anymore. She threaded through the small lanes of the town, avoiding taking any highways or main streets. She liked to drive past little corners, to discover a pond or a small patch of lonely woods. With Lakemore, she felt like she was always scratching the surface, trying to find something redeeming and good underneath the crusty film of destitution and violence.

She brought the car to a halt at a stop sign. On her side there was a park where some kids were playing on the monkey bars. They deserved better. It was only a matter of time before they would see what she saw every day. She had always had faith in Lakemore, staunchly defending it to critics. But it was ironic that during the most peaceful time there, her faith had begun to waver.

She pulled in next to an office building close to the Plaza, where Courtney's phone had last been active. It was a law office. Beeker and Associates. There was a small parking lot with many cars. Courtney drove a red Toyota Prius. It was still here.

She made a quick call to Peterson. She was used to having Justin Armstrong assisting her, the military-like junior detective, but he had recently earned a well-deserved promotion and become partners with Austin.

"Peterson, I found Courtney Montenegro's car. I'm sending you the address; bring a team here to go through it," she said. "Also, did you call her bank and flag her credit and debit cards?"

"Yes, they haven't been used yet."

"Have you heard anything about the other case?" she asked on impulse, and immediately regretted it. She didn't share the same level of comfort with Peterson she had with Justin.

"Uh, no... I haven't."

She hung up, embarrassed. Sophie had planted herself like a seed in her mind. Shrugging it off, she headed inside the swanky law office. The reception had a skylight and a row of fake plants with shiny plastic leaves in the front. The man sitting behind the desk with a headset didn't even blink when she showed her credentials. A law office was probably used to having visits from the police.

"Do you know this woman?" She handed him a picture.

He took his time and then nodded. "Yeah, I think she was here yesterday in a meeting with Mr. Beeker."

"She's missing. I need to talk to him."

He checked something on his tablet. "You can go right ahead."

She followed his directions to a room with the door already open. It was a corner office with wood-paneled walls. A large man with a goatee was seated at the desk with a phone tucked under his ear. When he saw Mackenzie, he frowned. But when she showed her badge, his face fell.

"I'm going to have to call you back." He hung up. "How can I help?"

Mackenzie took a seat. "I'm investigating the disappearance of Courtney Montenegro. She didn't return home last night."

He turned a pen between his fingers, looking contemplative. "I see..."

"She was here last evening. Her car is still downstairs," Mackenzie continued.

That caught him by surprise. "Her car is still here? Interesting."

"You don't seem very surprised that she's missing. What did you talk about?"

Beeker sighed. "Well, I hadn't signed her on as a client, so attorney–client privilege doesn't apply. She only came here for a consultation. I practice family law."

"She wanted to divorce her husband?"

"Yes." He nodded. "She wanted to discuss the details—child support, alimony, the lot."

Mackenzie frowned. "Did she mention why she wanted a divorce? Any accusations of abuse?"

"Nothing like that. She didn't really mention a reason, but I got the feeling she was bored of her life." He pressed his lips in a thin line. "I see this a lot. It's the seven-year itch, you know. She was in a rut, feeling stuck in the domestic trap."

"And what advice did you give her?"

"Told her to wait it out. To go on a vacation. Catch a break."

"Was yesterday the first time you'd met?"

"Yes, though we spoke on the phone around three days ago."

Mackenzie drummed her fingers on the armrest. After asking more routine questions and handing Beeker her card, she left the office. Outside, the light had grown softer, with billowing winds sending twigs dancing in the air. Why was Courtney's car still here? What if her husband had found out she was speaking to a family lawyer?

. . .

The sky was ominous. The moon played hide-and-seek behind wisps of floating cloud. The trees were silhouettes against the silver background, creaking and swaying in the gusting wind. But when Mackenzie looked around her, she noted the stark contrast. The carnival was in full swing on the grassy field. The lights were fuzzy. Old music blared from cheap speakers, intercoms announced the names of the winners of the ring toss, darts popped balloons, laughter rang in the air, and so did the screams of those riding the roller coasters.

Mackenzie was standing next to the Ferris wheel, watching a woman waiting in line with a kid, the two of them sharing a funnel cake. Her chest squeezed. She had never had maternal instincts; according to her ex-husband, it was why he'd cheated. Because he was hurt.

"Want some?" A cotton candy was thrust in her face, and Luna smiled at her brightly, blonde hair poking out of her pigtails, chubby face flushed pink, and sticky blue fluff stuck to her chin.

"Thanks, kid." Mackenzie took it and bit some off.

"This is the last one, Luna." Nick came from behind her. "I'm already on thin ice with your mom."

"Why are you on thin ice with Shelly?" Mackenzie asked as they began walking around with Luna between them.

"She thinks carnivals are grungy," Luna said.

"This is a bad idea. It's a school night, and there's no way you're sleeping if you get a sugar high." Nick reached for the candy, but she stomped her feet and whined.

"Remember when I got kidnapped, Daddy? Just think about that before you take things away from me. Oh! Spin the wheel!" She grinned and raced ahead.

Mackenzie was left speechless. Nick froze, his mouth hanging open.

"And you were worried she'd need therapy?" Mackenzie attempted to crack a joke.

He groaned. "I can't believe she's just nine. Anyway, any news on Courtney? I saw the case on the bulletin."

"Not yet. Her phone is off, and credit and debit cards haven't been used." She relayed her conversation with Beeker.

"The husband looked pretty convincing." Nick kept a close watch on Luna. "But we've seen some good liars before, haven't we?"

"That's what I'm thinking." She paused. "So, how did the meeting with Anthony go?"

Nick gave her a knowing look. She held his gaze. Eventually he gave up. "They didn't find anything in your car. No prints. No DNA. Nothing."

"I'll get it back then?"

He nodded. "Tomorrow."

"Anything else?"

He smiled. "Wouldn't you like to know?"

"Nick!" she moaned. "Please."

"They found muskrat fur on the rug. Don't know what it means. Have sent it for further analysis."

"Muskrat fur?"

"Yep. And Riverview sent over the tape they'd gotten from the bus station in Lakemore." He shoved his hands in his pockets. "We didn't catch anything on it."

"Can I take a look?"

Nick looked conflicted. "There's nothing there. I need to talk to Austin again tomorrow. Not looking forward to that."

Mackenzie felt deflated when he changed the topic. She picked at the torn hem of her jacket and watched Luna hop from one game to another. When she wanted to shoot balloons with a toy gun but was too short, she called for Nick to help her. Mackenzie watched them, that easy bond, that love and security that seeped down to the molecules, that tranquil happiness without any fluff or pretense. It was something she had lacked most of her life.

A strange thought crossed her mind. She imagined herself with Nick and Luna, and not just as a friend. As something more.

And for a moment, she felt like she was soaring.

She shook her head, snapping out of it.

Silly thoughts.

It was nothing. Just some meaningless fantasy as a result of being lonely. She wandered towards a patch of land outside the carnival, a few feet away from the dark woods. A gust of cold wind made her shiver, and she tightened her jacket around her. The sounds of the carnival were fainter here, and instead she could hear the rustling of the leaves ahead of her. She stared at the trees, lost in thoughts.

Then she noticed something.

A movement. Not from the wind.

She paused and blinked. It was dark. She squinted. A shadow was moving near the edge of the woods. Her feet carried her forward, her hand moving to the Glock tucked in the waistband of her jeans. She crept closer and closer, convinced that something—or someone—was there.

Just as she reached the edge, a woman stumbled forward and fell at her feet.

EIGHT

"Help me," the woman breathed. Her eyes rolled back in their sockets and she sank further into the ground.

"Oh my God!" Mackenzie bent down and grabbed her frail arm. "Can you hear me?"

The woman was limp, her head lolling like it was detached from her shoulders. Her thin lips were parted as she tried sucking in air, and she made a sound in the back of her throat.

"Shit." Mackenzie called 911 and relayed her badge number, requesting an ambulance. While she talked to the operator, the woman's eyes gained focus for a few seconds. Then they closed and she passed out.

Mackenzie checked her pulse. It was there, but faint. The woman was bony and small, wearing a tattered white dress. Dirt was tangled in her short black hair cut in a pixie cut. Her skin was covered in bruises and scrapes, some fresh and some old.

"Mack!" Nick called out. As he approached, he saw the woman in her arms and instructed Luna to stay at a distance. "What the hell is going on?"

"I don't know. She just came out of the woods and passed out."

He narrowed his eyes. "Was she running from someone?"

"I couldn't tell." She followed his gaze to the dark woods. The moonlight was blotted out by thick clouds. The woods looked like a bottomless pit. Like the world was cut off at the threshold and there was oblivion beyond it.

Within minutes, an ambulance pulled up and paramedics surrounded them. Mackenzie let them take the woman away and put her on a gurney. It terrified her how tiny she looked, a strange cross between a wraith and a child.

Mackenzie paced outside the hospital room. She could hear the faint murmur of activity behind the door—a monitor beeping, nurses talking, instruments rattling. Her mind raced, thinking about the moment she'd seen the woman stumble out of the woods. Before she'd passed out, she'd given Mackenzie a strange look, a look she couldn't identify but that stuck with her.

The door whipped open and a doctor with salt-and-pepper hair came out with a somber expression.

"Detective Price?" He closed the door behind him.

"Yes, I rode the ambulance with her," she said. "Is she going to be okay?"

He pressed his lips in a thin line. "I'm not sure. We definitely need to call in a psych consultant."

"What about her physical condition? Was she attacked?"

He dropped his voice and ushered her around the corner, away from some people lingering in the hallway. "The patient isn't cooperative at all. She hasn't spoken a word to anyone. As such, we can't administer a rape kit, even though I believe we should, considering her clothes were torn and there are bruises all over her."

"Did she tell you her name?"

He shook his head. "Like I said, not a word. We keep asking her questions, but it's like she's not there."

Mackenzie's throat tightened, thinking about how scared the woman must be. "Do you mind if I give it a shot?"

"Please. Be my guest."

Not that it mattered, but on instinct, Mackenzie fixed her hair and jacket. Her face wasn't gentle. She was always stiff. Everything about her screamed "unapproachable". But still, she tried to wear a softer expression when she entered the room.

The woman was on the bed with an IV stuck into her arm. A nurse practitioner stood next to her making a note of her vitals on the chart. She left the room when Mackenzie asked for privacy.

Mackenzie sat down by the bed. "My name is Mackenzie Price," she said carefully. "How are you feeling?"

The woman didn't reply. She just stared curiously.

"What's your name?"

No response.

She was dressed in a hospital gown now; her clothes had been bagged for the police. There was no longer any dirt tangled in her hair. Her skin looked cleaner, without any smudges. Some bruises were covered with white tape, while the milder ones had had glistening ointment applied to them.

"There's no need to be scared anymore. You're safe now."

Still nothing. She was like a wounded animal, watching Mackenzie with a curious reverence. There was no point in pushing anymore. Perhaps she needed rest. "Why don't you get some sleep? I'll see you again tomorrow."

The woman lay back on the bed and brought the blanket up to her chin. Like a child being tucked in.

As Mackenzie turned to leave, something caught her eye. The woman's bare foot was peeking out of the blanket. There was a tattoo around her ankle.

It was a barcode.

Mackenzie's chest filled with ice as she looked at the

woman, who mirrored her haunted expression. What on earth had happened to her?

NINE

APRIL 13

"The Lakemore PD is asking for assistance to locate a missing woman." Debbie spoke to the camera in her shiny dyed hair and newly crafted nose. "Courtney Montenegro was last seen two nights ago around the Plaza. She has not been heard from since." Courtney's picture flashed on the screen next to her. "Neighbors have expressed concern for the thirty-three-year-old accountant, who is a mother to two young boys. This also marks the first disappearance in Lakemore in over three months." Debbie's switch in tone from concern to alarming wasn't subtle. "If anyone has any information that can help, please contact this hotline."

Mackenzie closed the tab and shook her head.

"Debbie's planting the seeds for discord," Detective Troy Clayton chirped from her side. With his mop of red hair, he almost looked like a stick of carrot intent on using light-hearted humor as a veil.

"You should have seen her at that gala," she muttered. "Sniffing for a scandal. Even tried to pick a fight with me."

"I actually wouldn't know," Troy teased, swaying on his chair. "I wasn't invited. Not Lakemore royalty, you see."

"Yeah, Mack," Finn, Troy's partner, added from the other side. "Heard there was caviar. I've never had it my entire life."

"We had to settle for KFC. Again." Troy sighed dramatically.

Mackenzie gave them a bright, sarcastic smile while putting on her headphones. They got the message and stopped bothering her. The office complex had sent her the surveillance from the parking lot where Courtney was last seen. On one side the lot was bordered by thick foliage. She played the timestamp for when Courtney left the office according to Beeker. At eleven minutes past six, the woman appeared in the frame, digging into her tote bag, presumably for her keys. There was no one else in the vicinity. Mackenzie slowed down the speed. The image was slightly degraded, so she couldn't make out Courtney's expression. Had she left the lawyer's office contemplative or frustrated? Did she decide to just take a bus and drive away from the life that had begun to suffocate her?

Courtney put her key in the lock, and was just about to open the door when her head snapped toward the woods. Mackenzie leaned forward, the glow of the screen dancing across her face. Courtney started to walk towards the woods, her steps hesitant. Had she heard something? As far as Mackenzie was aware, it was just a patch of trees. On the other side was a pond and empty land. Courtney looked over her shoulder and then dipped into the woods, disappearing behind thick trees. The leaves rustled and then all movement collapsed into stillness. Hours passed as cars entered and left the lot, but her car remained stationary, with no sign of her.

"Detective Price?" Peterson cleared his throat.

"Oh, hey." Mackenzie paused the video and turned to him. "Did you find anything around the car?"

"No, ma'am." He looked uncomfortable. "I wanted to submit a request to the MUPU at Washington State Patrol to get a start on the missing persons posters for the victim, but it was denied."

"Denied?" She straightened. "By whom?"

"Sergeant Sully wouldn't sign off."

Mackenzie locked her jaw. "I'll talk to him. You did nothing wrong."

Peterson sighed, relieved. He was preparing for his detective exam, ready to take Justin's place on the team. Mackenzie gave him a pat on the back and headed to Sully's office.

She opened the door after knocking and found the beefy sergeant absorbed in his latest hobby. This time he was whittling a deformed-looking bird with a sharp knife. Over the years, Mackenzie had become used to his idiosyncrasies. It had taken her some time to realize that it was only when Sully was distracted with something else that he was able to think clearly.

"Why can't I get missing persons posters for my victim?" She crossed her arms.

Sully set the knife and the wooden bird on the table. "Because there is no definitive proof that there is foul play. And it hasn't even been seventy-two hours. She might get in touch."

"She's already been featured on the news!"

"Yeah, Debbie has sources everywhere." Sully rolled his eyes. "She's been bored these past few months and is creating a mountain out of a molehill."

"None of Courtney's cards have been used and her phone has been switched off," Mackenzie argued, placing a hand on her waist. "What do you make of that?"

"Her friends told uniform she was sick of her life, and she was consulting a lawyer to leave the husband."

"She left her two boys behind."

He gave her a flat look. "You're still surprised that not all mothers are good, after everything we've seen in our line of work?"

Mackenzie paused. She didn't have to look far to see how mothers could disappoint their children, how weak mothers bred strong kids.

"Mack, there's a budget crunch." Sully removed his glasses. "There was a surplus last quarter due to crime being at an all-time low. Which means that this time our budget was lower."

"Someone's life could be in danger, and we have to worry about budget?"

"Yes, we have to worry about the budget." He picked up the knife again, carving the bird almost angrily and further ruining the shape of its back. "This isn't a cop show. We have constraints."

"I have it on video that she walked into the wooded area by the parking lot. She was about to get into the car and then suddenly went off into the trees."

"Maybe she decided to take off on a whim." He shrugged, then looked at Mackenzie almost with pity. "Either find evidence of foul play or wait for seventy-two hours. Then I'll approve it."

Mackenzie nodded stiffly and left the office, feeling Sully's piercing gaze drilling into her back. On her way to her desk, she noticed some lingering glances and hushed whispers. The news of a body being found in her car seemed to still be the latest fodder.

She slumped at the desk and looked at Courtney's picture.

"Mack n Cheese, why are you even here? It's not like anyone wants to play you," she sneered, looking around the playground. "Are you getting mad at me?" Mackenzie fought back her tears. "I heard redheads have a nasty temper."

Mackenzie could still hear her piercing giggles. It was so strange. Over the years, she had forgotten about the girl who had bullied her. It all seemed so unimportant after everything that had happened in her life. Somewhere along the way, those tiny scrapes left by Courtney had healed, overshadowed by the deep cuts left by her family. Her life had taken a dark turn, and she wondered what Courtney was like now.

She heard voices, and spotted Nick in discussion with Austin outside. She could only see Nick's back, but she didn't need to see his face to read him. From his stiff shoulders, she could tell he was mildly pissed off. Austin's jaw ticked. He shook his head and marched away, scowling.

Mackenzie sighed. She had been exiled from a case she was invested in, and now her hands were tied in the case she had.

Courtney had a good life. Mackenzie's gaze traveled over the wall covered in framed photographs. From Courtney and Brett's joint graduation and proposal to their wedding and the pregnancy shoot. Courtney had gone to Vegas with some friends to celebrate her bachelorette. She'd gone to Amsterdam for her honeymoon. Last year, the family did a Disney cruise. Mackenzie wasn't naïve enough to believe that pictures reflected the truth. She knew that Courtney had felt suffocated. But still it made her heart twist that at least the woman had had that polish concealing her loneliness, a facade she could perhaps distract herself with, a lie the world could believe.

"The boys have been asking why their mom hasn't even called them yet," Brett said from behind her.

She met his red-rimmed eyes. "What have you told them?"

"That she's camping and doesn't get cell reception."

"How was your relationship with your wife? Any fights lately?"

He looked baffled. "Everyone fights. It's not unusual."

"Did you know she had gone to a lawyer the day she disappeared? To discuss leaving you?" Mackenzie studied his reaction. Brett had no criminal record. He was ex-military and now a simple family man. Even if he had snapped and hurt his wife, the likelihood of him lying like a seasoned criminal was very low.

His forehead crumpled. "What?"

"She never mentioned that she found her life a bit... boring?"

His eyes widened and his mouth fell open. He turned around, his hands on his head. "I... No. That can't be true."

"She never mentioned it?"

"No!" He licked his lips, frantically looking around the house like something here could fix his problem. "She wouldn't leave the kids. Not like this. Please believe me."

"Where were you that evening? When she disappeared?"

"Are you serious?"

"Yes," she said evenly. "I have to cover all my bases. Part of the job."

"I was at home," he snapped. "Waiting for my wife. Making dinner for the kids."

"Is there anyone other than your kids who can verify your whereabouts?"

He shook his head in disbelief. "Wow. No. There isn't."

She nodded slowly, making a note to pull up Brett's cell phone records to check if GPS could give a hint about where he'd been. Her own phone rang and she excused herself.

"Hello?"

"Detective Price?" Peterson said. "Do you have a minute?"

"Yes, what is it?"

"Tech just got back about the parking lot. They found something strange around the trees where Courtney was last seen. They found muskrat fur."

"Muskrat?" she repeated, drowning out Peterson's voice. Instead, it was Nick's voice that she heard, against the backdrop of screams and pinging of games at the carnival.

They found muskrat fur on the rug. Don't know what it means. Have sent it for further analysis.

Muskrat fur was found both on Sophie and around where Courtney was last seen. Could this be a coincidence? The tingle that rippled down Mackenzie's spine suggested otherwise.

TEN

Mackenzie carried a bag of fries and Diet Coke into the hospital. She checked her watch. There was only an hour until visiting hours were over. She slowed down, seeing Austin speaking to the doctor. When the doctor spotted her, he smiled. "Ah, Detective Price."

Austin looked over his shoulder, casting a curt glance at her.

"How's our patient doing?" Mackenzie asked.

Before the doctor could reply, his pager beeped and he excused himself, leaving Austin and Mackenzie facing each other in the middle of the hallway. The air between them was thick, cinched with palpable tension. The friendship they had built in the last months was now fragile. Mackenzie felt like she had gone back in time to when Austin had first arrived, when they'd treated each other like enemies, not realizing they were both hurting from a loss.

"So, you're on this case?" She tried breaching the cold silence. He nodded. "Has she spoken to you?"

He shook his head. "No one's reported her missing. She's consented to have her DNA tested and prints taken for us to check if she's on the system. She's Jane Doe for now."

"That's a start." Mackenzie tapped her foot. She wasn't the best at making small talk. It was always Nick compensating for her lack of social skills. "Where's Nick? I've been trying to get in touch with him."

"Port Angeles," Austin replied with an edge to his voice. "Chasing up some old leads."

Mackenzie opened her mouth to say something, even though she didn't know what exactly, but he was already walking away. The back of his coat swished in the air.

She tapped lightly on the door and pushed it open, peeking her head in. Jane Doe was lying on the bed, watching television dully. When she saw Mackenzie, she jerked upright, her chest heaving in deep breaths and eyes blinking.

"Am I disturbing you?" Mackenzie asked.

Jane Doe shook her head meekly.

Mackenzie smiled brightly and sat on the chair next to her, offering her fries and Coke. "The nurse told me you can have some. I can imagine hospital food is bland."

At first, the woman stared at the fries like she was waiting for them to attack her. Mackenzie picked up a fry and popped it in her mouth. Only then did Jane Doe follow suit. Initially she chewed hesitantly, but within a few minutes, she was eating like a starved animal. Mackenzie noticed that she looked better than yesterday, with some color returning to her pale skin. But she was still skinny like a whippet, with sinewy arms.

"What do I call you?" Mackenzie asked. The woman stopped chewing and stared at her. "Right now, we just call you Jane Doe. You must have a name." She shrugged and went back to drinking Coke.

"Jane Doe it is," Mackenzie muttered. "The detective on your case is very good. Austin Kennedy. I work with him." Jane Doe frowned, so she continued. "You can trust him."

Jane Doe looked away, watching the television.

"The nurse said you're getting discharged tonight. Do you know where you'll go?"

No response.

Mackenzie fiddled with her fingers, teeming with helplessness. She kept checking her phone, waiting for Nick to get back to her. She wanted to discuss the muskrat hair with him. She hadn't seen any forensic reports on the Sophie Fields case. But Nick was probably driving back from Port Angeles right now. She hoped that this coincidence would be reason enough to treat Courtney's disappearance more seriously.

In a few minutes, light rain began tapping against the window. Jane Doe muted the television and turned her head to look out into the bottomless darkness beyond the water-stained glass. The room filled with the soothing sound of pitter-patter. It massaged Mackenzie's brain. In the window, she saw Jane Doe's reflection. She had a soft smile on her face. Like she was listening to the rain after a very long time.

Later that night, Mackenzie was in her kitchen baking cookies, following one of her grandmother's recipes. She turned up the classical music and basked in the mouth-watering smell that filled the kitchen. A cool wind wafted inside from the open window, making the curtains billow. Outside, the squad car was visible. Whenever Mackenzie saw it, she was filled with annoyance and embarrassment. The poor guys on patrol were new and on the most unnecessary task. No one was going to hurt her. After everything that had transpired last year, she had become more cautious. But why was she unable to shake off that feeling? That one second of dread before a vase crashes to the floor. Except that one second was stretched into a perpetual state of being. She was always on edge, waiting for something to go very wrong.

When her phone rang, she jumped. "Shit. Hello?"

"Sorry, I just saw your missed calls," Nick said, sounding beat. "Traffic was a bitch."

"Remember you found muskrat fur on the rug?"

He sighed. "Mack, I'm tired. It was a long drive."

"No, I have something."

"I'm listening."

"Tech picked up muskrat fur from the place where Courtney was last seen. Few feet away from her car, just at the edge of a wooded area."

A beat of silence. "Muskrat fur? Are you sure?"

"I can share the crime lab's report with you. Think that's a coincidence?"

"I don't know..." he confessed, sounding far off. "How many people wear muskrat fur? Probably a lot, right?"

"In April? It's hardly the weather for it."

"We should compare the samples. If we can tell that they came from the same source..."

"That would mean that Sophie and Courtney's cases are related," Mackenzie said, unsure if she wanted there to be a connection. "Did you come across Courtney's name in your case? I don't remember seeing it when I helped Austin last summer."

"Not yet. I don't think their schools or jobs overlapped. Maybe the fur is just a coincidence. Why would they be connected?"

Mackenzie didn't have an answer. She hadn't delved too deeply into Courtney's life yet. "Sophie is Caucasian. Courtney is African American. Sophie is a Scorpio. Courtney is a Gemini." She recalled how she hated all Geminis when she was in fourth grade because of her.

"Sophie is two years younger than Courtney," Nick said.

Her phone began buzzing. "Nick, I'll call you later." She answered. "Hello."

"Detective Price," Peterson said on the line. "Sorry to

bother you at this time, but you need to come to the farmland on the border with Riverview."

"What is it?" She turned off the oven and picked up her leather jacket.

"We found Courtney."

ELEVEN

If Lakemore was a town with a good heart but rotten luck, Riverview was a place where everything was rotten. It was filled with delinquents and dilapidated structures. A prime reminder to people of how low a town could sink if it wasn't taken care of. Why a sense of community was important to keep the spirit alive.

The night was dark and wet. Thick woods surrounded the area, so dark and deep they blotted out any light. There was a red structure on the land behind a black fence with barbed wire atop. Once upon a time, it was a crime scene.

Mackenzie's car floundered over the dirt road before joining the squad cars parked nearby. The area was illuminated by flashing emergency lights and headlights. She got out of the car, her feet making squelching sounds on the wet earth.

Peterson came up, holding a flashlight. "There are no street-lights in this area. Must be a pain to find the way."

"I've been here before." She followed the path. "They should put up some lights, though."

"Land belonged to Riverview before Lakemore bought it," Peterson replied. "They didn't bother and then we didn't."

They navigated their way past uniformed cops trying to establish a perimeter. Peterson led her towards a bunch of teens in hoodies standing next to the barn, behind the crime-scene tape. "Kids from the community college come here for underage drinking. They were in for a surprise tonight."

The teens wilted, fidgeting and looking nervous.

"How old are they?" Mackenzie asked.

"Some nineteen and others twenty," one of the uniforms said, pointing at a pile of bottles on the ground. "We confiscated all this booze."

She pressed her lips in a thin line, glaring at them. They looked apologetic. "Did you see anyone else here? Someone running away?"

One of the boys shook his head. "We got here and turned on the lights and..."

"Did you touch anything?"

"No!" They all shook their heads.

Mackenzie nodded. "All right. Take their statements and let them go. Consider this a warning."

"But, ma'am..." the cop who had confiscated the bottles protested.

"Are you saying you never had alcohol before the age of twenty-one?" she challenged. When he fell silent, she turned away.

"I thought Mad Mack was a stickler for the rules." Peterson smiled nervously, like he was gauging if it was acceptable to joke with her.

"Rules that make sense. Don't tell me an eighteen-year-old can be trusted to get behind a wheel or decide who should run the country but not handle booze. It's all political lobbying."

Peterson pushed open the door to the barn. It made a creaking sound. Water dripped from the frame. The floor was sodden, the smell of hay and manure masked by the sweet tinge of wet mud. Mackenzie could only make out shadows, the darkness folding around equipment and doors.

When Peterson pointed the flashlight straight ahead, she gasped.

Courtney's body was slumped in a chair in the middle of the barn. She was still dressed in the clothes she was last seen in. Her head lolled back. Her hands were tied to the arms of the chair. Her ankles bound. Her lips parted. As Mackenzie crept closer, she saw Courtney's eyes. Blank and cloudy, they stared up at the dingy roof.

"Is Becky on the way?" she asked.

"Yes, she'll reach us in about ten minutes."

Mackenzie felt empty. She was transported back in time again, remembering Courtney as a young girl, mean and nasty, but alive. Never in a million years would she have imagined that this was how their story would end; that one day she would discover Courtney's body tied up in an abandoned barn in the middle of nowhere.

"Oh my God," Peterson whispered.

"What?"

The light wasn't pointing at Courtney anymore. It was directed to the wall behind the body. Mackenzie followed the beam and her blood ran cold. On the wall were words written in blood:

I will always protect you, Mackenzie.

TWELVE

"I will always protect you, Mackenzie." Melody wiped Mackenzie's tears. "Don't cry."

"He scares me," Mackenzie whimpered, unable to stop her body from shaking. "What if he hits me like he hits you?"

Anger flashed in Melody's eyes. She grabbed her daughter by the shoulders in an unforgiving grip. "Never."

Mackenzie shuddered out of the memory and wrapped her hands around the steaming cup of hot cocoa. She was in the conference room at the station. Again. A body had been found with a message for her. Again. The news was already spreading like wildfire. Again.

Nick dropped another blanket around her shoulders. "Are you feeling better?"

She still hadn't entirely snapped out of her daze. She was aware of her surroundings and registering conversations, but it was all diluted and hazy. Like it was a dream on the brink of being forgotten.

"How is she?" Rivera entered the room, dark hair tied in a messy ponytail and shirt inside out. She had clearly just rolled out of bed.

"She's processing. She'll be fine," Nick answered, drumming his fingers.

"What happened?"

"I got a call from Becky that Mack was staring at that message on the wall and not responding. She figured she'd gone into some kind of shock. I got there as soon as I could and brought her here."

"I don't blame her," Rivera said, pity coloring her tone. "Second body in less than a week with a message for her. What the hell is going on?"

"I don't know." Nick leaned forward, placing his elbows on his knees and interlacing his fingers. "Mackenzie?" he whispered. He rarely called her by her full name. She turned to look at him, realizing he was closer than she had expected. Lines of concern creased his forehead. His black eyes were like pools of ink. She knew what he saw in *her* eyes.

Fear.

But what she saw in his scared her more.

She pulled back, feeling too exposed and raw. "The homicides are linked," she said in a determined tone. "I want to be on the case." Rivera looked reluctant. She opened her mouth to argue, but Mackenzie stood up and spoke over her. "I won't sit this one out, Lieutenant. If you keep me off the case, I'll defy orders."

"Then I'll suspend you, Detective," Rivera countered.

"Do it. I'll work on it without my badge. But I'm not staying away."

The corner of Rivera's mouth pulled up in a smirk. "All right. You care too much and maybe that's a good thing. But I have a condition."

"What?"

She crossed her arms. "I'm hiring a profiler to act as a consultant." Mackenzie and Nick exchanged a pensive look. "Our budget doesn't allow us to keep one in-house, but given the nature of this case and how well we've done these last few months, my request for one wasn't denied."

"Is this necessary?" Mackenzie asked. "We've worked well without one for years. And Nick has been good at profiling."

"I need at least one cool head on this," Rivera explained.

"Nick *is* a cool head."

She chuckled, on her way out. "Not this time. Update each other on the cases. We'll have a briefing tomorrow with the profiler."

"What time is it?" Mackenzie asked when Rivera had gone.

Nick checked his watch. "One thirty."

She dropped her head back and groaned. "I lost all track of time. And I don't think I'm sleeping anytime soon."

He shifted uncomfortably. "Maybe we should talk about this."

Her head snapped in his direction. "This?"

"This." He made a general hand gesture.

"What's this?" Her heart picked up speed.

He huffed, mildly annoyed. "The murders and the messages for you."

"Oh. Yes." She blinked, relieved.

"What did you think I meant?"

"Nothing." She rubbed her eyes and began pacing the room. "It's just some psychopath. There isn't any depth to this, or hidden meaning."

Nick watched her, incredulous. "Are you joking? This isn't one of our run-of-the-mill lunatics. There must be a reason why it's happening."

"I don't know who it could be. First Sophie, and now Courtney..."

"And who next?" He stood up, raising his hands. "And why them?"

"I think you should discuss this with the profiler."

Mackenzie dodged his piercing gaze. "You know this psychobabble isn't my domain."

"Since when was trying to figure out a killer's motivation *psychobabble*."

"Since it involves me!" she cried. Tears of exhaustion swam in her eyes. "Can we please just focus on the facts and evidence?"

Nick stared at her for a few seconds before nodding. "Sophie's autopsy showed she was severely malnourished, though the tox screen couldn't pick up any drugs in her system."

"Which makes sense, since there was evidence that she was held captive."

"Upon further analysis, Becky mentioned that there were hesitation marks around her neck."

"Hesitation marks?" Mackenzie queried. "From when she was strangled?"

"Yes, the markings on the skin and bruises on the hyoid bone indicate that the killer hesitated while strangling her."

Her brain worked at full speed. "So it could be a novice killer. Maybe a first-timer?"

"Or someone who knew her well," Nick added darkly. "She was held captive for over a year, and there is no sign of sexual assault. It's very strange. But consistent with the logic of her killer being someone who maybe even cared about her."

Mackenzie connected the dots. "Is that what you and Austin were arguing about yesterday?"

He nodded. "I had to interview him again, and I... well, I asked some tough questions and he got pissed."

"Nick, Austin didn't do this. Why would he go to such lengths to search for her?"

"I know. I was just covering my bases. Following protocol and treating this like a brand-new case, just like Rivera ordered. And you know how it goes." He sat back down, crossing his legs. "The partner is always the first suspect."

"Did Becky say anything about Courtney? I tuned everything out."

"The body was stiff; rigor mortis had set in."

Mackenzie did a quick calculation. "She was killed on the night she disappeared."

"Forty-eight hours ago," he confirmed. "There was bruising around her neck. Seems like the cause of death."

"Just like Sophie. We have muskrat hair, senseless messages for me, and the same cause of death." Her head was already spinning. "I think it's safe to say that Courtney's husband had nothing to do with this."

Nick nodded. "Crime lab is doing a sweep of that barn. Hopefully they'll pick up on something new."

She bit her nails. Anxiety bubbled inside her. "Okay, we should exchange case files. I'll read up on it tonight."

"You need to get some sleep. Not that I care, but you should look in the mirror."

He was attempting to tease her, but it fell flat. Still, she turned to look at her reflection in the window, then staggered back, startled. Her red hair had sprung into curls. Her face looked washed out. Her eyes were baggy. Her steely, standoffish armor designed to hide deep-rooted vulnerability had melted away. Instead of rushing to the restroom to fix herself, though, she continued staring out the window. All she could think about was: who had been watching her? What did they see in her?

THIRTEEN

APRIL 14

"Come on, Mack. Just one more mouthful." The face of a gentle man hovered over hers. It was a face that could be trusted. Mackenzie made a fussy sound. "Even I don't like porridge, but we have to eat it. Do you want Dada to eat it too?"

"Yes."

He took a spoonful and made satisfied sounds. But he couldn't hide his frown.

Mackenzie giggled. "Robbie lies!"

"Robbie loves you."

Someone tapped Mackenzie on the shoulder. She stirred awake, the dream dissipating behind her eyes. She blinked groggily to find a young boy staring at her. He had dark curly hair and the longest eyelashes.

She frowned. "Who are you?"

"Robbie!" A man came running into the office. "Where have you been?"

Mackenzie straightened. She had dozed off at her desk, having barely slept overnight. "Robbie?"

The man was tall and lanky, with sandy hair, a square chin

and beady eyes. "Yes, this is my son, Robbie. Sorry he bothered you. Robbie, apologize."

"I'm sorry," Robbie said shyly.

"Oh, don't worry about it." Mackenzie smiled at him. "I had to wake up anyway. Can I help you two with anything?" Visitors weren't usually allowed in the office.

"Dr. Turner!" Rivera came in and removed her glasses, offering her hand. "Pleasure to meet you."

He shook her hand. "Sorry, I've got my son. The sitter cancelled."

"Don't worry about it. He can hang out around the lounge. A lot of vending machines there. Have you met Detective Mackenzie Price yet?"

Turner smiled. "Yes, yes, we just did. I'm Andrew. Robbie, will you be all right waiting in the lounge for me?"

Robbie nodded.

"It's a building full of cops. Safest place to be," Rivera said good-naturedly. "Let's head to the conference room."

Mackenzie pulled out a bag of Skittles from a drawer and offered it to the boy. "If your dad doesn't mind."

"Thank you." Robbie almost blushed before being escorted away by a uniformed cop.

In the conference room, everyone got settled in. Rivera introduced Andrew to Sully and Nick. Peterson organized his notes, swallowing hard, like he wanted to make a good impression at the meeting. Mackenzie sat next to him and gave him a reassuring smile.

"Dr. Andrew Turner is one of the best profilers in the Pacific Northwest," Rivera declared. "He's been wanting to consult with the Lakemore PD for months, but it wasn't on the cards until now."

Mackenzie and Nick looked at each other skeptically. No one ever came to Lakemore without an agenda.

Andrew seemingly sensed the surprise and interjected,

"I've been following a lot of your cases and how their outcomes are so closely linked to your town's culture. The cross-section between crime and society is an interesting topic, and Lakemore is a prime example, making it a fascinating study."

"Glad we can accommodate your academic pursuits," Mackenzie mumbled under her breath, and Nick almost choked on his coffee. Fortunately, no one else had heard her.

"Dr. Turner, you're aware of the case details?" Sully asked. "One of our own detectives is being targeted."

Andrew looked at Mackenzie curiously. "Yes, indeed."

"Do you think it could be someone I was responsible for imprisoning or something?" Mackenzie asked. "This is personal."

"I don't believe so." He shook his head. "Whoever this is doesn't hold a grudge against you or even despise you in any way." He opened his copy of the case files and pushed forward pictures of the two messages—the one on the wall and the other in Sophie's pocket. "*You're welcome, Mackenzie. I will always protect you, Mackenzie.* This is someone with an obsession with you."

Sully groaned. "Rotten luck, Mack."

"It's not luck." Andrew's eyes twinkled. "It's the documentary. Detective Price is not only famous in Lakemore, but also a familiar face around all of Washington. People often become obsessed with celebrities, and even go on to display violent tendencies like breaking into their homes."

"What does *I will always protect you, Mackenzie* mean?" Peterson asked. "The victim, Courtney Montenegro, was a former classmate of Detective Price."

Mackenzie stiffened. She hadn't told anyone that Courtney had bullied her. But Andrew picked up on her reaction, and a knowing smile curled his lips. "I think Detective Price can shed more light on her relationship with the victim. My guess is that it wasn't a good one."

All heads turned to Mackenzie expectantly.

She gritted her teeth. "She used to bully me."

"Why didn't you say anything?" Nick asked.

"Because it was in the fourth grade!" She rolled her eyes. "It's ancient history. I forgot she even existed."

Rivera pressed her lips into a thin line. "The killer did their research into you."

"This is absurd. It's not like Courtney was still a factor in my life."

"This person is killing people, Mack." Sully grabbed a cookie with his fat fist and munched on it, his stress-eating habit kicking in. "I don't think we should expect them to be reasonable."

"But why kill Sophie?" Nick wondered aloud. "Mack's never even met her."

Before anyone could venture a guess, the phone rang. Rivera put it on speaker. "Becky, you finished with the post?"

"Yes." Becky's voice filtered into the room. "Much like with Sophie Fields, there was no evidence of sexual assault. There was minor bruising on her arms and mastoid."

"Suggesting she struggled?" Sully asked.

"Yes. Based on the fracture pattern on her mastoid bone, I'd say the blow was strong enough to knock her out."

"Did you confirm the cause of death to be strangulation?" Mackenzie asked.

"Actually, no," Becky replied. "She was choked after she was already dead."

Andrew's eyebrows dipped. He opened the case file and began flipping through it with urgency. Mackenzie watched him, wondering what thought had popped into his mind.

"What was the cause of death then?" Rivera frowned.

"There was damage on the external auditory meatus."

"English, please," Sully said.

"Opening of the skull where auditory nerves feed into the

brain. The earhole," Becky explained, discomfort coloring her tone. "There were scrapings within the cranium and marks inside the parietal and occipital bones. My conclusion is that someone jabbed her in the brain."

Peterson's eyebrows shot up. "Through her ear?"

"That's correct. And then later they choked her. Most likely to confirm she was dead and not just brain-damaged."

Heavy silence descended on the room while everyone processed the details. Andrew's mind was visibly racing as he studied a piece of paper.

"Is there anything else, Becky? Any information on the weapon?" Mackenzie asked eventually.

"I've sent some particulates to the crime lab for analysis. You'll know in a day or two."

"Okay, thanks." Rivera disconnected the call and addressed the team. "So the cause of death isn't the same. But we still have the muskrat fur and the messages for Mackenzie. That's enough to combine the cases."

Andrew looked up at Mackenzie like she was a puzzle he was close to solving. "The first message was *You're welcome, Mackenzie.* And here it says that there were hesitation marks when Sophie was murdered."

"That's right," Nick said, sitting back. "What do you think?"

"I think you're looking at two killers," Andrew said darkly.

"Two killers?" Rivera narrowed her eyes. "There are two killers leaving these messages and the fur?"

"No, no, no." He shook his head, standing up. "I don't think the person who left Sophie's body for Mackenzie is the one who killed her... unless..."

"Unless what?" Mackenzie leaned forward.

He scratched his head. "I don't mean to probe. But how close did you and Detective Kennedy get this past summer?"

Mackenzie's face felt hot. Nick stifled a laugh behind his mug. "Not *close*. We were just friends."

"It's fair to assume that this killer has been watching you for a while. That's how they must have figured out about your involvement in the investigation into Sophie's disappearance. If they were under the assumption that you and Detective Kennedy were romantically involved, they could have perceived Sophie as a threat to that relationship."

"So they hunted her down, murdered her and left her for Mackenzie to find?" Nick said incredulously. "How the hell did this killer find Sophie when we couldn't?"

"That's your domain." Andrew shoved his hands in his pockets. Tilting his head, he gazed at Mackenzie. "And I can tell you one more thing. Courtney Montenegro won't be the last victim."

FOURTEEN

"I finally get why you used to smoke," Mackenzie confessed, poring over Sophie's phone records.

Nick offered her a cigarette. She took it from him and tossed it in the garbage. She had spent an entire year getting him to quit. He had mostly behaved, but had a habit of playing with his lighter and case, especially when he was deep in thought.

"There's nothing here," he hissed, shutting the file he was reading. They were looking into each other's victims, hoping to find something new the other had inadvertently missed. "Which makes sense, because it seems our killer isn't anyone with a personal connection to either victim."

"And none of the witnesses reported anyone strange lurking around." Mackenzie rubbed her eyes, to ease the budding ache.

"Our only hope is forensics."

Mackenzie swiveled on her chair to face him. "Were you able to figure out why Sophie had come to Lakemore? I never found out."

He shook his head. "I went through all the statements again, including her texts, but she never mentioned Lakemore to anyone."

Mackenzie pulled out a copy of a ticket. "But she bought a bus ticket to Lakemore a week before she arrived. She never told *anyone* about it. Why would she hide something like that? Planning a surprise?"

"She had no connection to Lakemore—" Nick broke off when Jenna interrupted them.

"Nick, I found Ethel Gedrick." She handed him a piece of paper. "She's in Seattle. Spent the last few years in Ohio, but moved back two years ago."

"Who is Ethel Gedrick?" Mackenzie asked.

Jenna turned on her heel and clacked away without acknowledging her.

"I guess I shouldn't have spoken at all." Mackenzie mumbled, exasperated.

Nick made a sour face. "Yeah, ignore her. Her attitude is getting worse. Ethel was an old family friend of Sophie's. From the notes I got from Riverview PD, she called several times showing interest in the case, but nothing came of it."

"Didn't she just contact Austin?"

He shrugged. "Apparently not. Austin said he'd never even heard her name before. But she's the only person associated with this case I haven't spoken to yet." He stood up, collecting his keys and wallet. "Come with?"

"You can't keep me away now."

The drive to Seattle was painful. Cars and trucks clogged the freeway. Even though they mostly moved at snail's speed, Mackenzie felt bile swimming in the base of her throat. As she popped a couple of Gravol tablets that Nick kept in his glovebox for her, she looked out the window at the car next to them. A wrinkled old man with a hunched back had one hand on the wheel and the other holding his wife's hand. He was bony and withering away, but still more alive than Mackenzie in many ways.

"Did I tell you I saw Sterling the other day?" Nick said out of nowhere.

"He's an ADA. We see him around a lot."

"No. At Frankie's. Saturday night." He hesitated, gripping the wheel a little tighter. "It looked like he was on a date."

A giggle bubbled out of Mackenzie. Her shoulders shook as she laughed until she almost had tears in her eyes.

"Are you having a stroke? What the hell was that?"

She wiped a tear, reining in her laughter. "No, no. At least he's going on dates when he's not married to me anymore. He's learned his lesson."

Nick frowned. A flash of fury crossed his face. "He hasn't. He'll do this again. People don't really change."

Mackenzie imagined Sterling on a date with another woman. Holding her hand, telling her she was beautiful, everything he had done with Mackenzie. She waited for her chest to feel heavy. But she felt nothing.

She asked suddenly, "Weren't you supposed to be with Luna on Saturday night?"

"Yeah, but Shelly wanted to take her to visit her grandmother and they ended up staying the night there."

Her chest felt prickly. Like it was filled with needles. "So... you went to Frankie's?"

"Yeah. With my cousin. For a beer."

"Oh!" She sighed, the prickly feeling evaporating and leaving confusion behind it.

"Here we are. Finally," he said abruptly.

There was a row of houses in front of them—white and blue—occupying a small space on the wetland. They looked old, something from the sixties. An old man wheeled his cart on the sidewalk, his gait frail and his cart broken. He whistled a forgotten tune. It was as though time was frozen in this part of town—or at least moving as slowly as the man.

They marched toward a house with a broken flowerpot lying on the porch.

"Our last lead with Sophie," Nick admitted, checking his reflection in a window.

"Let's hope we catch a break." Mackenzie knocked on the outer door, which had frosted glass.

There was a squeak and a click. The wooden door behind opened, the hinges protesting. A short, pudgy woman glared at them from behind the frosted glass.

"We're looking for Ethel Gedrick." Mackenzie flashed her badge.

The woman opened the outer door—a new installation in the otherwise ancient and disintegrating house. "I'm Ethel. What—" Her eyes widened at the broken flowerpot on the porch. She looked over her shoulder and barked, "Tom! Control your stupid cat! If you don't train her, I'll put her down myself!"

Tom shouted back something incoherent. Ethel rolled her eyes and focused back on Mackenzie and Nick. "Yes?"

"We're following up on the disappearance of Sophie Fields," Nick said.

Ethel's face didn't change, but her grip on the door tightened till her knuckles were white. "Did you find her?"

"Yes," he answered apologetically.

Her face fell. She took out tobacco and popped it in her mouth. "Guess I shouldn't be surprised. What are the chances of a young woman being alive after all this time?"

"You said you were a family friend," Mackenzie said, watching Ethel closely. "But we found no trace of you in Sophie's life. She never mentioned you to her fiancé."

"She had a fiancé?" Ethel asked, and gestured to them to move back. Closing the door behind her, she limped toward a brittle-looking swing and sat on it. "It's my hip. Standing for too long is painful. I knew Sophie and her family when they lived in Colorado."

"When was this?"

"Oh, Sophie was around twelve years old when they moved. We lost touch."

"So you never spoke with her or had any contact with her after that?" Nick asked.

"No. When I heard from mutual friends that she was missing, I called the police a bunch of times, but they had no answers for me."

Mackenzie and Nick looked at each other, disappointed. They had been hoping that Ethel would perhaps know something new, but it seemed like another dead end.

"You don't know yet who killed her, do you?" Ethel spat out the tobacco next to her feet and drew a pack of cigarettes from her pocket. "What a fucking shame. That entire family got destroyed." She growled when she couldn't find a lighter. Nick held his out. "Thanks. Poor child. What a fate. First her sister, then her parents and now—"

"Her sister?" Mackenzie quizzed. "Sophie didn't have a sister."

Ethel took a drag, her eyes sharpening. "Oh, she did. A twin. Aria. She went missing when she was only eleven. That's why the family moved away."

"What happened?" Nick asked.

"She didn't come home from school one day. There was a huge search. She was never found. A year later the family left Colorado to escape the painful memories."

The wheels in Mackenzie's brain spun. Could Sophie's murder have anything to do with her missing sister? But something else niggled at her. Why wouldn't Sophie confide in her fiancé about her sister? Or was Austin hiding something?

FIFTEEN

"The disappearance of Courtney Montenegro has come to a heartbreaking end," Debbie said to the camera with a rehearsed concern etched on her face. "The Lakemore PD confirmed her demise. Although the details are being kept under wraps, we have been told that Courtney was found murdered in an abandoned stable near the border with Riverview. Our sources have confirmed that this homicide has a personal connection with the Lakemore PD, even though the nature of that connection currently remains unknown. Meanwhile, in good news, the Lakemore Sharks have started shooting an ad for the sports entertainment company chaired by Rafael Jennings..."

Mackenzie walked past the lounge. "Didn't I see this segment a few hours ago?"

"Jesus, are all the other reporters dead?" Nick shook his head. "They've been replaying her segment on a loop."

"If she finds out that the connection is me, she'll crucify me." Mackenzie shuddered, remembering the sour looks Debbie was throwing her way at the Mayor's party.

They saw Andrew standing by the espresso machine, trying to work the buttons. The machine kept making a grating sound.

"There's a trick to this," Nick said, and banged his fist on top of it. A stream of hot coffee gushed into Andrew's cup.

"Thanks." He smiled and nodded at Mackenzie.

"Where are you staying?" Nick asked.

"I got a cabin here."

"Oh?" Mackenzie arched an eyebrow. "In Lakemore? That's weird."

"It's so cheap here. Like I said before, I've been hoping to work with your department," Andrew said with a giddiness in his voice. "I bought the cabin a few months ago. My way of manifesting that, I suppose."

Lakemore's failures and instability had attracted voyeurs from all over the place. Mackenzie didn't know whether to be upset by the spectacle the town was becoming or flattered by the curiosity. She had always been wary of attention; the intentions behind it were generally dubious.

"How's your son?" she asked.

"Adjusting well. He still goes to school in Olympia, so there hasn't been a significant change for him. Thank you for asking. I'm supposed to head to the Miller Lodge motel in about an hour. Do you know how far that is?"

"Miller Lodge?" Nick asked. "For what?"

"Sergeant Sully told me about a female victim you discovered a few days ago?" Andrew's voice was slightly high-pitched and uneven, like his vocal cords were getting scrubbed against sandpaper when he talked. "I was told she's unresponsive."

"Yeah, I found her at the carnival," Mackenzie said. "I visited her yesterday at the hospital. She hasn't said a word to me."

"It's a coping mechanism following serious trauma. I'll get a better understanding when I meet her."

Jane Doe was not in the system. Her prints and DNA were not on any database. Her dental scans revealed nothing of her identity. Even her age was unknown. Based on her appearance, she was perhaps in her mid-twenties.

Austin came around the corner, thumbing his phone furiously. Mackenzie's back snapped straight and she looked at Nick. He nodded in understanding.

"Austin!" he called out. "We need to talk."

Austin eyed the three of them like he was being cornered. "What is it? Did you find anything?" he asked with a clenched jaw and fists in his pockets.

"Have you heard of a woman named Ethel Gedrick?" Nick asked.

"No." His eyebrows stitched together. "Who is she?"

"She was an old family friend of Sophie's," Mackenzie said. "Didn't Sophie ever mention her?"

"No. Why?"

Mackenzie sighed, glancing at Nick, who nodded. "Did Sophie ever tell you about her twin sister?"

"*What?*" Austin's face twisted in disbelief.

"She had a twin called Aria, who disappeared when they were only eleven years old," Nick said. "A year later, the family moved from Colorado to Washington."

But Austin wasn't listening. He was stumped, fidgeting and blinking vehemently, like he was still stuck at that first revelation. "You must be mistaken."

"Well, we've contacted the authorities in Colorado and requested student information from the school they attended," Nick said. "Are you sure she never mentioned this?"

"No! I knew she lived in Colorado, but she didn't give me any particular reason for why they moved." Austin dragged his hands down his face. Mackenzie noticed the subtle changes in him since Sophie's body had been discovered. The perpetual lines on his forehead. The scruff of hair on his usually clean-shaven jaw. The sunken cheeks.

"If I may," Andrew interjected politely. "Did you ever feel

that Sophie was hiding something from you? Acting cagey? Dismissive?"

Austin was about to deny it when something flashed in his eyes. "She rarely talked about her childhood. But I always thought it was because it was painful for her to remember her parents."

When the three of them continued staring at him distrustfully, he cried with eyes ablaze, "What are you getting at?"

"It's strange that your fiancée wouldn't tell you about her missing twin." Nick hitched a shoulder.

Austin's nostrils flared. "So what? That means I killed her?"

"No," Mackenzie insisted. "We're not implying that."

"Then what *are* you implying?" he snapped. "My fiancée disappeared, and then she was killed and left in *your* car, and I'm the one who is being treated like a suspect."

She was taken aback. Despite her tall, broad frame, rivaling Austin's, she almost cowered seeing the fire in his eyes. "You think I have something to do with this?"

"I think this is all happening because of you." He lowered his voice, but his words were razor-sharp and cutting. "Everyone knows about the message left with the other victim too. Maybe if it weren't for you, Sophie would still be alive."

"Don't." Nick glared, his eyes turning black.

But Mackenzie was left splintered. Austin had voiced the thought she had been pushing to the back of her mind. He had spoken the words that perhaps everyone had been thinking.

"Enough!" Sully roared from behind them, cracking the bubble the four of them were in.

It was then that Mackenzie noticed several people watching.

"Kennedy, you're supposed to meet with the DA," Sully said sternly.

Austin's gaze never wavered from Mackenzie. Grinding his jaw, he stomped away like a storm unleashed.

"Don't listen to him," Nick said with a deep scowl. But Mackenzie was still shaking like a leaf on the inside.

This is all happening because of you.

"You two need to head to the news studio right now," Sully said with a twitch in his eye.

"What happened?" Mackenzie asked. Sully had mastered the art of a certain detachment in this job. He was diligent and thorough, but he was also aloof. But now he looked almost afraid.

"Apparently Debbie Arnold is missing."

SIXTEEN

Debbie Arnold had started her career as an air hostess, but had caught the eye of a media mogul, who offered her a job as a weather person. She'd packed her bags and moved to Los Angeles, only to find out that the man expected her to sleep with him. After trying her luck in LA and failing, she moved to the rainy town of Lakemore, one of the few places in Washington she could afford on her dwindling bank balance. A stint on the *Lakemore Latest* yielded a permanent job. But Debbie was hungry. Not satisfied with her segment on celebrity news, she waited and bided her time. And when, over a year ago, the first domino fell in Lakemore, she picked up the ball and ran with it. While other reports displayed sensitivity and professionalism, Debbie understood that news wasn't just about spreading facts; it was showmanship and theater. It was a seduction. People didn't want to interpret information and reach their own conclusions; they wanted to be told what to believe. Then they wanted those beliefs validated and engaged and dramatized.

That was why Debbie called herself a storyteller.

"Did you read her book?" Mackenzie asked, closing the Kindle app on her phone.

Nick scoffed. "No thanks. Have you seen the cover?"

"Yeah. It's a close-up of her face. You can see every pore."

"Sometimes it's okay to judge a book by its cover."

The studio was lit up like a light bulb against the black backdrop of the sky. Inside there was a hum of activity—mostly people scattered in groups and whispering frantically to each other. There was camera equipment and spools of wire everywhere, bright lights pointing at the stage, and screens with reruns from various channels.

A stocky man with thinning ginger hair, wearing a headset and carrying a clipboard, came up to them.

"Lakemore PD? I'm Dave. I called."

Nick showed his badge. "We were told—"

"She's not here!"

Mackenzie suppressed a groan. "Did you try calling her?" It was Debbie. Everyone knew she was acting too big for her boots.

"Yes. She isn't answering. Something is wrong." Dave's eyes widened. "She was supposed to start recording a special an hour ago. That's why we've been airing her old footage. It was an interview with someone important from London. She wasn't going to miss that."

An intern interrupted them, whispering something in Dave's ear.

"Think she's just throwing her weight around?" Nick muttered.

"Her office was locked from the inside. Please come take a look." Dave led them to some rooms in the back of the studio. "She usually retires here for hours. Has a bed in here as well. We just got a few guys to break the door down..."

He paused in front of the open door. Mackenzie and Nick went in and froze. The large suite had red walls and wooden furniture. There was a bed in a corner, but mostly it was couches and tables with vanity mirrors and a slew of makeup products.

Everything was a shambles. Two lamps were on the floor with their bulbs smashed. A table had been turned over. The couches were out of alignment. Makeup products were scattered on the floor. The futon on the bed had been ripped. And the window was open, curtains fluttering in the chilly wind that permeated the room.

"What the hell." Dave cursed and began shouting at some intern about security protocols.

"Call it in," Mackenzie said, treading carefully through the room, finding a phone on the floor. "This is a crime scene."

"No one heard anything?" Nick asked Dave, who was standing by the door white as a ghost. "There was clearly a struggle here."

"It's always loud in the studio. And Debbie had a habit of blasting music..." Dave ran a hand through his hair. "I need water."

"We need security tapes from all the CCTV cameras around here, and no one leaves until we take their statement," Mackenzie instructed, inching closer to the open window and peering out. It overlooked one of the many lakes in Lakemore. The water looked like ink, perfectly still on this windless night. The moon was full, a sparkling silver disc reflected on still waters. Like a painting.

"Second disappearance in less than a week after months of peace," Nick said in a quiet voice dripping with panic. "Think this is a coincidence?"

"Debbie is a public figure. She rubbed a lot of people up the wrong way." It felt like a lie. But maybe she was just being paranoid. Especially after Austin's words.

"Yeah, but the timing is suspicious as hell," he continued, while Mackenzie struggled to contain her anxiety. "And she hates you."

"She hates a lot of people."

He raised an eyebrow. "I'll ask tech to look for muskrat hair first thing."

Mackenzie tried swallowing the lump in her throat, hoping that this disappearance had nothing to do with her. "If it's related... Courtney was killed immediately after she was taken."

"Debbie might have no time."

SEVENTEEN

APRIL 15

Mackenzie's feet slapped against the concrete. As the sun floated up the horizon, drenching the sky in a rosy glow, it ignited all the colors around her. The rich browns of pine trunks. The silver-cream lake. Green wands of grass. A cocktail of scents assaulted her nostrils. The air had lost its bite. She threaded through the woods this time, taking a different path from her usual route. The ground was swathes of waving green. Her bare arms brushed against the vibrant tips of leaves and flowers. The dappling sunlight made the morning mist blanketing the grass look like crystalline flakes. It was all picturesque and idyllic. But as she kept pushing forward, the light began changing. The ground became uneven and the trees crowded together. She had to squeeze her way through. The trickling sunlight was blotted out by thick leaves and branches.

And then there was a patch of darkness. Even the sun couldn't reach here. The shadowy trees looked menacing, as though they didn't like her being here.

She took out her earbuds and listened for sounds. No leaves rustled. No birds cawed. Her breathing was the only sound in this part of the woods where she felt like a trespasser.

When her phone rang, she jumped out of her skin. "Hello?"

"Mack?"

"Yeah, I'm here."

"You're breaking up," Nick said. "Where are you?"

Good question. "Just out for a run. Bad reception. But I can hear you fine. What's up?"

"I'm patching Anthony through. He got something for us."

Anthony worked at the crime lab in Seattle, an old, lanky man with clumps of white hair around his head, and large eyes. "We picked up muskrat fur from Debbie's bed," he said. Mackenzie's heart sank. "We compared it to the samples obtained from Sophie Fields and Courtney Montenegro. They come from the same source."

"How can you tell that?" Nick asked.

"They're colored by the same dye, which was patented by a men's track company. In fact, it's a specific jacket. I'm sending you the information."

"This is great." Mackenzie nodded. "Maybe we can track down the buyer."

"Did Mack say something?" Anthony asked. "I can't hear her."

"Yeah, she probably ran into the middle of nowhere," Nick replied. "But this is good news, Anthony. Maybe we can track down the buyer."

"That's your department," Anthony said, ending the call.

Mackenzie tried retracing her steps, away from this strange pocket in the woods she had wandered into. Her heart careened from beat to beat. In this silence, there was only one thought blaring loudly in her head. Debbie Arnold had been snatched by the same person who'd killed Courtney and Sophie. One more person had been targeted because of her.

Her phone buzzed with a text message from Nick: *Don't get eaten by coyotes.*

She knew it was his attempt to get her to smile, realizing

that Anthony's conclusions would have sent her down a rabbit hole. But he was probably too late. She was teetering on the edge, barely hanging on by a thread.

The sound of Sully filing his nails grated on Mackenzie's ears. She saw the shavings fall onto his desk and resisted the urge to clean them up.

"So, third victim. Same evidence left behind," he commented dryly.

"Turner pointed out that it's possible Sophie was killed by someone else." Nick rubbed the back of his neck. "I don't buy it, though."

Sully's eyes zeroed in on Mackenzie, who stood like a statue with her back pressed to the door.

"You can talk to Turner if you want. If you need help."

"Help?" she scoffed.

"Yes. Help. This case is personal. If it isn't affecting you, then I'm even more concerned."

"Noted." A layer of cool sweat covered her back. There was surprise on Sully's face when she didn't argue.

"Following protocol for this one?" he asked.

"Posters will be up soon. Debbie's information has been entered into NCIC." Nick was referring to the National Crime Information Center. "Riverview and Olympia PD have been forwarded the information, so they'll be on the lookout."

"Have the transportation department pull up any traffic cameras around the TV station."

Mackenzie made a note of it.

There was a knock on the door. Peterson peeked his head in. "Sorry, but Debbie's girlfriend, Noor, is here."

Mackenzie and Nick followed him out of Sully's office.

"This is the jacket we believe our killer was wearing when they took the victims." Mackenzie handed Peterson a hard copy of the information Anthony had forwarded to them. "Try to get a list of the buyers. It's a long shot, but we need to cover all bases."

Peterson nodded. "You know the largest jacket measures over forty-two feet from collar to hem."

Nick gave him a quizzical look.

"It's his thing," Mackenzie explained. "Good to know, Peterson. Get going now."

"What's his thing? Jackets or random facts?"

"Random facts," she said. "He could become a millionaire if he did trivia."

The light banter between them died the second they saw Debbie's girlfriend sitting in the lounge. She was a tiny woman with dark skin and stringy light brown hair. Mackenzie was taken aback at how different she was from Debbie. While Debbie wore bright colors and high-end jewelry, her girlfriend dressed like a college student.

"Do you know where she is?" Noor's lower lip quivered.

"Not yet," Nick said.

Tears streamed down her face. She covered her mouth, squeezing her eyes shut.

"Did you or Debbie notice anything strange? Someone watching you?" Nick asked.

She shook her head. "No."

"Did she mention anything out of the ordinary?" Mackenzie asked.

Noor's blazing eyes turned to her. "*You.*"

"Sorry?"

"Why are you working this case?" Noor bit out. "Debbie exposed your true colors to this town. How you're just an attention-seeking cop playing the woman card to get ahead in life."

Mackenzie's mouth opened and closed repeatedly, unable to form a coherent sentence.

"Ms. Khan." Nick tried to placate her, but Mackenzie could

hear the edge in his voice. "We're just doing our job. And I can vouch for Detective Price. We're professionals."

"Why would she want to find Debbie?" Noor crossed her arms. "I bet she hates her. I bet she's glad that Debbie is missing. I don't trust her."

Mackenzie clamped her jaw tight and spoke in a measured voice, "I'm extremely sorry for the emotional distress you're experiencing right now. I sympathize. But firstly, I'm standing right here, so please don't refer to me in the third person. And secondly, you'll find that I have one of the best records in this department for closing cases."

Noor licked her lips and nodded curtly. After answering more routine questions, she left, sniffling and sobbing.

"That was intense," Nick said. "You okay?"

Mackenzie nodded, stifling a growing uneasiness. Fortunately, at that moment their phones rang with another notification. It was the analysis of the particulates found on Courtney's body.

"Microscopic traces of calcium carbonate." Nick frowned. "What's calcium carbonate?"

"Chalk," Mackenzie replied. "Why was there chalk on her?"

"There wasn't any in that barn," he confirmed after checking. "There was also some glitter in her hair." He pulled up a picture showing red and blue glittering specks tangled in Courtney's hair and sticking to her scalp.

"That's odd." Mackenzie checked the statements from Courtney's co-workers. "There was no party at her workplace. Why else would she have glitter in her hair?"

"There's something else too." Nick showed her the page. "Strands of yarn made of cotton and polyester."

She took the picture from him. It showed a zoomed-in snapshot of Courtney's scalp with the strands circled with red. "Yarn?"

"Yarn. Glitter. Chalk," he listed, squeezing a stress ball. "They weren't found at the barn, or at her work or the lawyer's office."

"Could she have been in contact with them before that? At home?"

He shook his head. "According to the husband, she took a shower and left for work early that day, and he was in charge of breakfast and packing the kids' lunch. It has to come from wherever she was killed."

"But there was nothing like this in the barn. So she was killed elsewhere? Why was she moved then?"

"Obviously the killer wanted her to be found with that message to you." Nick tossed the stress ball between his hands. "Maybe they took her to their house and killed her there. The scene of the murder might implicate them."

"Why not just kill her at the barn then?" Mackenzie echoed her doubts.

"They hadn't decided where to leave her for us?" Nick clicked his tongue. "Never mind. If they can look into your life enough to find out about your grade-school bully, they should have planned enough ahead."

"My grade school bully..." She repeated his words, her random thoughts assembling into a coherent picture. "Blue and red are the colors of my school. Lakemore Elementary. The chalk, the glitter... I think I know where Courtney was killed."

EIGHTEEN

The wheels of the car chomped on the gravel lane before finally coming to a halt. Lakemore Elementary sat like a rectangular box on a green field surrounded by ancient and twisted oaks. It shared grounds with Lakemore Secondary, another matchbox-looking building right across from it. The sky was darkening early, beckoning a storm. Gray clouds whirled above with flashes of thunder, lightning illuminating the clouds from behind.

Mackenzie took a shaky breath, climbing out of the car and narrowing her eyes against the gusting the wind.

She had come here before several times. But today felt different. Today felt like she was stepping into her past. A nine-year-old Mackenzie dressed in her blue raincoat, her red hair in high pigtails. Tears streaking her cheeks. She blasted out through the doors and ran in the wind, her backpack bouncing. She was faint, translucent. Like a ghost. Mackenzie felt a jolt of pain. The pain left behind by cruel words on the malleable mind of a child. The pain of a thousand paper cuts.

"Mack?" Nick's voice boomed over the wind.

"Sorry." She shook her head. "Did you call ahead?"

He nodded, walking on. "The principal. She said we can talk to the caretaker. He'll give us access to look around."

"The caretaker?" She remembered the caretaker and wondered if it was the same man after all these years.

It was.

At the door stood a scrawny old man with no hair, dressed in baggy clothes and waving his hat at them.

"It's Boothby," Mackenzie whispered.

"Here you go, little one." Boothby handed Mackenzie a lollipop. "Why aren't you playing with your friends?"

"I don't have any friends," she said in a small voice, watching the others play tag.

"Special people belong to a special tribe. That's hard to find."

"Mr. Boothby?" Nick said as they entered the building and shut the door behind them. "I'm Detective Blackwood, and this is my partner—"

"Little one." Boothby smiled. "I remember you."

His skin was dotted and hanging loose. His eyes looked ghostly. Like very slowly life was leaving his body.

Mackenzie couldn't help herself. She hugged him, feeling how frail he'd become. Despite his age, he gave her a good squeeze back. When she pulled away, Nick was watching them, puzzled.

"Mr. Boothby, I can't believe you're still here."

"This school is my life. I was so proud to see you in that documentary." He chuckled and looked at Nick. "I always knew she would do something great."

"You know why we're here," Mackenzie ventured.

"Courtney." He nodded, his smile dropping. "I remember every kid. Especially that one. She was nasty. Still. Horrible what happened."

"We believe she might have been brought to the school," she said. "I remember we used to make pompoms from yarn. Blue and red. Do the kids still make them?"

"Yes, yes." He gestured them to follow. "In the crafts room."

"What was that?" Nick whispered to Mackenzie as they walked.

"What?" She pretended not to follow, knowing where he was going with this.

"Mad Mack doesn't go around giving people hugs."

"I'm not a robot!"

"I know." He rolled his eyes. "But since when do you hug people?"

She stopped in her tracks. "Do *you* want a hug?"

"N-no." He frowned hesitantly.

"Then quit complaining."

"Here it is." Boothby unlocked the door, pushing it open.

The room was just as she remembered. A chalkboard. Tables with tiny chairs painted in different colors. A supply shelf with glue, glitter, yarn, paintbrushes, craft paint and markers. Another shelf showcasing the creations of students.

"It would have been April 10," Nick said. "How do you think someone would gain access to this place?"

"All doors are locked," Boothby insisted. "And none of them were broken down. The windows can be opened, though."

There was a window across the room. Nick crossed to it and tried opening it.

"Looks like you found your special tribe," Boothby said to Mackenzie in a low voice.

"Sorry?"

He looked at Nick pointedly.

Nick pushed open the window. Wind whooshed in, disturbing sheets of paper lying around. He closed it again. "That was easy. Figure that's how they could have gotten in. What about CCTV?" he asked Boothby. "We'll need the tapes. The principal gave us the go-ahead."

Boothby nodded. "We store everything."

While Nick and Boothby discussed the security tapes from

the premises, Mackenzie looked around the room. It was here that Courtney had bullied her most of all. It had put her off crafts. Even after all these years, seeing this room did something strange to her. She took out a small bottle from her pocket and shook it.

"Do you mind?" she asked. "It will detect blood."

"Sure. But don't you use UV light?" Boothby asked.

"Blood doesn't fluoresce in UV light. That's a TV trope."

She sprayed the floor to see if there was any cleaned-up blood. Close to the supply shelf, a blue stain appeared. She paused, her skin tingling in anticipation. The stain grew larger and larger.

"That's a lot of blood," Nick said. "No one could survive that."

"This is where she was killed."

NINETEEN

"This is sick." Nick shook his head, his eyes spelling fury. "Murdering someone in a *school*."

"As opposed to murdering someone... in the woods?" Mackenzie suggested.

They were back at the station late in the evening, while the CSU went over the crime scene with a fine-toothed comb. They hoped they'd be done collecting samples by tomorrow morning, but it seemed like the room would be sealed off for a few days at least.

"No. Kids go there," Nick said with a cup of coffee in his hands. "Imagine Luna folding paper in there with all that blood around her."

"Luna would probably find it fascinating." Mackenzie tried to lighten the mood. It made him crack a smile. "Any news of Debbie?"

"None." He sighed. "Jenna went through all the security tape surrounding the news station but didn't catch anything. Patrol and sheriff's office are still on the lookout."

"Are the posters out?"

Nick hesitated and took a sip of his coffee. "There was a bit of a delay. All hell will break loose tomorrow."

Mackenzie was looking over the evidence photographed at Debbie's office. "Why?"

"Because it's Debbie Arnold, Mack," he said, like it was obvious. "She's our very own Anderson Cooper or Tucker Carlson."

She thought about it. "More like the latter. Just based on the colorful language."

She heard a grating laugh and turned her head to find Andrew chatting to Peterson by the water cooler outside the office.

"What do you think of him?" she asked Nick.

He shrugged. "Nothing."

"Isn't it weird that he was trying hard to come to Lakemore?" She leaned forward. "Who does that?"

"People who realize Lakemore has more to offer than football. Like a template for everything that can go wrong in a town so that they can learn from us."

Mackenzie shot him a flat look, but he just grinned. Despite her spending many years away from Lakemore, she had a fierce loyalty toward it. In some ways more than people who had never left it.

"Detective Price." Peterson approached them holding a photo. "This is one of the items retrieved from Debbie's office."

Mackenzie and Nick peered at the image of an orange wristband with little black Vs printed on it.

"We haven't been able to trace where it came from," Peterson said, hooking his thumbs in his belt. "Uniform asked her co-workers, and they have no idea what it is."

"It looks like one of those bands they hand out at nightclubs or concerts," Nick said. "Did you ask Noor?"

"Not yet. I will." Peterson's shoulders tensed like he'd been caught out. "In fact, I could go now and—"

"You're doing fine. Were you able to get a list of the people the jacket has been sold to?" Mackenzie asked.

His face reddened. "The store shut down a year ago. It's an old website with no address. I've asked Clint to track down the domain address."

"Detective Price." Andrew joined them, his hair ruffled. "I was hoping I could borrow you for an hour."

"An hour?"

"It's Jane Doe," he said softly.

Mackenzie's chest pinched, remembering the meek woman who had fallen into her arms. "Of course. I just have to use the washroom. I'll be back."

"Wood frogs can hold their pee for up to eight months," Peterson said. All heads slowly turned to look at him, bewildered. "Sorry," he mumbled and hurried away.

Jane Doe had been housed in a motel, with a squad car always parked outside. It was an unusual situation. Doctors had declared that she was definitely an adult, even though she looked and behaved like a child. But she didn't exist anywhere. There was no record of her. No one had reported her missing. Even NamUs, the national database for missing persons, yielded nothing. Mackenzie chewed on her fingernails, wondering how a woman was found injured in the woods, too traumatized to converse, and nobody cared. Jane Doe was just a blip in this world. A speck. Someone inconsequential and invisible.

"Sorry about the mess." Andrew jutted his thumb to the back seat. The car went over a pothole and Mackenzie almost bumped her head against the roof. "Sorry again."

"It's fine." She looked behind her at the food wrappers littering the seat. "He likes Twizzlers."

"Yes, yes, he does." Andrew smiled, dimples denting his cheeks. "His mom used to eat them when she was pregnant."

"Is she in Lakemore too?"

"No." Sadness crossed his face. "She died."

"I'm really sorry." She looked out the window at the blurry green of trees passing by.

"Yeah, sometimes I feel it would be nice for Robbie to have a mother," he continued, and Mackenzie shifted uneasily at how personal the conversation was getting. "I have a sister. She is very kind to Robbie. But it's different."

"Yeah, must be hard."

"You didn't get to spend that much time with your mother, am I right?" Andrew asked, narrowing his eyes. "You were thirteen when you left for New York?"

"How did you know?" The question came out sharply.

"The documentary. You talked about it."

"Oh." She rubbed her temple. "Right. I forgot."

He spoke again after a beat of silence. "You're on edge. It's natural. Someone knows a little too much about your life. All this unwanted fame must be rattling."

"How would you recommend dealing with it?" She didn't put much stock in therapy. Her question wasn't meant to extract any useful insight from him, but to study him, to judge this new addition to the team.

"Normally I would have suggested the typical steps of tightening your inner circle, dedicating allocated time to a hobby and so on." He shot her a probing gaze before returning his eyes to the road. "But truth be told, since my wife passed away, I feel there's more than we imagine that's out of our control."

"We can never control what happens, just how we respond to it."

His face twitched with uneasiness. "Yes, but maybe sometimes it's best not to fight it. Let the chips fall where they may."

"What is that supposed to mean?" she asked, irritated at his riddles.

"Everything happens for a reason, Detective Price." He smiled.

The words echoed inside her as she calmed her breathing. Luckily, she didn't need to elaborate or reply, because they had reached the motel. She followed Andrew as he climbed the stairs to the dingy floor poorly lit by flickering lights. A constant hum buzzed through the air, coming from a giant refrigerator. Mackenzie disapproved of this motel. It gave her the wrong vibes. Like horrible things could happen behind closed doors here. But the Lakemore PD budget was tight.

"Why me?" she asked suddenly when he stopped in front of a door.

"I mentioned you yesterday and her eyes lit up. She still isn't talking, but I think with you there, we might get close." He knocked on the door and raised his voice. "It's me. Dr. Turner. I'm with Detective Mackenzie Price."

Mackenzie braced herself. It felt like a huge responsibility somehow. It pained her to realize that this was the first time someone had relied on her emotionally.

A click. Another click. Jane Doe clearly liked to lock herself in. The door opened with a creak and her face appeared in the crack. Her dark eyes were soulless. But when they landed on Mackenzie, there was a spark. She opened the door and stepped aside, letting them in.

"How are you?" Andrew asked cheerfully. She didn't reply.

Mackenzie looked around the spacious room. There was a four-poster bed, a television, a mini fridge, and a balcony. It was a standard room decorated with cheap showpieces. There was nothing of Jane's. Not even a suitcase. She was wearing a ratty old T-shirt with poppies on it, and baggy track pants.

"Do you need anything else?" Mackenzie asked. "I can bring you more clothes, maybe a phone?"

Jane shook her head and crossed her arms, bowing her body inward. But her eyes wouldn't leave Mackenzie.

"I thought it would be nice for Detective Price to join us." Andrew settled in an armchair. "What do you think, Jane?"

She nodded mutely, not even throwing him a glance, then sank onto the bed, while Mackenzie sat on the other chair and shrugged off her jacket. Jane's eyes veered all over her yearningly, from toes to throat.

"Mackenzie, why don't you tell Jane what you were doing at the carnival when you met?"

"I was there with my partner and his daughter," she explained, following Andrew's lead.

"Detective Price has a knack with kids." Andrew smiled. "Do you like kids?"

Jane shrugged, playing with her tattered sleeve.

Andrew looked at Mackenzie, resigned, before turning his attention back to Jane. "How about tomorrow I bring a drawing book? We can do some art together."

The hem of Jane's pants rode up, revealing the barcode tattooed on her ankle. Once again it made Mackenzie shiver. Like a string of live wire had grazed her skin, leaving sizzling burns. What did it mean?

"I have a scar," she blurted. She raised the bottom of her pantsuit and twisted her leg to show the bullet wound from over a year ago. It was a small scar, a permanently bruised patch of skin. A remnant of a betrayal that cut deep. The culmination of a decades-old lie. "It doesn't hurt anymore. But it's there."

Jane's eyebrows knotted and she raised her ankle, pointing at the tattoo.

"Yes, I can tell that means something to you," Mackenzie said. "Mine is the price I paid to learn the truth. The price I paid for closure. What does yours mean to you?"

It was the first time she had heard Jane's voice. She had

expected it to be soft and mouse-like. A voice that would suit her demeanor and appearance. But instead it was throaty and rough. Like she was a smoker. Or someone who had screamed a lot. She said only one word that evening.

"Prison."

TWENTY

APRIL 16

Mackenzie felt the shift in the air that morning when she arrived at the station. It was electric. She parked her car and climbed out, immediately despising the balmy air that formed a thick paste on her skin. As she crossed the lot, she spotted a throng of reporters and camera crews outside the entrance to the building.

"Shit." She slowed down and tucked her chin inside the collar of her light jacket.

"Debbie Arnold went missing two nights ago..."

"Her partner, Noor Khan, has alleged that the Lakemore PD isn't doing enough..."

"Sources have confirmed that there hasn't been a ransom demand yet..."

Mackenzie heard only tidbits before she went to the rear of the building and entered through the back door. Chaos was slowly mounting, and they were no closer to figuring out where Debbie was.

When she reached her floor, her feet stopped. A group of people including Rivera were engrossed in the television. On the screen, a man and a woman were in animated discussion.

"The disappearance of Debbie is an attack on free speech in this town," the man declared.

"Why would you say that, Bob?" The woman was scandalized.

"Debbie is the only person in this town who has the balls to criticize the big shots. She called out the police when they were being incompetent and corrupt. Last year, when the mayor was lazy and too focused on re-election, she was the one with the sensitivity to suggest dedicating a bench to those kids who were killed."

"But the free speech argument is a bit of an exaggeration."

"Don't you think the police will have bias against this victim? Don't you think things are easier for them now that the person who criticized them on a daily basis has mysteriously vanished?"

The woman laughed nervously. "What exactly are you suggesting? That Debbie's disappearance is part of some conspiracy?"

"The police won't say anything, will they?" he scoffed. "But I can guarantee you that anyone who speaks up against them isn't safe."

Rivera switched off the television and spun on her heel. "Show's over! Back to work!"

They all dispersed in different directions. Rivera was left standing in the middle of the room, quaking in anger.

"We should tell them." Mackenzie approached her.

"Tell them what?" Rivera sounded annoyed.

"That Debbie's disappearance is related to the two other homicides. Otherwise they'll crucify us. Did you see the reporters downstairs?"

Rivera crossed her arms and squared her shoulders. "I won't be bullied by unprofessional news anchors and reporters. We will treat this case like we treat any other. I'd rather focus on finding Ms. Arnold alive than worry about what to tell the media."

A seed of insecurity planted itself inside Mackenzie. Rivera's reaction was the one she herself should have had. But she hadn't. Was this case actually getting to her?

"Keep your head in the game, Detective Price," Rivera advised sternly. "The only way to get all this to stop is to focus only on one thing. The bastard behind it all. The rest is just noise."

Mackenzie nodded curtly. Rivera clapped her arm and left the room.

Nick showed up and handed her a cup of iced tea. "We got some updates. Clint tracked down the domain information from the website selling the muskrat jacket. Peterson reached out, but the email address now belongs to someone else."

"A dead end?" Her shoulders dropped.

He pressed his lips in a thin line. "Unfortunately. He's working hard to redeem himself and figure out where that wristband came from. Noor doesn't know anything about it."

"Did we find out anything about Sophie's sister?" she asked.

"Yes, we did."

She followed him to his computer. He pulled up a PDF file containing some forms and pictures.

"Look at this. Aria Fields was registered at the same school Sophie attended in Colorado. It's a cold case. There's even a picture and some newspaper clippings."

Mackenzie angled the monitor better. There it was. A yearbook picture of a young girl with blonde ringlets around a cherubic face. Her lips curled into a naughty smile. The tip of her nose was slightly upturned. She had a little mark on her cheek shaped like Africa. She looked like she was up to no good. That girl who was always smiling. And she'd gone missing over fifteen years ago.

"Oh my God." Mackenzie clicked her tongue. "Poor Sophie. Her entire family was destroyed. Didn't Riverview get into her computer and her search history?"

"Yeah. She randomly booked a ticket to Lakemore. Didn't even bother to really look it up."

"I think we need to look at that again. See if she was investigating her sister's disappearance."

"What are the chances that her abduction and murder could have anything to do with that?" Nick sounded doubtful. "I mean, we know the connection is you."

"I know, but this is just too strange to pass on. Something feels wrong about it."

His lips quirked into a smirk. "Since when does Mad Mack rely on her gut?"

She'd always known that Nick had a nice smile, but she was still flustered for a second before gathering her bearings. "Right. Yeah. Good plan."

"What?"

Blood rushed to her cheeks. "Is there a picture of her and Sophie in the case file? Can you get me a hard copy?"

"Sure." He printed it out and gave it to her. "Here you go."

Sophie and Aria—identical twins. Except Aria had a birthmark on her cheek and that mischievous look. Whereas Sophie looked like the good girl. The one who finished her homework on time and ate all her vegetables. It was one of the last pictures taken of them together before Aria vanished.

She went to Austin, who was working at his desk. She stood next to him, waiting for him to notice. When he finally looked up, his face hardened. It made her stomach sag.

He cocked an eyebrow.

She gave him the photo. "This is Sophie and Aria."

He dropped the pen he was holding. His tense manner dissolved, and vulnerability shone through. With shaky fingers, he clasped the picture and stared at it as if it might come to life and give him answers. "I can't believe this. She never said anything."

"I'm sorry. I'm sure it was because it was painful for her to remember that time in her life."

He gave her a baffled look, like he hadn't expected her to say that. She was surprised herself.

It was like Mad Mack had finally cracked.

"Mack!" Nick called. "We got the CCTV."

"Right." She glanced at Austin. "I'll see you later."

She could feel his curious stare as she walked back across the room.

"Which ones?" she asked, pulling her chair next to Nick's.

"From the school. I asked for the tapes the night Courtney went missing and the next day just to be sure."

"How many cameras are there?"

"Two." He clicked on the icons and the screen divided into two sections, each displaying footage from a camera. "One facing the front door. One facing the back."

The video played from five in the evening onward, showing staff members leaving the premises and cleaning crew entering. Mackenzie rubbed her eyes, watching the grainy scenes blur into each other.

At around seven, an hour after Boothby left the building and locked the door behind him, there was a flash of light.

Mackenzie slowed down the speed. A few seconds later, a car entered the frame of the camera that faced the back door of the school. It slowly rolled out of the frame without stopping.

"What was that?" Nick asked. They waited for the car to show up again, but the time stamp kept inching later into the night and there was no sign of it.

"That car wasn't just passing by." Mackenzie replayed the video. "It's on the premises. And it was too close to the building." She did a quick calculation in her head. "This was an hour after Courtney went missing from the parking lot. It would take twenty minutes to get to the school from the lawyer's office, but there's probably some downtime to account for."

Nick froze the screen where the car was driving away. "We got a license plate."

TWENTY-ONE

Mackenzie's boots landed in a puddle, and she grimaced at the mud-soaked leaves now sticking to them. It was a dim afternoon, with the sun sometimes shining and other times hiding behind the drifting clouds. After running the license plate through the DMV, they'd found out that the vehicle was registered to a limited liability company called King of the Road. The address was in Tacoma, an hour's drive away from Lakemore.

"This looks like it." Nick removed his sunglasses, the wind playing with his hair.

It was a strange structure to find in the middle of the woods. They'd had to take winding roads after getting off the highway, and finally a stretch of dirt track. Mackenzie was convinced that the GPS had lied and they were going to be stranded in unknown territory in one of the hiking trails without cell reception. The single-story modern rectangular building was made of glass and white stone. A stark contrast from its lush natural surroundings. Too clinical and synthetic.

"Why would you have an office here?" She pushed open the door. The first two things she registered were the aroma of eucalyptus and the sound of classical music. The walls were paneled with white screens. The floor was made of white marble. The layout was airy and structured. Rows of cubicles contained people working diligently. There was a reception desk with a logo—a crown on wheels—in blocks on the wall. Fake plants sat atop the counter, hiding a man wearing a headset.

"Lakemore PD." Mackenzie tapped on the desk with her badge.

He had sandy hair, gelled stylishly to his scalp. Dressed in a button-down Oxford shirt, he looked like he was part of the golf club at an Ivy League school. Mackenzie noted his artful features—almond-shaped eyes, scruffy squarish chin and broad jaw matching a wide forehead.

"I'm Tag. How can I help you?" He removed his headset and cracked his neck.

"What company is this?"

"It's an exclusive car rental service. We don't advertise our address anywhere, though."

"Then how do you get clients?" Mackenzie asked.

"Strictly word of mouth."

"We're looking for one of your cars." Nick slipped him the license plate number.

Tag smirked. "Can't help you there, I'm afraid. Company policy."

"Sorry?" Mackenzie asked.

"Privacy is our motto." He shrugged. "Our clients pay a huge amount of money not only for our premium services, but also for our discretion. It's in the contract that we keep all information to ourselves."

"I don't think you fully understand." She tucked her hair behind her ear. "We are investigating a homicide and we have reason to believe this car was involved in the crime. We need to know who rented the car during that specific duration, and access to the said car."

Tag didn't even flinch. "Then get a court order. Sorry, my hands are tied."

"Where do you keep your cars? I don't see a garage here."

"Our garage is located elsewhere. This is just the office. And no, I'm not allowed to give you its location."

"Can we speak to your boss?" Nick tried a different approach.

Tag grinned. "Don't think so. I have to get back to work now. Excuse me, please." He slipped his headset back on and began typing on his computer.

Mackenzie glanced at the employees in their cubicles. Not one of them had glanced up. Clenching her jaw, she walked out of the building, slamming the door shut. "What the hell was that?"

Nick rubbed the back of his neck and took out his phone. "This is shady as fuck. I really didn't think we'd need a court order for this. I'll get Jenna to start preparing an affidavit right away. Hopefully by this evening we can get it to a judge."

"This is a very exclusive establishment." Mackenzie searched on her phone, leaning her elbows on the hood of the car. "It has no internet presence."

"*Tag* said it's solely word of mouth."

"I'll get Peterson to do a background search on Tag too." She dawdled. "Do you think your dad would know about this rental service?"

Nick's nostrils flared. "Seriously?"

She shrugged innocently. "He's a senator, Nick. If there's anyone who knows about such... secret services, it's politicians."

"No. We're doing this the right way."

She didn't argue. Nick had never gone to his father for help. Their relationship was healthy, but it was a matter of integrity for him. He had rejected several lucrative job offers in big cities, knowing very well that they were only interested in having the son of a senator on the force.

"Are we looking for someone powerful and well connected, then?" Mackenzie voiced her concern.

"Not necessarily. The car could have been stolen."

She chewed the inside of her cheek, considering. "This car wasn't reported stolen."

"I don't think they would." He rocked on his heels. "If they're that secretive about their books, they wouldn't go to the police and risk disclosure."

"But this is a town car. It's expensive."

"Look at this." He hitched his thumb over his shoulder, pointing at the office. "Their clients are paying a shit ton of money. Losing a client over a car is the worst business decision here."

"That means that if we want to get to the bottom of this, we need to access their records and find who rented the car. Let's hope that court order goes through fast."

"Can't wait to rub it in Tag's face," he muttered, exasperated.

"We need that car to lead us to Debbie." Mackenzie tensed, remembering the chaos that was building in Lakemore. She could feel it in the air. A bite. A snap. Like a page was turning.

"Courtney was most likely transported in that car to the school." Nick perched an unlit cigarette between his lips.

"We can check the traffic cams. We have the license plate and the approximate time frame from when Courtney was abducted to when the car reached the school."

He nodded, catching her drift. "And hopefully one of the cams caught a picture of our perp."

"If not, then at least it might give us a clue as to where the car was headed after leaving the school."

By the time night rolled in, there was a full-blown storm in Lakemore. Every few seconds there was a booming sound and

Mackenzie jerked from the vibrations she felt underneath her feet. She was seated at her kitchen island, reading over the case files again and hoping to pick up something new. There were three victims. Sophie, Courtney and Debbie. Two were dead and one missing, likely dead too. The thought was like smog. Engulfing and dizzying. The stakes were high. Every move of Mackenzie's was being watched. Lakemore was at tipping point; its sanity balanced on the edge of a knife. She pushed away those thoughts. Her job was to find Debbie, not worry about what it meant for the town.

When she came across Courtney's picture with her family, she wondered how good a father Brett would be now to their kids. Whether he would be as good a father as Robert was. She touched his watch on her wrist, a certainty blooming inside her.

The doorbell chimed. She checked the time, not expecting anyone at this hour.

Outside, she found Andrew and Robbie huddled under an umbrella.

"I'm sorry to show up unannounced!" Andrew yelled over the lashing rain and growling thunder.

"Come inside."

"No, no. I have to go and see our Jane Doe." He clutched his son's shoulders tightly. "My sitter cancelled because of the storm, and our cabin has no power. Do you mind watching Robbie for an hour?"

"Of course." She blinked.

"Thank you." He smiled and then glared at Robbie. "Behave. I don't want any complaints!"

The boy nodded, and then grinned at Mackenzie with a warm glint in his eyes.

Once Andrew had left, Mackenzie shut the door and turned to see Robbie standing in the foyer, playing with his fingers shyly. His dirty shoes had smeared the floor with mud and water. But for the first time, the mess didn't irk her.

"Do you want to take off your jacket and shoes, kid?"

He nodded, giving his jacket to Mackenzie to hang in the closet. The only other kid she was used to being around was Luna, who was three years older than Robbie and vastly different. While Luna was sassy and chatty, Robbie was reserved and meek.

"Do you want something to eat?" she asked.

He shook his head.

"Twizzlers?"

He grinned and nodded eagerly.

"You don't talk much, do you?" She tossed him some candy. "Do you like Lakemore?"

"It's okay." He was focused on ripping open the wrapper. "Dad says it's like a person."

"A person?"

"Yes, it has moods. He wants to study the moods."

She thumbed through the files. "Every place is like that, I suppose. I lived in New York for a few years. Have you been there?"

He shook his head. "Do you have pictures?"

"I do!" She remembered that she still had a photo album in the attic. She hurried upstairs, suddenly overcome with excitement. The album was dusty, with the cover yellowing at the edges. When she returned, Robbie was sitting on the couch, his feet dangling.

She settled next to him, flipping through the pages, which hadn't been touched for years. She showed him her grandmother, their old house, her school trips to Central Park, the view from the Empire State Building, the Freedom Tunnel, where she would go to seek refuge from stressful days, the hidden platform under Grand Central Station where she first tried a cigarette and coughed a lung out, that family-owned bakery in Little Italy she loved, and many, many other places. She told him stories, recalling snippets from her time there that she didn't realize she still remembered. Memories buried deep still burned bright, like all this time all she had to do was light a match to see them. It almost brought a tear to her eye. She had spent so many years consumed by thoughts of Melody, and what had transpired that night in Lakemore, that she never realized she had lived a life. She had cried and laughed and danced and shouted, unaffected by the night she buried a body with her mother. All those moments when the past didn't have its claws around her bones, holding her captive like a puppet.

The hour passed quickly, and Andrew returned.

"Hope he wasn't a bother."

"Not at all. It was nice to catch up," she said without thinking.

"Can I use the restroom?" Robbie asked.

Mackenzie showed him where to go, while she and Andrew waited in the foyer. "How was Jane Doe? Did she say anything?"

"Nothing of use to the investigation into what happened to her." Andrew flattened his mouth, disappointed. "It appears her PTSD has triggered selective mutism."

"How long do you think it will take her to... heal?"

He shrugged. "There are no rules. Every mind is different." Mackenzie frowned. "You're not a fan of psychology, are you?" he asked, amused.

"I just don't enjoy how abstract it is."

"That's a challenge!" he said cheerfully.

Before leaving, Robbie gave Mackenzie an unexpected hug. She felt something tug at her heart. A force trying to thaw the frozen muscles. He gave her that smile again—like they shared a deep secret.

She went back to work feeling lighter. If it weren't for Robbie, she probably wouldn't have realized that the evidence of a life lived had been sitting in this very house all along. A reminder that she was more than her mistakes and her violent past. She had spent so long focusing on her future without realizing that her past wasn't something to run away from. Amidst the darkness, there was light there also.

Turning to Sophie's browser history in the weeks before she went missing, Mackenzie noted nothing out of the ordinary. But then she saw it.

Aria Fields.

Aria Fields Colorado.

Aria Fields found.

Aria Fields disappearance.

Three weeks before Sophie vanished, she'd begun looking up Aria on the internet. Before that, there wasn't a single search about her. What had prompted her to think about her sister again? It only solidified Mackenzie's suspicion that Sophie's disappearance was linked to Aria.

TWENTY-TWO

APRIL 17

"The Lakemore PD's lips remain sealed when it comes to the disappearance of Debbie Arnold, who was last seen two nights ago retreating into her office." A shiny new face had replaced Debbie, a younger version with a squeaky little voice, lacking Debbie's boldness. "The news station has tightened security around the premises. But while we as a network continue to provide support to Debbie's partner and volunteer in on-foot searches, the Lakemore PD has refused to provide any updates, claiming that they don't want to compromise an ongoing investigation. We are now joined by Lakemore's very own Vincent Hawkins."

The camera panned to Vincent, a gangly gray-haired man with a pencil-thin mustache capping his narrow lips. Dressed like a college student in loose T-shirts and pants, with a pen tucked behind his ear, he looked nothing like the man who'd broken the biggest news in Lakemore a year and a half ago, catapulting him to fame at a national level.

"Mr. Hawkins, you have played a key role in exposing corruption in this town. A lot of people are worried that history is repeating itself."

"As shocked and saddened as I am by Debbie Arnold's disappearance, I really don't believe there's any conspiracy at hand. We all like stories with a clear villain, but that's not always the case."

"But don't you think the Lakemore PD should make a statement, considering the victim in this case is a public figure?"

Hawkins' lips twitched in amusement. "That doesn't make a lot of sense, does it? The minute they give her preferential treatment and maybe risk her safety, it will be you calling them out again."

Mackenzie sighed and closed the tab on her computer.

"The new one sucks, doesn't she?" Troy chewed the end of his pen, making Mackenzie scowl.

"She has big shoes to fill."

"It's good news for you." He grinned. "If she keeps embarrassing herself and shoots herself in the foot, maybe we won't be hated as much."

Mackenzie nodded faintly. She'd skipped dinner last night and still hadn't had breakfast. Her appetite was dead, but her stomach was growling. The thought of eating anything made bile rise in her throat.

"Sorry," Troy said softly, playing with his wedding band. "You know no one blames you, right?"

Did she? Courtney's husband, Brett, hadn't been informed of the message left for Mackenzie. He was calling every day, asking if they were any closer to catching whoever had murdered his wife. It ate away at her, one sharp bite at a time.

"Thanks," she mumbled half-heartedly.

Before Troy could reply, Nick stormed into the office and slammed a file on his desk. "The court order didn't go through."

"*What?*" Mackenzie gasped.

"Judge Hamilton refused to sign it." He loosened his tie.

"Why?"

"His clerk said that Hamilton felt we didn't make a good

enough case that the car was part of the crime. Apparently a lot of cars drive past the school. Not enough reason to get a company to reveal confidential information, especially one that is notoriously private."

"But we need access to the car to confirm if it was used to take Courtney there."

Nick raised his eyebrows. "Yeah. Chasing our own tails."

"We'll send it to some other judge. Tag's background check was clean. No trouble with the law. Only graduated from high school three years ago."

"I've asked Jenna to submit the affidavit again." He ran a hand through his hair. "But I'm pissed off. This is an unnecessary delay."

Mackenzie paled, thinking about where Debbie was right now. She imagined her face-down in a puddle of water. Her hair noodling around her neck. Lifeless and stiff.

"I don't think she's dead yet," Nick said, reading her thoughts.

"Why? Courtney was killed almost immediately."

"Then where is she?" he challenged. "This person wants us to find the bodies and the messages for you. So they're not dumping them in a lake or burying them in the woods. And with the massive ongoing search, I think we would have come across her by now."

"Why would they kill Courtney immediately afterwards, but not Debbie?"

"I think there are two possibilities," Andrew interrupted them. "From what I've seen, Debbie is a resourceful and shrewd person. She may have found a way to keep herself alive longer, by humanizing herself or perhaps trying to negotiate her survival."

"And what do you think is the other possibility?" Nick asked.

Andrew cast a reluctant glance at Mackenzie. "She's being tortured as we speak."

Mackenzie's stomach contracted. "Courtney wasn't tortured. Neither was Sophie. Why would Debbie be? That's not the MO."

"Because Debbie has targeted you recently," Andrew said. "Courtney was only a kid when she bullied you all those years ago. It's possible that the killer... cut her some slack."

"How generous," Nick muttered under his breath.

When Mackenzie's computer pinged with a notification, she steeled herself, hoping for new information. "Oh, I think Peterson tracked down the vendor for the wristband."

"He did?" Nick couldn't hide his surprise.

"It didn't match any club in Lakemore or neighboring towns," she read aloud from the email. "But there's a shop in Lakemore that sells these wristbands."

Nick was already picking up his jacket. "If we couldn't find the owner of that muskrat jacket, then maybe we can find where the wristband came from."

"Can I come along?" Andrew asked brightly. "It'd be fun to be out in the field."

The tires hissed on the hot tarmac before coming to a halt. "What is this place?" Andrew asked from the back seat.

Mackenzie's skin prickled as she looked out the window. This was Tombstone—a nickname given to a small neighborhood in Lakemore because local legend said it was haunted. Every child in Lakemore grew up listening to the old folktale about a handsome man who lured a woman there every year, promising her riches, only for the woman to never be seen again. But even as the years went by and more and more women went missing, the man never aged. Some said he feasted on the flesh of beautiful women to nourish his youth.

Over time, the stories about this place had changed, twisted, and blurred into one another. Pieces were lost and new pieces were added. The truth was long forgotten and unrecognizable, that line between fact and fiction too fuzzy. Not even the truth stood the test of time. But one thing stayed the same in Tombstone.

Fear. It permeated everything about this place. From the sharp texture of the air to the eerie way light fell on the shapes here. As Mackenzie stepped out of the car and her boots landed on the asphalt, she felt it in the air. A heaviness and haze. Like invisible ropes had reached out to render her motionless. Like she had stepped into a place that didn't exist in the normal world.

Box-shaped stores surrounded them in a semicircle. They were all shut down. Some were boarded up. There were no other cars around. Overflowing dumpsters were filled with cats scavenging for scraps of food. Rumpled newspapers glided on the rough concrete in the wind. It was just the three of them.

"Lakemore is like a hidden treasure," Andrew exclaimed, straining his neck to look at the hill extending behind the shops. "This neighborhood must experience a lot of crime."

"No." Nick removed his sunglasses and jolted when the dumpster next to him shook.

"No?" Andrew was surprised.

"No one comes here. They're too afraid," Mackenzie said, noting her own apprehension.

"Fear is like a ghost in a children's story—an illusion," Andrew declared.

"An illusion that holds so much power that it has vanquished empires and minds," she countered, but then her words died on the tip of her tongue and her thoughts flew out of her head.

Another memory conjured up. It was around nine years ago when she had returned to Lakemore from New York. Her throat had closed. Her mind had flooded with memories of that wretched night that led to her being sent away. And for some reason, she had found herself here. In Tombstone. If she could tolerate being here, she would be fine in any corner of Lakemore.

"Have you been here before?" Andrew picked up on her expressions.

"Yes." Nick answered for her, trying to hold back his laughter. "This is where Mack and I met. She hit me with a pipe."

"Ow! Fuck!" Nick roared, falling to his knees.

Mackenzie stood behind him, panting, holding the pipe in a deathly grip. The adrenaline pounding more wildly than the rain.

"He was wearing a hoodie, and it's a scary place. I thought he was going to mug me," Mackenzie said defensively.

"I'm so sorry!" She dropped the pipe, remorse ticking in when Nick removed his hoodie. "You came out of nowhere!"

"Why were you carrying a pipe?" Andrew wondered.

A gust of wind blew across, the sound bouncing between the concrete structures, creating a haunting whistling sound.

"Never mind," Andrew muttered, his expression of curiosity faltering.

Nick frowned at his phone and then pointed to his left. "It's that one, according to Peterson."

It was a yellow-painted store with a garage door. The windows weren't boarded up like the others, but they were laced with cobwebs. Nothing about it indicated that it was open. As they came closer, Mackenzie bent and peered through the window. Inside she could make out a dusty room containing figurines, rolls of yarn and wool, paper crafts, dollhouses, and cans of dog food. An eclectic mix with no common theme.

"Looks like nobody's home." Nick banged on the garage door.

"What a shame. I was hoping to catch someone in a chase,"

Andrew said. "Sorry. The life of a psychologist isn't very exciting."

"Someone's here!" Mackenzie exclaimed as a light turned on inside the store.

A frumpy man with a drum of a belly, dressed in a wife-beater, emerged from the storeroom and dawdled his way to the front to open the door. "We're closed."

When Nick showed him his badge, the man didn't budge. "What is it?"

"Do you recognize this?" Mackenzie held out a picture of the wristband.

The man pulled a face and rubbed his grubby jaw. "It's ours. Why?"

"Who do you sell these to?" Nick asked.

He took out a cigarette, settled it between his lips and lit up. After taking a leisurely drag, he said, "What's in it for me?"

"Not being in lockup for obstruction of justice." Mackenzie gave him a sweet smile.

The smoke zigzagged out of his nostrils. "There's a guy who places an order for them from time to time."

"What's his name?" She took out her notepad.

"I don't know."

"How does he pay?" Nick asked.

"Cash."

"What does he look like?" Mackenzie pressed.

The man shrugged. "A regular chap. Tall and young."

Mackenzie tapped her pen to the notepad, a hunch rising inside her. She took out her phone and pulled up Tag's picture, which she had saved from the DMV records. He didn't look as preppy and sophisticated as he did now—his floppy hair fell on his forehead and he still had acne on his cheeks—but it was clear enough.

She showed it to the owner. "Is it this guy?"

The man wrinkled his nose and took another puff. "That's

him all right. Comes here in a big shiny car and takes around fifty of these bands at a time. Pays in full. No small talk. Good customer."

"Who is he?" Andrew asked.

But Mackenzie and Nick exchanged a solemn look, thinking the same thing. Another path in the case led back to King of the Road rental services.

TWENTY-THREE

Mackenzie clipped the three pictures on the whiteboard in the conference room. Sophie Fields, Courtney Montenegro, Debbie Arnold. She scribbled everything she knew about them underneath. After returning from their excursion, she had felt the need to take a shower and cleanse her skin. But there was no time to waste. The clock was ticking and there was no news about Debbie. With each day that passed, the noose around Mackenzie's neck tightened further.

You're welcome, Mackenzie.

I will always protect you, Mackenzie.

Nick pressed a hot cup against his forehead.

"Didn't you sleep last night? You've been yawning all day."

"I didn't." He cracked his neck. "I kept hearing footsteps."

"Footsteps?" She frowned.

"Yeah, like someone was walking around in my house. But I checked and there was no one. It was a weird dream."

Nick clearly didn't think much of it, but an alarm was ringing in Mackenzie's head.

"I can hear you thinking," he said dryly.

"It's just..." She chewed her lip. "You don't have weird dreams. Do you think someone was actually in your house?"

"Like I said, I checked and nada."

But she wasn't convinced. That pecking feeling was back. Suddenly she remembered how a year ago, she hadn't felt safe in her own house. As though someone had been lurking in the shadows, watching her. And now there was someone killing women in her name...

"Mack." When he held her shoulders, she jolted out of her spiraling thoughts. "I know you're on edge. We all are because of this case. But you're being paranoid. Everything's fine."

She pushed those thoughts away as he searched her eyes. Maybe he was right. Moreover, being a woman, her antenna was more active than his.

"We have three victims." She changed the topic and capped her marker. "The forensic evidence connecting them is muskrat fur."

"We were able to trace the specific jacket, but that shop shut down, so we don't know who bought it." He crossed off *muskrat fur* on the whiteboard with a red marker.

"We know from her Google searches that Sophie had started looking into Aria's disappearance. And then she arrived in Lakemore... But from what I dug up on the internet, Aria had no connection to Lakemore. So why did Sophie come here?"

There was an inches-thick stack of news clippings about Aria Fields' disappearance on the desk. Mackenzie had spent last night highlighting anything and everything important. But the case had generated no promising leads.

Nick folded his lips over his teeth, contemplating. "There are a lot of details that are never publicized. There could be some information that Sophie was privy to from the detectives on the case during the investigation."

Mackenzie made a note on the board. *Request case files and check for a link with Lakemore.*

"Now the messages for you." He shoved his hands in his pockets and tilted his neck. "The note in Sophie's pocket had no fingerprints or anything of significance. And the message left on the wall in Courtney's blood, nothing there either."

"That's what baffles me." She bit her lip. "We have two bodies and one abduction site, but there isn't enough physical evidence, or any witnesses."

"To be fair, Sophie went missing a long time ago."

"But she was killed recently. Do you think Turner is right? That we could be looking at two killers?"

Nick shook his head. "Yeah, and our killer took her body from some freezer? That's a lucky shot."

Something didn't sit right with Mackenzie. In a way, the link between the victims was undeniable. A glaringly clear string of motivation behind the brutal targeting. But consistency was lacking. The methods didn't align. The time between abduction and killing wasn't the same. Then there was Sophie—the only victim with no history with Mackenzie. It was almost like tasting an ingredient in a dish that didn't belong there, whose taste had seeped into the entirety. She just needed to figure out that one aspect. That one truth that once revealed would slot everything into a neat picture as opposed to the mess it was right now.

"If we add this wristband evidence to our affidavit to get the rental company to open its books for us, we have a better shot, don't you think?" Mackenzie pondered. "That company is associated with two victims now. Can't rule that out as a coincidence."

"I agree." Nick crossed his arms. "And we have uniform picking up Tag. If we can get something out of him, that will help."

"Clint wasn't able to spot the car anywhere else?" Mackenzie asked.

He shook his head. "Not even on the cams on the freeway.

He checked an hour-long window from when we saw it on the CCTV at the school."

"They're that prepared, huh," she said glumly. "They know which streets and areas to avoid."

"Planned everything to a T."

Mackenzie felt a heavy weight on her chest. She'd never been interested in participating in that documentary, facing a camera and giving strangers a glimpse into her psyche. But her bosses had pressured her, desperate to rehabilitate Lakemore's problematic image and hitch their wagon to the female-empowerment movement that was sweeping the Western world. Never had Mackenzie imagined that the attention would be more than an inconvenience. That somewhere out there someone was watching a little too closely.

"I haven't been to that neighborhood in a very long time," Nick said, cutting the silence in the room. "Have you?"

"Not since I attacked you." She snorted. "When were you there last?"

"When Luna was four." He leaned against the wall and crossed his ankles. "She was refusing to sleep, and I'd tried everything. Thought of this crazy idea that I'd drive around Tombstone close to sunset and freak her into submission."

"What happened?"

"She loved it and asked to go back every day for weeks." He flattened his mouth. "I should have known then."

She chuckled. "Sounds about right. Nothing fazes her."

"You have something under your eye." Before Mackenzie could react, he reached out with his thumb and swiped something off her skin. She lurched back in reflex. His eyes widened. "What?"

"Nothing."

There was a knock on the door. Their heads turned in that direction, and Mackenzie's heart galloped again.

"Sterling?" She frowned.

Dressed in a dark blue suit, Sterling looked all business. He was tall, with broad shoulders, a muscular frame, and hair in tight curls. His eyes were icy blue—a sharp contrast against his dark skin. "Did I interrupt something?"

"No." Mackenzie moved away from Nick. "What are you doing here?"

He arched an eyebrow. "Need to prep you for your testimony. Your blackmail chain case is going to trial in a couple of weeks."

Mackenzie had completely forgotten about it. Sterling had contacted her two weeks ago, informing her that he was the prosecutor.

"You can take the room." Nick picked up his stuff and walked past Sterling without sparing him a glance. It had been over a year, but the tension between them was still as visceral as ever.

It was Nick who had discovered that Sterling was cheating on Mackenzie. Sterling had promised he'd come clean to her within a week, but he hadn't. When Nick discovered that he had lied—again—he'd punched him in the face for good measure.

"How've you been?" Sterling asked, setting his briefcase on the table. "I can imagine Debbie going missing has made things complicated."

Mackenzie sat on the farthest chair. "When are they not complicated? How are things in Olympia?"

"Complicated." His lips twitched in a smile. "I heard."

"About what?"

"That these disappearances are related to you." He paused. "Is it true?"

"How did you know?" Concern coated her voice.

"People talk."

How long was it going to be before this news was made

public? It could hinder the investigation, and she would become the town pariah, Courtney and Debbie's loved ones coming at with her pitchforks. Even Austin couldn't hide his contempt when he looked at her. It was a grudge that was never going to die.

She straightened. "I think we should focus on work."

Sterling smiled fondly. "Remember the first time I questioned you on the stand? It was then I realized that I needed to coach you beforehand."

Mackenzie's directness and fierce responses had thrown him off guard and made him stammer and fumble his words. But it hadn't stopped him from asking her out later.

"I've changed." She sat back.

"I can tell. You look less scared."

"That's ironic." She couldn't stop herself. She was terrified. In moments of silence or inactivity, fear arrested her ability to think straight. It had her in its fist, applying pressure every now and then. A shadow trailing her that swallowed everything around her.

"You're less scared of yourself," Sterling corrected.

She pulled her eyebrows together. "What does that mean?"

"You were always so afraid." His gaze was piercing, like he was seeing her for the first time. "You were always rigid and at times hard-hearted, but it wasn't just a way to keep others out so that they didn't hurt you like your parents did. You were also hiding from yourself, refusing to feel. The past few months, I've noticed this change in you. Like you've finally accepted it."

"Since when did you become such a sage?" She tried to lighten the mood.

"We were together for six years. I was a jackass, but not clueless." He gave her a timid smile and opened a file.

Mackenzie spent the next hour discussing work with him. The man she had once loved and married. The man who had cheated on her and broken her into a million pieces. She had let go of the anger, but now she waited for the awkwardness to seep in. That lingering *what if*. But when Sterling shook her hand, she felt only peace.

"Mack, uniform picked up Tag." Nick walked in. "He's in the interrogation room."

TWENTY-FOUR

There was no reason for Tag Stuart to be in the interrogation room. He wasn't a suspect yet. It was too late to issue a warrant since it technically wasn't an emergency one. But as Mackenzie took a sip of hot tea and felt the welcome burn trickle down her throat, she sighed in satisfaction, watching Tag squirm on the other side of the glass.

"Not smirking now, is he?" Nick said. "If we weren't desperate, I would have let him sweat it all night long."

The room was cold, clinical, and sterile: white walls, linoleum flooring, and a minimalistic steel table and chairs. It was designed to isolate and intimidate. And it was working. Because despite the chilly temperatures, beads of sweat popped under Tag's hairline.

"Let's try to break the kid." Mackenzie set down her mug and followed Nick.

When she entered the room, she schooled her face into impassivity.

"Why am I here?" Tag asked, annoyed, masking his apprehension.

"We are the ones who ask questions here." Nick clicked his

pen and opened a file. "So, Tag, when did you begin working for King of the Road car rental services?"

Tag narrowed his eyes, his gaze bouncing between Mackenzie and Nick. "Am I under arrest?"

"We told you. We ask the questions here." Mackenzie evaded the question. He was free to leave and not answer any questions. But pressuring him to keep talking was a ploy they often used to get probable cause for a legal arrest.

"You've been working there for three years. Straight out of high school. Was it your lifelong dream to be a receptionist at a car rental company?" Nick asked, trying to get a rise out of him.

Mackenzie saw the gleam in Tag's eyes before it diminished. "Those high school reunions will sure be fun," she added.

"You're being dicks." Tag's head bobbed in jerks, his lips curling in a sneer.

"We don't mean to be." Mackenzie's voice dripped sarcasm. "Of course, you're doing the best you can. Not every young man has goals."

Nick shrugged. "To each their own. If I were in your place, I would have liked more responsibilities, made plans—"

Tag gritted his teeth. "You don't know me! I got plans."

"I'm sure you do," Mackenzie snorted under her breath.

It was the straw that broke the camel's back. Whatever insecurities Tag was concealing beneath his groomed exterior were spilling out.

"You don't know anything," he spat, tipping his chin up. "My job isn't just to answer phones. If you must know, I set up their whole online banking system. I took computer classes at the community college during high school."

"Really?" She raised an eyebrow. "Is that all?"

"And I build important relationships with our clients and make any necessary arrangements."

"What relationships do you need to build? You're a car rental company." Nick egged him on.

"We're not just any company," Tag replied haughtily. "We organize events too."

"Exclusive events?" Mackenzie asked.

"Yes. Not that you'll ever get an invitation," he scoffed, sitting back and puffing out his chest.

They were playing him like an instrument. It didn't hurt that he was a twenty-year-old kid too full of himself.

"Do we need one of these for it?" Nick showed him a picture of the orange wristband.

Tag's eyebrows dived low. "Where did you get that from?"

"A crime scene. A different one this time." Mackenzie clicked her tongue. "Doesn't look good, does it?"

"Unfortunately for us," Nick said, "King of the Road has no virtual presence and is very difficult to find out about. Unfortunately for *you*, you are clearly top dog there, so we can just focus on you. Makes it much easier."

"So what? I'm under arrest now?" Tag challenged, but there was panic rising like a tide behind his eyes.

"You must have been watching the news. Debbie Arnold is missing."

A beat of silence. Tag's face changed like he'd connected some dots. "This is related to her?"

"You tell us. Was Debbie at these exclusive events you speak of?" Mackenzie met his eyes. "Did she rent out of one your expensive cars?"

Before Tag could answer the question, the door to the room clicked open and a short, bald man in a tweed suit walked in. Mackenzie instantly recognized him as defense lawyer Tom Cromwell.

"Don't say anything, Mr. Stuart," he ordered.

"What are you doing here?" Mackenzie asked, reeling from the whiplash of Cromwell appearing out of nowhere. Despite always being cheery, he was ruthless and only had high-profile clients.

"Representing Mr. Stuart." Cromwell remained standing. Tag glanced at him, visibly regaining confidence. "You haven't arrested him. He is under no obligation to answer your questions or even stay here."

Tag stood up, smirking. "Such bullshit."

"Next time you wish to speak to my client, do not do so without me. And no more tricks." Cromwell waggled his forefinger like he was scolding children for stealing candy.

"And how exactly is he affording your expensive services?" Nick demanded.

"Pro bono!" Cromwell cackled. "Your move." Just as quickly as he had arrived, disrupting their process, he whisked Tag away.

Mackenzie's brain stuttered. She felt like she'd been trampled on. "What the hell just happened?"

"I think we rattled someone's cage. The question is, whose?"

TWENTY-FIVE

APRIL 18

The sound of the blender filled Mackenzie's home. With exhaustion threatening to force her eyes shut, she struggled to watch the berries dissolve in the green slush. She looked over her shoulder at the open case files, with several pages spilled out onto the floor. Debbie's financial records. After returning home from yet another disappointing day at work, she had decided to immerse herself in the woman's credit card statements. Debbie had made a lot of money in the last two years, far more than Mackenzie ever would. And her contribution to Lakemore was to rile them up for that one-hour special she did every night. Meanwhile Mackenzie risked her life and worked twenty-hour days to clean up the streets.

Waves of sleep were reaching out, trying to take her under. Even the shower hadn't helped. She was guzzling her smoothie, trying to get energized, when the doorbell rang. She wasn't expecting anyone that early in the morning. She hesitated, then wrapped her hand around the knob.

"Austin?" she almost squealed.

He shouldered past her, despite not being invited inside. "We need to talk."

"Okay..." She noted that he was still dressed in the same clothes as yesterday. Yellow stains peppered his collar, like he'd accidentally dropped instant noodles on himself while eating.

"Do you have any updates?" he asked guardedly.

"You know I can't discuss the progress of an ongoing investigation."

He groaned and pressed his lips in a tight line. "You owe us answers."

"Us?"

"The families of the victims." His words cut her deep. "Three women have been hurt in your name. No fault of their own. I don't even know why Sophie was killed."

"I can't control someone else's actions!" she said hotly and turned away. "I didn't ask for any of this. It's not my fault."

"It's not about blame. It's about compassion." His eyes bored into hers. "Sharing a few details with a trained officer who can help won't hurt the case. But I guess I should have known that Mad Mack doesn't bend the rules."

Mackenzie craned her neck to release the building tension. "Is that why you came here? To give me more shit when I'm working day and night to find out the truth?"

"No." He glanced at the files on the kitchen island, then slid his gaze back to her, finally registering her palpable exhaustion and sleep deprivation. "I came because I might have something."

"What?"

"I saw that kid you were interviewing yesterday. I figured it was something to do with the case. So after he left, I followed him."

"Of course you did." She fell onto a chair, resigned. There was no point in reprimanding or reasoning with Austin. In front of her stood a man who had the means to find closure dangling in front of him.

"I thought I'd talk to him." He began pacing. "Maybe get

him to tell me what you guys talked about. But then I saw him get into this town car that was waiting for him in the parking lot."

"Was it Cromwell's?"

He shook his head. "Cromwell got into another car."

"Tag works for a car rental company. They must have sent him a ride."

He rocked back and forth on his heels. "Yeah... I didn't know that, but I was curious about him. So I followed him."

"Where to?"

"Tombstone."

The word sparked a fetid feeling inside Mackenzie's stomach.

"Where exactly in Tombstone?" she asked.

"I don't know the area well. I've never had to go there in the year I've been in Lakemore. But it was on a hill. A big colonial-style house. He went inside. I waited in my car for about fifteen minutes before I had to leave because of work."

There was a hill. Mackenzie had seen it yesterday. From a distance, it was just an expanse of green; she never knew that there were houses up there.

"Did you get the house number?"

"No. But I took a picture." He showed her his phone eagerly.

The exterior was made of rich red brick. Intricately designed panel doors in the center, with a decorative crown above the entry. A medium pitched roof with square-cut weaves. There was a faint glow around the building, which was otherwise surrounded by thick woods where light seemed to die.

Mackenzie remembered Tag's background information. His address was listed as nowhere near this place. He lived in Olympia. This house clearly shouted money, and someone had sent a car and taken him straight there.

"I'll look into it," she promised, her heart jackhammering at this new flicker of hope.

Mackenzie took pride in not having any vices. Which was why today seemed like a big day. The day another thing about her changed. In the break room, she sipped on black coffee and gagged. Austin's words kept playing in her head.

You owe us answers.

Three women have been hurt in your name.

It was like a monumental weight on her shoulders. Logic dictated that this wasn't her fault. Logic dictated that she needed to compartmentalize and focus on her job. But why did logic fail so often in the face of fear? Fear of more people dying. Fear of irreparable hurt. Fear of spiraling guilt.

"Who would have thought?" Nick's voice came from behind her, and she jumped.

"Jesus, Nick."

"How the mighty have fallen." He rummaged through a basket of snacks. "What's the story?"

She swallowed a few more sips before emptying the cup in the sink. "Disgusting. There's no story. I'm running on very little sleep, and we have that meeting in a few minutes. You're hoarding."

He had candies and chips in his arms. "Turner brought his kid to work. They're waiting for his sister to pick him up. Poor guy isn't feeling too well."

"Robbie's here?"

"Yeah."

She hurried after Nick, eager to see the boy again. He was in the lounge, concentrating on an iPad, his little tongue poking out. Seeing him loosened something inside Mackenzie's chest.

"Hey, kid."

He looked up and smiled brightly, revealing a gap in his teeth. "Mack."

"You lost a tooth!" She raised her hand. "That's great."

He gave her a high-five. "Are those for me?"

Nick put the snacks next to him. "Yup. I don't know what you like, so here's everything."

"Are you not feeling well?" Mackenzie asked.

"Just a stomach ache."

"How did you lose your tooth?" Nick asked.

Robbie grinned and began telling them an animated story about how his tooth had come out at school. A smile was plastered on Mackenzie's face, which collapsed when she saw a familiar figure approaching them.

It was Jane Doe. Timid and tiny, hiding behind Andrew and trying to dissolve into the baggy hoodie she wore, she glanced around at the cops with suspicion swimming in her eyes. She kept chewing her dry lips and let her dark bangs hide her face. But when she saw Mackenzie, she looked up, not hiding anymore.

"Morning." Andrew smiled. "I thought I should bring her to the station to have a look around. She's been cramped at that motel."

"Hello," Mackenzie said. "This is my partner, Detective Nick Blackwood."

Jane Doe eyed Nick with total disinterest. It was not the reaction Nick usually elicited from women.

"Are you from Lakemore?" he asked.

She turned to Mackenzie and pointed at her watch. "Nice watch."

"Thank you." Mackenzie touched it. "It was my... father's."

"Would you like some snacks?" Nick asked.

Jane Doe sat on the chair next to Robbie. He offered her a pack of Skittles, which she gladly accepted. She didn't seem to flinch away from the boy or pointedly ignore him. Perhaps it was his innocence that made her feel safe.

"How's she doing?" Nick asked in a low voice.

Andrew didn't look happy. "I'm getting more one-word responses, but she still goes catatonic when I ask her who she is and what happened. The comment about your watch, Detective Price, is the first time she has initiated conversation."

"I can imagine she feels safer around me, since I'm a woman," Mackenzie guessed. "The way I found her, with all those bruises and torn clothes... It doesn't take a genius to deduce what she went through."

"It is a possibility I strongly considered, which is why I brought her here. We were in Lieutenant Rivera's office, but she didn't seem interested in the lieutenant. She wasn't as jumpy as before, but she was still quiet and mostly non-responsive."

"I don't know what to make of this," Mackenzie confessed.

"She's anchored to you," Andrew said simply. "You were the first person she saw after she escaped whatever ordeal she was running from. You saved her. It's the only thing that explains this attachment."

"Well, at least I'll have an ally if this town decides to burn me alive," she muttered. "We're getting late for our meeting. We'll see you in a bit."

"I told you to avoid the news," Nick said on their way to Sully's office.

"Sterling knows the killings and disappearances are related to me."

His eyebrows shot up. "How?"

"People talk." Her chest tightened. "How long do you think before someone slips it to the media?"

Nick didn't reply. His silence was blaring, and his muscles had gone rigid.

Entering Sully's office, she noticed crayons of different colors on his desk. A coloring book was open, and the sergeant was feverishly filling in the shapes. Rivera sat across from him, thumbing her phone, used to Sully's nuances.

"We just got off the phone with the sheriff's department and with the Riverview PD." Rivera removed her glasses. "There's no trace of Debbie. The woods around the news station have been thoroughly searched. Riverview PD had a few tips, but they're all bogus. What do you have?"

Mackenzie updated them on the connection with the car rental company. "It's the only tangible link we have between the two cases."

"The only way is to get into the company's books," Nick said. "If we can get the client list and who the company belongs to, we can get to the bottom of this. With Tag's involvement, our affidavit is stronger, so we're hoping—"

"We got nothing," Sully said, still coloring in the book.

"What do you mean?" Nick inquired.

"Didn't you hear? Our servers went down last night. When they came back up, random files had been deleted." Sully's face was grim. "Including the surveillance video from the school showing the car."

Mackenzie's mouth fell open. "*What?*"

"Clint's been trying to salvage the missing data, but he's got nothing. Why do you think I'm coloring?" He lifted the book to show a half-finished peacock. "Even the Special Investigations Unit was hit."

"What about backup servers?" she asked.

"Those were hit too." Rivera glowered. "A lot of ongoing investigations have been compromised."

"We'll contact the school again to get the footage," Nick said.

Rivera sounded annoyed. "Do you have any other leads?"

"An address." Mackenzie spoke up. "We believe it's linked to the rental company."

"How did you get it?"

"The shop owner who sold the wristbands. He remembered something later." Mackenzie conjured the lie in a heartbeat, knowing it was best to keep Austin out of this until things cooled down a bit.

"Okay. Follow that up," Rivera ordered.

"One more thing." Nick shifted uneasily. "I think we need to tighten measures around here."

"What do you mean?" Sully picked up a pink crayon.

"There have been leaks. I'm concerned that whoever is talking might speak to the media next. I suggest we crack down on the source and suspend them." Fire raged in his eyes. "Send a real message as opposed to empty warnings."

"Okay, I don't want anyone losing their job over this." Mackenzie placed a hand on his shoulder.

"He's right, Detective Price." Rivera raised an eyebrow. "Nobody will lose their job. But there will be consequences. Everything will plunge into chaos if we just sit around."

The car weaved along the winding shingly road up the hill. The afternoon sun was invisible behind swollen clouds ready to burst. Whooshing breezes blew leaves and sticks onto the windshield. Tall trees swayed, bending at angles, as if the wind was trying to uproot them from the ground. The higher Mackenzie got, the more isolated she felt.

"Can't complain about Austin's transgression if it leads us somewhere," Nick said with an unlit cigarette hanging from his lips. "By the way, what do you think of Jane Doe?"

"I feel sorry for her, I suppose." She sighed. "We circulated her information all around Washington, but no one recognizes her. She has refused to let her picture be printed in the papers for any family or friends to reach out."

"She's probably scared out of her mind that whoever hurt

her will find her again if she agrees to that. Such a backward world we live in."

A few houses came into view. But they were rickety, nothing as posh as the one Austin had seen Tag walk into. "Who even lives here?"

"They look abandoned."

The houses appeared to be decades old, with wear and tear that had never been repaired. Over the years, storms had caused a lot of damage, but no one had bothered to fix anything. Some of the doors and windows were open, almost as if the residents had left suddenly.

The house finally came into view.

"There it is." Mackenzie pointed ahead.

Nick slowed the car and whistled. "That's fancy. Wonder who it belongs to."

The spacious house had been maintained well. It looked like extravagant Southern architecture.

When they climbed out of the car, Mackenzie gasped. There was a sharp chill in the air. Currents danced on her skin.

"Maybe there is some truth to this place being haunted," she whispered.

"Don't tell me now that you believe in ghosts."

"So you don't feel anything?"

He looked uncomfortable. "That doesn't mean anything."

"I don't know, Nick. Some places have weird energies." Mackenzie had never been the superstitious type. But she couldn't deny how starkly different this place was.

They walked up the empty driveway and rang the bell. No answer.

Nick drew a frustrated breath and pounded his fist on the door. The sound was carried by the wind. But there was still no response. Curtains were drawn in all the windows, blocking the view inside.

"Looks like no one's home." Mackenzie shoved her hands in her pockets.

"Well now at least we know the exact address." Nick took out his phone. "I'll ask Clint to find out who this house is registered to. As soon as I get some signal in this goddam place."

While Nick wandered about trying to catch some bars on his phone, Mackenzie circled the house, hoping to find a window that would give her a peek at what was inside. But the building was just as opaque as the woods surrounding it. There was no backyard either. Why anyone would actually live here was beyond her. She was walking back to the front when she saw someone from the corner of her eye and jolted.

"Oh my God!" she gasped, her heart jackknifing in her chest.

An old woman wearing a long, tattered black coat stood a few feet away from her. Her skin was wrinkled and sagging. She had thin lips and a bulbous nose with black spots. Her gray hair was in dreadlocks around her face, and her back was slightly bowed. She looked like she had crawled out of a hole in the ground. The only striking thing about her were her dark blue eyes, which were wide and blazing.

"Hello, ma'am." Mackenzie stepped closer, then stopped. The woman smelled like death. "I'm Detective Price from the Lakemore PD. Do you know who lives in this house?"

"Nobody." Her voice sounded like she was being strangled.

Mackenzie's eyes drifted to her neck. Strange marks, X-shaped grooves, were branded on her skin. A group of ravens flew across behind her, making a deep croaking sound.

"We're looking for a missing person," Mackenzie explained, hoping the woman would be more cooperative. But she only stared at Mackenzie as if the latter were a ghost.

"They come here sometimes," she whispered. "They'll be here tonight after the sun goes down."

"Who?"

"Mack!" Nick's voice boomed.

Mackenzie was about to respond when the woman stepped forward and wrapped her icy hands around her wrist, making her heart climb up in her throat.

"We've been waiting a long time. This land can't handle any more spilled blood."

Mackenzie wrenched her arm free and stumbled back. The woman stood frozen like a statue.

"Nick!" she cried, turning and running in the direction of his voice.

When she reached him, he grabbed her shoulders. "Mack. You're as white as a ghost. What happened?"

"There's this old woman. She was saying such strange things." She pulled him behind her. "Come with me."

But when she turned the corner, there was nobody there.

"What the hell?" She looked around, seeing no sign of the woman. She had vanished without a trace. "She was right here!"

"Where did she go?"

"I..." Cold sweat matted her scalp. Her teeth chattered as her eyes scanned her surroundings. "I don't know. But we need to come back here after sunset."

TWENTY-SIX

Nick's laughter rang around the car. Mackenzie crossed her arms and pouted. He looked at her expression and snickered again.

"It's not funny." She ground her jaw.

"An old lady appeared out of nowhere, grabbed your hand, and said, 'This land can't handle any more spilled blood.'" He wiped a tear.

"I should not have told you."

"Boy, you must be really sleep-deprived to be full-ass hallucinating."

"Yeah? Then why are we here?"

The sky was darkening to a dusky shade. Light drained away as the last rays of the sun peeled off. The sound of nocturnal animals was beginning to grow louder. If it were the city, there would be a stream of lights and sounds. But on this hill, there was nothing but stillness.

They had parked a bit away from the house, behind one of the abandoned buildings. They had a good view of the house without being seen themselves. Furthermore, the lack of streetlights helped them stay hidden.

"Clint needs more time to figure out who the property belongs to," Nick admitted. "The person it was registered to in the county records has been dead for the last twenty-plus years. He's going to hunt down whoever's paying for utilities. Clearly someone is." He gestured at the lit-up windows.

"Aha, so you're not entirely dismissing what happened."

"Technically anything is possible. Even if the chances are less than one percent. It's not like we have any other solid leads to follow up on at the moment."

Right on cue, a light appeared, shining bright against the darkness. Soon, two headlights came into view.

"Look at that." Mackenzie watched through binoculars. A black town car had driven up the road and stopped in front of the house. She recited the number plate, which Nick typed into his phone. The door to the back seat opened and someone got out. "I can't tell who it is. It's too dark."

"Can you tell if it's a man or a woman?"

"Maybe a man? But I'm not sure."

The shadowy figure knocked on the front door, which opened a sliver before being pulled wide. The figure slipped inside and the town car drove away.

"We can definitely just go in now, don't you think?" Mackenzie asked, unbuckling her seat belt.

But then another car arrived.

"Wait. Let's see what happens," Nick suggested.

In the next twenty minutes, fifteen more cars swarmed up to the house, dropping off people whose faces Mackenzie and Nick couldn't make out in the dark.

"Guess my hallucination was correct." Mackenzie couldn't stop herself from rubbing it in.

"Look." Nick pointed through the windshield.

She peered through the binoculars. Someone had stepped out of yet another car. He was on his phone, and the glow from the screen illuminated his face long enough for

Mackenzie to recognize him. "Isn't that Mayor Rathbone's chief of staff?"

"Shit," Nick hissed.

"I feel like we've just walked into something we shouldn't have."

He tapped the wheel to some random tune. "We've had seventeen cars drop off seventeen people. Are they having a meeting?"

"Could be. I don't know. We'll have to go in and ask." She was about to open the car door when her phone rang. It was Peterson. "Hello?"

"Detective Price." Peterson's voice was laced with unease, and there was a drone of mutterings and movements around him. "You need to come to the quarry."

Her stomach folded in on itself. "Why?"

"We found Debbie."

TWENTY-SEVEN

It was a sticky night. One of those nights when the air swelled with moisture, becoming soupy and viscous. But it just wouldn't rain. Even the blackness around them felt dense and thick. The beams from the headlights illuminated the way ahead, but all Mackenzie saw was the abyss in front of her. It was so close, within reach of her fingertips. Like no matter which path she continued to go down, all roads led to there. It didn't chase her. It wasn't a predator. It was an inevitability. Nick was silent next to her. But she could feel the worry radiating from him. His hands fidgeted on the wheel. No voice came out of her either. Nothing went on inside her brain. All she could focus on was the feeling of being smothered.

Three women have been hurt in your name.

Three women had been *murdered* in her name.

Austin, Brett and his two children, and now Noor. One more innocent person whose life had been torn apart. One more innocent person who would have to learn to re-stitch the fragments of their life around a giant gaping hole left by the loss of someone they loved.

Nick finally came to a stop. She realized they had reached

the quarry. Ahead of her were three squad cars, their red and blue lights illuminating the area. Uniforms were spread around, some of them standing in groups, peering down into the giant hole in the ground. Artificial lighting had been installed, the beams all pointing to where the body must be.

"Detectives." Peterson nodded, coming up to them as soon as they exited the car.

"Who found the body?" Nick asked. "I thought we'd covered this area."

"Patrol did. We searched here yesterday."

"At least we know when it was dumped," Nick said.

Mackenzie's feet carried her closer to the edge, dreading what was waiting for her. She gazed down. Debbie was sprawled against the slabs of jagged rock. Unnaturally contorted. She was wearing the black dress she was last seen in. Her blonde hair gleamed in the lights. She looked like a doll on stage under a spotlight.

"It looks like the killer rolled the body down the quarry, but it got stuck on the way," Peterson said. "We're waiting for the techs to arrive to take pictures before we bring her back up."

Mackenzie paced, biting the pad of her thumb as the crime-scene unit arrived behind the coroner's van. Her limbs felt shaky. Nervousness bubbled inside her. What message was she going to find this time?

"The quarry." Nick came up to her, a muscle ticking in his jaw. "Last time the body was left in that barn, which was also one of our cases."

"The quarry was your case, though. I wasn't here at the time."

"Yes, but it's related to our case from last year. You mentioned it in your documentary."

For the next thirty minutes, they waited as the techs put on protective gear and climbed down. Uniform unrolled the yellow crime-scene tape. Investigators placed evidence markers close to the quarry edge, around the disturbed soil.

Finally the body was transferred onto a gurney and lifted slowly so as to not compromise the remains.

Becky removed her skullcap and mask as she approached them. "That's Debbie all right."

"Can you tell anything yet? How long has she been dead?" Nick asked.

"There's lividity, and she's cold. I'd say around eighteen to twenty hours." She inspected Mackenzie. "She's almost as pale as you look right now."

"Is there a message?" Mackenzie asked, her voice breaking.

Becky nodded. She gestured to the techs carrying the gurney to pause next to her.

When Mackenzie saw Debbie's face, her breath tore inside her throat. It wasn't just that it was unnaturally white. There were words written on it in blood. A sentence. The first two words on her forehead. One on each cheek. And the last on her chin.

My. Gift. To. You. Mack.

TWENTY-EIGHT

Mackenzie's senses were diluted. She had tunnel vision. All she heard was the drumming of her heart in her ears. She had barely registered Nick dropping her off at home or whether any conversation had happened. She entered her home, locked the door behind her, and took off her clothes, still dizzy from the sight of Debbie's body and the message left on her face in blood.

Everything was hazy and buzzing with tension and unpleasantness. Like the air itself was cinched with something putrid. All she wanted to do was scrub it off, get inside her head and scrape away the parts of her brain that held those memories. She wanted a clean slate.

Steam rose around her. She rubbed her skin, applying soap three times, until she felt clean. She felt like this case and this killer had dirtied her. Each time she blinked, she could see the faces of the CSI and uniformed cops, and how they looked at her and whispered to each other. How Debbie was murdered as a *gift* to Mackenzie.

Once she was finished, she analyzed her naked body in front of the mirror. The water had been almost boiling hot. Patches of her skin were red. Angry lines ran across from her scratching herself clean. Her reflection reminded her of some tragic sculpture. Underneath all that aggression, there was a frightened woman.

The tears didn't come. She crawled into bed still naked, hating the feeling of being trapped—in this case, in this body, in this life. For the first time in years, she regretted coming back to Lakemore.

Why hadn't she stayed away? Those women would still have been alive.

As sleep pulled her in, she found herself in the living room. Stunned, she paced around, then stopped dead in her tracks. Sophie stood in front of her.

Mackenzie wheezed and clutched her throat. Her hands flailed, knocking over the lamp. She turned around to run up the stairs, but almost bumped into Courtney.

"Please... please..." she choked, hot tears streaming down her cheeks.

She made a run for the front door. She didn't care; she'd run screaming down the street if she had to. But Debbie popped up there, blocking the only way out.

Spinning on her heel again, she realized that Sophie, Courtney, and Debbie had disappeared. She was alone in her living room. But she didn't feel alone. There was something wrong about this silence.

She wasn't alone.

Sitting in the armchair was a shadowy figure. Someone whose face was too fuzzy. They were eerily still. And even though Mackenzie could make out nothing about them, she was hypnotized and rendered still. Too scared to move. Too scared to breathe. Completely and utterly at the mercy of this shadow.

She felt like she was floating. Her bones weighed nothing. It wasn't gravity holding her in place, but the shadow.

She sat across from it and met its stare evenly. Eventually her hammering heart beat to a steady rhythm. Her dashing pulse slowed. The cold numbness tightening her skin evaporated. Finally she was able to move. She stood up and walked away. There was no fear holding her back.

She'd won.

April 19

Mackenzie woke with a jolt. Both the events from last night and the nightmare washed over her. Morning light filtered through the slats of the blinds into her bedroom. She checked her watch. It was already eight o'clock. There was no time to go for a run to clear her mind. Once she was showered and dressed, she came downstairs—and screamed.

"Ah!" She grabbed the railing, almost falling.

Nick was asleep on the couch on his stomach, his blazer on the floor and one arm hanging freely. He stirred awake and looked up with sleepy eyes. "What?"

"When did you get here? What's going on?" Her voice came out shrill.

He sat up, rubbing the slumber from his eyes. "Well, last night I told you I was crashing, since you looked like you were... possessed."

"Huh?" She had no memory of it. "Really?"

"How do you think I got in?" He fixed his tie and went to the kitchen sink to splash water on his face. "Kind of offensive if you think I broke in to sleep on your uncomfortable couch."

To Mackenzie's horror, she realized she had slept naked last night. If she didn't remember him spending the night on her couch, what if she'd forgotten taking a trip to the kitchen in the middle of the night to fetch water? "So... you just slept? Nothing happened?"

He turned on the faucet and filled a glass with water. "What would happen?"

"Oh, I mean I didn't bother you?" When he drank the water slowly, she got annoyed. "Well?"

"No, you didn't bother me," he replied, bemused. "Your car is still at the station. I need to go home and shower first."

"I'll take a cab to work."

He smoothed his collar and sleeves and was about to head out when his phone trilled. "It's Clint... Hello?"

Mackenzie watched his expression change. The laziness dissolving into indignation. He hung up and clutched the phone tightly in his hands, making the cords in his arms strain.

"What did he say?"

"Clint traced the account being used to pay for utilities at that house," he said. "It belongs to Sylvia Hamilton."

"Who's Sylvia Hamilton?"

"Judge Hamilton's wife."

TWENTY-NINE

Lieutenant Rivera looked sharp as she approached the podium and nodded at the throng of reporters flashing cameras at her. "The Lakemore PD is disheartened to share that the remains of Deborah Arnold, more commonly known as Debbie, were found yesterday evening. Ms. Arnold's partner, Ms. Khan, was informed last night and is being kept in the loop. There is clear evidence of foul play; however, at this stage of the investigation we don't have any suspects. We request the residents of Lakemore to come forward with any information pertaining to the investigation and hope the coverage of this case is dignified. Our deepest condolences to Ms. Khan and the colleagues and ardent viewers of Ms. Arnold."

Sully closed the video. "We're all going to be in for a bumpy ride."

Mackenzie was seated across from him. Sully hadn't mentioned anything about the message left for her on Debbie's face. She was waiting for it. Having worked with her boss for nine years now, she knew that the man wasn't a fan of uncomfortable conversations.

"Nick and I are going to talk to the judge today," she said.

"Now that we know he has a connection to the case, it explains why he refused to sign the warrant."

Sully drummed his fingers on the table. "But in your warrant, there was no mention of the house, right? How did you find out about it?"

Mackenzie faltered, scratching her head, trying to scramble for an explanation. But she couldn't lie. It all had to go into a report anyway. When she related the story to Sully, she waited for him to bark a laugh like Nick had.

"Oh! Her!" Sully's mouth fell open, and a look of wonderment crossed his face. "She's still alive?"

"You know her?"

He grinned. "Why, yes. That's Mallory. Gray dreadlocks, you said?"

"Yes!" Mackenzie perked up. "How do you know her?"

"It was over twenty years ago—I had just joined the force straight out of the academy. A young woman had gone missing, and I went to Tombstone to ask around. Mallory appeared out of nowhere, and said something cryptic about how the woman I was looking for was long gone and now wasn't the right time."

"Guess that's her MO, to speak in riddles. Did you find that missing woman?"

He shook his head. "We didn't have much hope anyway. She had a history of running away. But a creepy encounter like that, especially in your first year, stays with you." He popped some gum in his mouth. "Other people have run into her too."

Mackenzie felt a burst of relief that there was a logical explanation. "Well, that settles it."

"Regarding Debbie." Sully finally approached the topic while trying to fit a thread through a needle—his latest hobby. "Everyone who was there last night has been ordered not to disclose the message found on her face. We have requested that the crime-scene unit and medical examiner's office share case files only with senior staff who can be trusted. We're doing everything we can to ensure the details aren't leaked."

"Oh, don't worry, Sully." She crossed her legs, trying to make light of the situation. "I won't sue the department if the information gets out."

He paused and set the needle aside. "It's not about lawsuits, Mack. It's about your safety."

"We're back at that."

"If word got out that Debbie was murdered as a *gift* to you, how many people do you think will come after you?"

The Hamiltons lived in a modest apartment in Lakemore. Judge Hamilton had been a vocal advocate for mental health since he was a young man in law school. Over the years, while other older people had refused to learn basics like how Facebook made money, Hamilton had adapted and used social media to hone his image and further important causes.

"Everyone likes Hamilton," Nick said, walking up the carpeted staircase. "He's one of the good ones."

"Yeah, I guess posting things on social media makes you a nice person." Mackenzie tightened her ponytail.

Nick stopped at the landing and turned around. "Spit it out. What happened with Sully?"

She paused a few steps below him. "How do you know?"

"Just your typical tendency to resort to sarcasm when you're stressed out."

Sully's warning had stuck with her. Just when she was trying to be brave and face her fears head on, something else would happen that would almost undo her efforts.

"Sully told me that there might be serious consequences. Not just for the town, but for me personally."

Nick didn't say anything. He crossed his arms, brooding, before turning to knock on the door.

To Mackenzie's surprise, the judge opened the door himself, dressed in tennis attire—white shorts and red polo. In her experience, whenever she visited high-profile people of interest, it was usually a lawyer or a secretary who greeted her.

"Judge Hamilton," she said. "Your clerk told us you were working from home today."

Hamilton was a short, lean man with gray hair but fairly young-looking skin. He had a gentle face, big doe-like eyes, a small nose and thin lips. Something about him screamed that he was a reliable person. Like he didn't belong behind a bench, but in a classroom teaching young kids about the civil war.

"Yes, yes, I have a migraine today." He gestured them to follow him to his office.

On the way, Mackenzie noted how basic his living arrangements were. The walls were covered in family pictures. The furniture was IKEA. The Persian rug was faded, with loose threads. He pushed open the double doors to his office. Floor-to-ceiling shelves were filled with thick-spined law books. There was a large wooden table in the center with scratches and chipped polish.

"It was my great-grandfather's." Hamilton sat behind it, noticing Mackenzie's interest. "Are you here about those warrants I didn't sign? This is a bit unorthodox."

"Actually, no." Mackenzie pulled a chair next to Nick. "Do you own a house in Tombstone?"

She felt Nick glare at her. Even she hadn't been expecting to dive into the topic right away. Usually when interrogating people familiar with the system, it was better to be tactful and manipulative. But her patience was wearing thin. She was done being pushed into a corner. She was ready to show some teeth.

Hamilton's eye twitched. "Yes. I do."

"Why?" she asked.

"What do you mean, *why*?"

"Real estate is usually a good investment, unless it's in

Tombstone. Prices will never go up there, and it's hardly a place to get away."

Hamilton glanced at Nick, who just shrugged. "That house has been in my wife's family for three generations. We haven't been able to sell it for the reason you just said."

Nick cleared his throat, a sign to tell Mackenzie to cool down. "Judge, you know the case we're on. There is a link to your house."

"Dear God." Hamilton looked appalled. "How?"

"That car rental company we mentioned in our warrant. King of the Road," Nick said. "One of its key employees was seen entering that house after we had pulled him in for interrogation."

"And last night, during surveillance, we saw many people enter the house. All of them came in town cars registered to that company."

Hamilton's forehead bunched. "What are you implying?"

"What went down last night?" Mackenzie asked.

"What went down?" He barked a laugh that didn't reach his eyes. "Around once a month, some of us get together for a poker night. A few friends hanging out like a gentlemen's club. That's all that house is for. I don't have enough space in this apartment and others can't host at home, since they have wives and families they don't want to disturb."

"Then why was there a car waiting for Tag that took him straight to your house from the police station two nights ago?" she volleyed back. "Was there another poker night that he was invited to? He doesn't look like the type who hangs out with the likes of you, Judge."

Hamilton rolled his eyes and sighed. "I don't know who this Tag is. Besides, I'm not the only one with keys to the house. Every man in our gentlemen's club has a set."

Mackenzie and Nick exchanged a look.

"Where were you two nights ago?" Mackenzie asked.

"Presiding over a trial. The jury returned a verdict in two hours. Please go ahead and confirm."

"Then we would really appreciate a list of the members of your club," Nick said.

Hamilton fidgeted in his seat. "I'm afraid I can't do that."

"Why not?" Mackenzie asked.

"Why do you want it? To find out who knows this Ted person?"

"Tag," she corrected. "Yes. We need information about that company and Tag seems to be our only feasible link, especially since it was *you* who refused to approve our warrant."

"Detective Price, you are free to go to other judges. Just because *I* refused doesn't mean you've hit a dead end. I would have approved, but circumstances are different now."

"Circumstances?" Nick leaned forward.

Hamilton pursed his lips, wrestling internally with something. "Look. There's an... expectation now. Lakemore's economy has taken heavy casualties following the outcomes of some of your cases. Surely you know that." Mackenzie already hated where this was going. "Things in this town are looking up, but they're not as good as your mayor has been portraying them to be. It's all to attract investments like Rafael Jennings."

"I don't follow." Nick shook his head.

"Your town cannot afford to lose more business, Detectives," Hamilton declared firmly. "You have a reputation for being anti-business."

"We're not anti-business. We're trying to put murderers and rapists in jail!" Mackenzie raised her voice.

"The unemployment rate had reached ten percent, Detective Price! We've had to undo the damage." His voice boomed. That gentle quality had evaporated from his face. "It's easy to declare that justice has been done when you're not collateral damage, when you're not the one who lost your livelihood and have bills piling up."

"So what are we supposed to do? Let rich killers walk free because they're kind enough to pay salaries?" she snapped.

"Of course not." He scowled. "Definitely not. But if you think people above you in the food chain, people who have been elected, aren't going to step in and try to fix things, you're mistaken."

"Are you saying that judges have been told to protect businesses in criminal investigations?" Nick rubbed his jaw.

"No, Nick. Nothing of that sort. All this is hypothetical." Hamilton winked. "Do your jobs better. And if you think I'm being unreasonable, you are free to send your warrant to other judges."

"Why won't you give us the names of your friends then?" Mackenzie asked. "Your gentlemen's club isn't a business. It's a social gathering."

"Because I don't want to piss people off," he huffed. "Our poker nights are an escape. It's private. They wouldn't appreciate unnecessary intrusion."

"Three women have been murdered and you are worried about offending your—"

"Detective Price, can you actually tell me that some low-level employee of the car rental company coming to the house is hard evidence that will lead you to your killer? Why stop there? Why not find out where he gets his hair cut?"

"Like we said before, your friends all arrived at your house in cars registered to that company," Nick said.

"Coincidence." The archaic-looking landline on the desk rang. Hamilton picked it up. "Hello? Yes... okay... I'll get on it. Give me a minute." He hung up. "Look, that company provides good cars. One person must have recommended it to the rest. That's how these things go. But like I said before, feel free to take your argument to another judge. And if you want the names of everyone in our gentlemen's club, get a warrant. Now, if you'll excuse me, you can see yourselves out."

Mackenzie's stare remained pinned at Hamilton, who opened some documents, ignoring her completely. She followed Nick out of the apartment, clicking the door shut behind them.

"Is it just me, or did Hamilton sort of make sense?" Nick said as they headed down to the car. "I mean, think about it. The killer is obsessed with you. Something tells me they're not some sixty-year-old man playing poker."

Before Mackenzie could manage a response, her phone rang. It was Becky.

"Hey, Becky, are you done with the autopsy?"

"I am. You and Nick need to come down here right away. I found something inside Debbie's stomach."

THIRTY

Becky held up an evidence bag containing a small black disk covered in reddish juices. Mackenzie brought her face close and peered at it.

"What is it?" she asked.

"It's a memory card," Becky said. "I know keto diet is all the rage these days, but it doesn't involve eating memory cards. Please take this."

Nick grabbed the bag. "Clint will know how to clean it up. Can't wait to see his face when he sees it. Do you have anything else?"

They were in Becky's office, which was next to the room where she cut open dead bodies. Despite the labs being renovated, the offices and hallways were still squalid, with yellow walls, as if the building was permanently jaundiced. Behind her, books were spilling out of shelves and her framed certificates hung crookedly.

"Cause of death was a gunshot to the chest." Becky showed them a picture of the bullet wound in Debbie's ribcage. "A .38."

"That's different from Courtney," Mackenzie mused. "She was jabbed in the brain through the ear."

"And Sophie was strangled," Nick added.

"Our latest victim was tortured too." Becky displayed two pictures of Debbie's body. The first showed purple marks criss-crossing her bare back. "She was flogged." The second was a view of her mouth, opened with gloved hands, her tongue outstretched with forceps. The tip was missing. "Her tongue was cut. Blood aspiration there tells us that this was done while she was still alive."

Mackenzie's gut felt hot, like it had been torched with gasoline. She squirmed in the chair, fighting a wave of nausea.

My gift to you, Mack.

"They're escalating." Nick played with his lighter. "Courtney was killed immediately. But Debbie was kept alive and tortured."

"Debbie had been badmouthing me lately. I bet in the killer's twisted mind they thought the punishment should fit the crime."

"I've bagged everything else and sent it to Anthony. This is all I could get from her," Becky said with pity swimming in her eyes. "Mack, I'm sorry."

"Everyone should play nice with me now." The words poured out of her. "Otherwise, one more body for you to cut open."

A part of her felt like a sullen child throwing a tantrum. But there was a stinging truth to the words she spewed. The killer was still out there, getting bolder. And Mackenzie was a police officer who had plenty of enemies for them to pick next.

"Close your eyes," Andrew instructed.

Mackenzie did as she was told, welcoming the blackness. Sully had taken one look at her after she'd found out Debbie's fate and sent her to Andrew for a session. To ensure them privacy, he had lent them his office while he attended a meeting.

"What do you think they look like?" Andrew asked in that therapist tone she had come to identify. A cross between curious and mollifying.

"Who?"

"The person who is hurting those who hurt you."

She dug her nails into her palms. "You mean the *murderer*."

"Yes," he said after a pause. "Can you picture them?"

"No."

"Why not?"

"It humanizes them." She had refrained from thinking about them. She was already entangled in the case, already occupying real estate in the mind of someone deranged. In an effort to hold on to the little power she had left in this situation, she had decided to put as much as distance as she could between her and the killer, to not let them take over her thoughts, which was perhaps what they wanted.

"Surely you've seen worse. You've dealt with child killers. Do you hate this killer more because they're making this about you?"

"Yes," she blurted, her eyes still closed. "I know it's narcissistic of me—"

"No, no, it isn't. They're the one who made it about you," he assured her kindly. "But if you refuse to humanize them, that means you refuse to understand them."

"Such people don't deserve to be understood." She gritted her teeth. The bruises left on Debbie's back and her cut tongue flashed in her mind.

"I may be new here, Detective Price." Andrew sighed. "But I know you wouldn't have earned your reputation for being a good detective if you weren't analyzing the criminals."

Mackenzie remained quiet.

"It is natural to want to understand human nature. It's a way of understanding yourself."

"I don't know what that means."

"That's why I'm asking—how do you picture them?"

What *did* they look like? Was it some unhealthy, ugly man living in his parents' basement? Or was it someone around her? A friendly face, intelligent and charming, hiding someone completely unhinged? Despite the options floating through her head, whenever she closed her eyes all she could picture was a shadowy figure. Someone shapeless made of black smoke. Sitting across from her, completely placid.

"Get closer to them," Andrew said. She must have described the figure aloud.

She wasn't in Sully's office anymore. She was in her living room again, bathed in a golden light. Andrew was next to her, both of them facing the shadow in the armchair.

"If you don't go after them, they'll keep coming after you." She felt Andrew's hot breath in her ear.

Her legs carried her forward. The shadow remained still. But as she got closer, an Arctic chill swept through her. Lowering herself level with the shadow, she could see patches of skin behind the swirling smog. "I know her."

"*Her?*" Andrew sounded surprised.

"I thought I had to save her." She waved her hand over the face, clearing away the smoke. Wisps of it dissipated, revealing Melody. "Mom?"

She opened her eyes and snapped out of it. "What the hell?"

"You said *Mom*?" Andrew was sitting across from her. She was in Sully's office.

"What just happened?"

"Hypnosis. It's a way to reach to your subconscious. And it's interesting that you thought of your mom. I thought she passed away a very long time ago?"

"Yes. She did." Mackenzie stood up. "I have work to do."

She ignored Andrew calling out to her and almost sprinted away. Catching up with Nick by the water cooler, she griped about the session.

"What a waste of time."

"Reach any interesting conclusions?" He poured himself some water.

"Of course not. I don't believe in that mumbo-jumbo." She crossed her arms. "Read too much into anything and anyone can find *some* interpretation of it."

Nick's lips twitched in amusement. "My mother was a psychologist."

"Shit!" she gasped. "I didn't mean... I'm sure there is..." When he started laughing, she widened her eyes. "Very funny. Hilarious, actually."

"I had to."

Clint appeared at the end of the hallway, along with Peterson. "I got something."

Mackenzie and Nick chucked their cups in the garbage and followed him to his office downstairs.

"The memory card isn't completely damaged," Clint told them. "I was concerned because Becky told me that stomach acid can be extremely acidic. She said Debbie must have swallowed the card right before she was killed."

"Something must be on that card," Nick said, excited. "Debbie was always a smart one."

They waited as Clint opened a folder.

"Using data recovery software, I was able to retrieve one file. There are at least twenty more. I will need time and access to proprietary software and then maybe I'll be able to get more. But I can't promise anything. Some of the data is definitely lost for good."

"What kind of file did you get?" Peterson asked.

"Two pictures." Clint opened them side by side.

It was a piece of land captured from two different angles. Surrounded by tall pine trees cut into conical shapes. There were weeds sprouting out of the ground, but the rest of the foliage had been removed. It was evident that this vast area right in the middle of the woods had been artificially created.

"What's the significance of this?" Nick frowned. "Was it cleared for construction?"

"I know this area," Peterson said suddenly.

"Where is it?" Mackenzie asked.

Sweat beaded his nose, making it shine. His eyes bounced between Mackenzie and Nick before he finally answered. "Tombstone."

THIRTY-ONE

It was the third time Mackenzie had returned to the most wretched place in Lakemore. It was a full-moon night, the silver orb ominous behind floating wisps of clouds. The stain of darkness had almost completely spread over the sky. Mackenzie, Nick, and Peterson walked carrying lanterns.

The deeper she moved into the woods, the more her skin tightened and tingled. She hadn't expected it to be this eerily quiet. Usually, an owl would hoot, or crickets would chirp. Even leaves would rustle. But it was deadly silent. The only sounds were made by their feet as they padded on the wet soil, following Peterson, who looked around nervously.

Mackenzie felt like she was one of the ghosts that legend said still haunted Tombstone. She was a part of the legend now. A phantom who roamed the woods.

"Here we are," Peterson announced, pointing ahead. "This is definitely the place."

"How did you know?" Nick asked.

"When I was a kid, I was foolish enough to come here. Never believed the stories, except I heard a woman wail. I ran like my life depended on it and never returned."

Mackenzie cast her light around, trying to spot anything of significance in the dark. "I don't get it. Debbie swallowed the memory stick right before she died. So it must have been important, something that could help us. She was smart enough to know that checking stomach contents is part of the standard autopsy."

"It's possible that the other information on the stick is what's important. The photos are just... random," Nick said, his voice almost wobbling. "What is it about this damn place?"

Mackenzie didn't know. But she felt it. They all did. Something both violent and tragic. Like something had reached out of the ground and latched onto their souls. She took in the clearing and was turning around when she caught a glimpse of that same old lady standing in the surrounding woods.

"Ah!" She let out a scream and fell on her ass.

"Mack!" Nick rushed to her. "Are you okay?"

"Yeah... I just tripped." As she tried to push herself up, she felt something under her hand. In the lantern light, she saw that it was a ring. An old silver ring with black spots from oxidation. But it seemed like it was still attached to something. She tried yanking it free.

"What are you doing?" Nick asked.

"There's this really old-looking ring here." She grunted and finally pulled it free. "Fuck."

Her blood ran cold.

Sticking out of the disturbed soil was a finger bone. There was a body buried here.

Everything happened in a blur.

"Peterson, call dispatch," Nick ordered. "We need CSU here."

Mackenzie stared at the white bone without a shred of

tissue or skin. Nick helped her up and pulled her away. "Mack, you need to move. You can't compromise the remains."

The remains.

In no time at all, it seemed, the crime-scene investigators arrived, along with a group of deputies. All of a sudden, they weren't alone in the woods. Lights were erected around the clearing. The perimeter was marked by tape. Technicians in gear gathered around the finger in the soil.

Mackenzie looked at the ring in her palm and then at the spot in the woods where she had seen Mallory standing. But there was nobody there. It had probably just been her imagination.

Officials roamed the clearing and the edge of the woods carrying portable scene lights. One of the technicians brought out ground-penetrating radar and scanned the entire area. And then the technicians weren't just centered around that one spot. They broke into groups and soon they were spread all around.

"What the hell is going on?" Mackenzie couldn't shake off a terrible feeling.

"No fucking clue," Nick muttered.

Anthony removed his skullcap and goggles and ducked under the tape, heading toward them wearing a haunted expression. Mackenzie had never seen him like this. The tall, lanky man was usually wry and bored.

"Now I know where the name Tombstone came from," he said somberly. "There are nine bodies buried here. This is a mass grave."

THIRTY-TWO

APRIL 20

"This house will never be good, Mackenzie." Melody scrubbed at the hardened caramel on the bowl. She scrubbed so hard that Mackenzie was concerned her skin would peel off.

"Why?" Mackenzie sat at the table in the kitchen, watching her mother slog by the sink.

"There's something about violence, sweetheart." Melody turned on the faucet and rinsed the dish. "It leaves a mark. Not just on people, but also on places. It changes something in the air."

Mackenzie emerged from the water in her bathtub and blinked away the memory. The water was now lukewarm. The bubbles sizzled against her breasts. She thought about what her mother had said all those years ago. How violence always lingered, leaving something behind. Her own house had seen violence. Someone had died here after they tried to kill her.

Should she move?

When her phone pinged, she answered, "Hello?"

"Mack, can you pick me up?" It was Nick.

"What's wrong with your car?"

"Long story. I need to change the tire and don't have a

spare. When can you get here?" Sounds of keys clanging and drawers opening and closing filtered through.

Mackenzie propped herself up, leaning forward to begin draining the tub. "Give me twenty minutes. We have a meeting with the mayor, don't we?"

"Yeah." He paused as the water started to drain. "What's that?"

"Oh yeah, I was taking a bath. Just getting out now," she replied without thinking.

He cleared his throat. "Yeah. Okay. Cool. See you later." He hung up before she could utter another word.

By the time Mackenzie rolled the car into Nick's driveway, she felt more centered. Last night, after the discovery of the mass grave, she had returned home and showered vigorously. When she'd woken this morning, though, something fetid still clung to her skin. It had sharpened her soul.

She noticed Nick's car standing ahead of hers and climbed out to check the tires. One of them was completely flat, making the car lean to one side. She knelt and spotted a tiny hole drilled into it.

"Hey." Nick came out fixing his tie. "I could have taken a cab but figured you'd be driving by my place anyway."

Mackenzie was tracing the tiny hole. "Who did this?"

He shrugged, but his forehead was creased with lines. "Probably some prank by delinquent teenagers. Really hope Luna doesn't grow up to be like that."

"When did you notice it?"

"This morning." He checked his watch impatiently. "Come on. We gotta go."

Mackenzie stood up slowly. "Has this ever happened before?"

"What? This?" He pointed at the punctured tire. "No."

The thoughts hissing through her brain made her stomach swoop in fear. "First you hear someone walking around at night in your house, and then someone pops your tire—which, by the way, could have caused a serious accident if you hadn't noticed."

"Come on, Mack. It's just a coincidence." He shrugged nonchalantly and turned around to head to Mackenzie's car. She stepped forward and yanked his elbow.

"No, it's not!" she cried, worry taking over. "I'm being watched. That's how they knew when to leave Sophie's body inside the trunk of my car. The people who have hurt me have been targeted."

"Have I ever hurt you?" he challenged.

"Of course not."

He bit back a smile. "Then why would this person come after me?"

"Maybe we should ask for a security detail to be assigned to you." She was already forming a list in her mind.

"You're overreacting," he groaned.

"You did the same with me!"

"The day there's a body left in my car, we can talk about this." He dropped his voice, realizing they were arguing out in the open.

Her skin was burning up. *Was* she overreacting? A potent haze was permeating the corners of her mind. What if Nick was also being watched? What if he was in some kind of danger?

When he lightly touched her shoulder, she was anchored back to the moment. "I'll be careful. The first sign of any real trouble and I won't fight you over this. Nothing will happen to me."

Mackenzie nodded through the fluttering in her throat, hoping that the sickening feeling of someone lurking around Nick was just an illusion.

. . .

Rathbone was a man Mackenzie could never figure out. He'd had the most tumultuous term as mayor in the history of Lakemore. But there was nothing about him that was leader-like. No charisma and no passion, and not even a semblance of being effective. He reminded Mackenzie of someone who'd gone into politics with no ambition or desire to make a change but who was there purely for the perks. But then by accident someone had made him mayor, and he was stuck in this position, living a destiny that wasn't meant for him.

Inside Sully's office, Rathbone stood by the open window puffing a cigar, while Sully was relegated to sitting on a chair that wasn't his.

"I know it's a bit cramped, but I'd rather talk here." Rathbone sat on Sully's chair, facing Sully, Rivera, Mackenzie, and Nick. "Your conference room is too public, and you don't have the best track record of containing leaks. Did you see the media circus outside?"

Mackenzie had seen it when she reached the office. It was worse than before. She couldn't even bear to listen to the radio. Debbie's brutal murder had made for front-page fodder.

Lakemore Latest's *Debbie Arnold murdered.*

What is the Lakemore PD hiding?

Is this an attack on the media?

Free speech in danger in Lakemore.

Who killed Lakemore's own Debbie?

"Debbie was a local celebrity," Sully said, pushing the delivery box containing whatever his latest hobby was under the table, away from Rathbone's sight. "It will take time, but things will settle down."

"When?" Rathbone put out his cigar, his hand almost trembling. "This was supposed to be peacetime in Lakemore. Until you catch Debbie's killer, this town will continue to plummet into chaos—and I guess we know *why*." His eyes found Mackenzie and narrowed, like he was trying to decipher her.

"You're the reason. If only I'd known featuring you in that documentary would make things worse... Talk about a publicity strategy going wrong."

Mackenzie's ears burned. But Rivera brought the conversation back on track.

"Mayor Rathbone, as I informed you earlier, we found a mass grave in the Tombstone neighborhood."

Rathbone's lips pursed in discomfort. "Yes. Yes. A mass grave. Just what I need."

"Dr. Angela Weiss has been kind enough to consult on this," Rivera went on. Weiss was Washington state's forensic anthropologist, whom Mackenzie had seen correctly estimate a victim's favorite sport within five minutes of a visual examination. "She will be flying to Lakemore from a convention in DC, but she has already confirmed over Skype that based on the pubic arch, all nine sets of remains belong to women. Looking at the pubic symphyses and sternal rib ends, she's also been able to tell us that at least three of the victims were under the age of twenty. For the rest, she'll need to access the remains."

Rathbone stroked his jaw. "Could this be related to a story Debbie was working on?"

"We checked her computer and phone, and no," Nick said.

"And you have no leads." The mayor sat back, shaking his head. "How is it that you have multiple victims and no leads?"

"We do have leads, except our warrant was rejected, and then a shutdown wiped out some of our stored evidence," Mackenzie said. The IT department was still trying to access the deleted files. Meanwhile Mackenzie and Nick had requested another copy of the CCTV from the school, but they deleted all files older than five days. That video was effectively erased for good.

"You lost evidence?" He was appalled.

"Could be avoided if we had funding for solid backup systems," Sully said.

"And why was the warrant rejected?" Rathbone ignored Sully's jibe.

Mackenzie told him about Judge Hamilton's house, which coincidentally wasn't far from the mass grave.

"I can't interfere in the judicial process." Rathbone flicked his hand dismissively. "And there are a lot of places around there. You don't have enough to force people to open their books."

"I guessed you'd say that. Your chief of staff is part of that gentlemen's club." Mackenzie crossed her arms.

Rivera shot her a warning glare. Sully groaned. Nick stiffened next to her.

Rathbone's face hardened. "This entire police force is taking flak from the media to protect *you.* Have you thought about giving a statement to the public?"

"What?" Nick was pissed off. "Absolutely not. She'll put herself in danger. Mob mentality will take over and they'll come after her."

"Based on what Dr. Turner told me this morning, this killer has a strange reverence for you," Rathbone continued, ignoring Nick. "Why don't you just make an appeal to them to stop the madness?"

"That is the dumbest thing to do." Nick scowled. "I'm sure Dr. Turner has also told you that the killer is deranged. They're not reasonable, so they can't be negotiated with."

"*Because* they're deranged, maybe they'll listen," Rathbone countered. "Besides, the risk is worth the reward. We can provide protection for you, Detective Price. I believe you should do everything you can to stop the killings."

"I will do everything I can to catch this killer. I *will* catch this killer." Mackenzie tried to keep her voice steady. "But I refuse to be a scapegoat for your problems."

"Scapegoat?" Rathbone sneered, rubbing his lips. "You're

not a scapegoat, sweetheart. You're the cause of all of this. But if you choose to hide—"

"I'm not hiding." She stepped forward, fists clenched. "I'm the one who has cleaned up the mess *your* friends caused in this town in the first place. And I will fix this too. Even if your friends are making things harder than they need to be."

Everyone in the room was motionless. Tension swelled, like they were all gauging Rathbone's reaction. He drummed his fingers on the table, his eyes pinned on Mackenzie.

"I'm not the enemy, Detective Price. While your last few years have been rough, trying to lock up my *friends*, as you call them, I've had to take care of this town through unemployment, corruption investigations, debt, protests, and re-elections. All the while trying to be there for my son, who has leukemia." His voice cracked on the last sentence. "It's easy to be low on the totem pole and believe those who are higher have it easy and don't do anything. We're all doing the best we can."

"Then we're on the same team," Mackenzie replied calmly, despite her tongue feeling like iron inside her mouth.

He swallowed hard and made an approving grunt in the back of his throat.

After Rivera assured him that they were redoubling their efforts, Rathbone left and the meeting ended.

Andrew was waiting outside. "I need to talk to you both."

"What's up?" Mackenzie checked her watch. She didn't think Andrew's contribution had been significant. And their session had ended on an awkward note, leaving her feeling raw and jaded.

"Sully told me about that mass grave." He rubbed his temples. "Sorry, I've been busy with Jane Doe. But I thought of something."

"What is it?" Nick asked.

"That message left on Debbie's face—*My gift to you, Mack.* I believe the killer is getting closer to you."

Mackenzie noticed how Nick's posture changed instinctively. He crossed his arms and positioned himself like he was guarding her. "What does that mean?"

"Look at the progression of the victims," Andrew explained. "Sophie—assuming it was the same killer, though as you know, I have my doubts—had nothing to do with you. Second victim was Courtney, who bullied you many years ago. The latest was Debbie, who has been badmouthing you for the last two years."

"So the next victim will be someone who has hurt me recently?" She shook her head. "I'm a cop. People are pissed off at me on a daily basis."

"Yes, but this is personal. It will be someone you are or were close to. Someone who has hurt you more than Debbie has. And the killer went from calling you Mackenzie to Mack. In their head, they're building a relationship with you, which gets stronger as they eliminate more of your enemies. Can you think of anyone who could be the next victim?"

Mackenzie could. To her horror, she could. But before she could say anything, Peterson approached them wiping his brow.

"Christ, Peterson!" Troy guffawed as he walked past the four of them. "Why are you sweating already? It's a cool sixty-five degrees."

"Did you know that sweat is like a fingerprint?" Peterson said. "Its composition of compounds is unique for each individual."

Mackenzie's heart sank down her chest. She knew what he was going to say.

"Get on with it," Nick urged.

Peterson blinked at Mackenzie, his mouth opening and closing before he finally said the words.

"Detective Price, we just got a call. Sterling Brooks has gone missing."

THIRTY-THREE

"We are now boarding passengers traveling with children and those who require assistance."

Mackenzie looked over at Sterling clicking away furiously on his phone. His eyebrows were pulled in a knot. His lips moved silently as he typed his message. It was a habit he didn't realize he had. She found it adorable. Spotting a crumb stuck to the corner of his mouth, she brushed it away with her thumb.

He paused and looked at her. "Mrs. Brooks, was that a romantic gesture in public?"

"Okay. Go back to work."

She fidgeted in her seat, tapping her boarding pass and eyeing the strange faces around her. The nervous middle-aged woman panicking every few seconds and checking her passport was still in her purse. A group of teenagers giggling and poking each other. An old couple holding hands and looking out at the runaway.

Her mind wandered back to work. Her cases were temporarily reassigned to Nick and Troy. She pulled out her phone and texted Nick.

Interview Candice's housekeeper with Alex. She has a

language barrier. Might feel more comfortable talking in Spanish.

"We are now boarding passengers seated in first class." The announcement echoed in the gate. The movement around her spiked. People started gathering their luggage, shouting orders to rowdy children, and making a beeline for last-minute washroom trips. Her phone vibrated.

Don't be a buzz kill on your honeymoon. Have a safe flight.

"Ready, Mrs. Brooks?" Sterling kissed the back of her hand.

"I'm still not used to that."

He intertwined his fingers with hers and pressed his lips into her hair. "You have a lifetime to get used to it."

The souvenir from their honeymoon in the Bahamas sat right in the center of the coffee table. A ship inside a bottle. Mackenzie had bought it from the local market in Nassau. Sterling had never got rid of it. She stood in his first-floor apartment. Her first time visiting since he moved out and they got a divorce. She floated around the one-bedroom unit, trying to think like a detective and not an ex-wife. Trying to look for clues related to his disappearance and not poke around to see how differently he lived.

Did he procrastinate in emptying the dishwasher?

Did he still use a bathrobe instead of a towel?

Did he still not care about pairing his socks correctly?

"Who made the 911 call?" she asked Nick.

"According to the first responders, it was someone by the name Ivy Pierce. She's outside."

She could feel him watching her expression closely, and sighed. "I don't care, Nick. I left him a year ago."

"I know, I know." Nick shoved his hands in his pockets. "You shouldn't care. Guy was a cheater."

"Sometimes I think you hate him more than I do."

"Sometimes I think you don't hate him at all."

"All right. Let's talk to Ivy Pierce." Mackenzie automatically ran a hand through her hair and tightened her ponytail, making Nick chuckle. "It's vanity. Sue me."

Outside Sterling's apartment, they found a meek woman with dark wavy hair containing blonde highlights, wearing a summer dress and carrying a large tote bag. She had big eyes and a giant nose.

Mackenzie couldn't help but draw comparisons. This was the first woman Sterling had actually *dated* since their divorce. The first woman he must have seen potential in. The first woman he liked enough to make him decide to move on from Mackenzie.

"Ms. Pierce?" Nick made the introductions.

Ivy's eyes widened. "Oh, *you're* Mackenzie. Of course you are!"

She had an Australian accent and very large teeth. When she smiled, her gums were visible. But it was endearing. A kind of radiance that was natural.

"Sorry, I'm not a stalker." She blushed. "I watched the documentary and... well, you're famous here."

"Right. So how did you realize that Sterling was missing?" Mackenzie asked.

Ivy tightened her hold around her bag. "I came by because we'd decided to get breakfast together before work. But when I arrived, the door was open. He didn't answer his cell and then the apartment was empty. I called his work, but they said he wasn't there yet. I went down to parking and confirmed his car was still there. I waited for twenty minutes, thinking maybe he'd show up... but he didn't." Tears misted her eyes. "What happened? It's not like him to disappear like this, is it?"

"It's not," Mackenzie answered abruptly, and then bit her tongue. "When was the last time you talked to him?"

"Last night, over the phone. That's when he told me to come by. He sounded totally normal."

One of the uniforms called to Mackenzie and Nick. "I think we found something."

Ivy tried hurrying after them, but Mackenzie instructed her to stay put. They followed the deputy to the refuse room. Outside, a garbage bag was on the ground with half of its contents spilled. "We canvassed the neighbors on this floor. None of them recognize this bag, and they didn't hear anything."

Nick leaned down, examining the contents. "Could it be Sterling's? How will we know?"

"It's his," Mackenzie said, her throat dry.

"How do you know?"

"That's the milk he buys." She pointed at the contents. "Those socks with holes in were a gift from me. And... that's the condom brand he uses."

"Damn it," he muttered. "So someone got to him when he was putting out the trash." He stood up and looked at a metal door to one side. "What's that?"

The deputy pushed it open. Beyond was a concrete hallway that led to the docking area.

"Looks like that's how they got in, since there's no way to enter the building without being buzzed," Nick said.

"Then how did Ivy get in?" Mackenzie asked.

"She has a fob." He shrugged, and then his eyes snapped to her.

"Relax, Nick. I'm fine." She turned to the deputy. "We need all surveillance footage from this building for this morning, especially the cameras covering the docking area. And get the CSU here. This area might be a crime scene."

"Yes, ma'am." He nodded and left.

"You're taking this pretty well," Nick commented once they were alone.

"Which part?" She leaned against the wall. "That my ex-husband has gone missing or that he's in a relationship just a year after our breakup while I haven't even come close to getting laid." She clasped her hand over her mouth. "I can't believe I just said that."

Nick's grin was wide. "One of those problems can be solved. I can help you."

"*Excuse me?*" she shrieked, his words making butterflies take flight in her stomach.

"I can set you up with someone."

"Oh!" She patted her cheeks, trying to stop herself blushing.

"Why? What did you think I meant?" His voice was innocent, but mischief danced in his eyes.

"Nothing." She tried playing it cool and failed miserably.

"Oh! You thought I—"

"Shut up."

"That's very flattering." He grinned.

"Please stop talking."

"I'll have to think about it."

She stomped her boot on his shoe and he cried out in pain. "Now that we're over this, I'm thinking that we shouldn't assume that Sterling's disappearance is related to our case. He's an ADA and has made enemies."

"I'll ask Jenna to inquire at his work. But I guess you can change your mind about Andrew now."

"What do you mean?"

"I know you were underestimating him, but his prediction was right about this one."

She spotted Ivy fretting about in the hallway as Peterson attempted to pacify her. "If only he'd thought of it sooner."

THIRTY-FOUR

Sterling had been missing for less than twelve hours, but his disappearance had the full force of the Lakemore PD behind it.

"There is no obvious crime scene. No blood or even a sign of a struggle. He's an adult male. Are we sure about declaring this a missing person yet?" Rivera had questioned.

"We need to move fast. We've lost three people already. Two on our watch. I don't think this is the time to follow protocol," Nick argued.

"I just don't want anyone getting a whiff of this. They'll say we're showing favoritism to someone from the DA's office." Rivera sighed. "Apparently we can't do anything right these days."

"I think we need to stop giving a shit," Sully recommended, munching on Doritos.

Mackenzie didn't stop for breath. She pestered the sheriff to spread the word and recruit volunteers. She personally contacted the Washington State Patrol to get the missing persons posters out immediately. She made the calls to Riverview PD and Olympia PD, including the DA. Even the mundane things that she would normally assign to Peterson or a junior detective, she took upon herself. Her brain had gone into overdrive.

"I'll ask Clint to give us the last known location of Brooks' phone," Jenna pitched in.

Mackenzie looked up from crossing one more thing off her list. "Already did."

Jenna scoffed. "Didn't expect you to be this hands on when it came to your ex-husband."

The activity around Mackenzie froze for a heartbeat before resuming. She glared at Jenna, resurrecting that side of her that made people wilt. "Just because he's my ex-husband doesn't mean I want him dead. Now if you want to be useful, you'll follow up on the CCTV from the apartment building."

Jenna blinked, dazed. Her head nodded in jerks as she made her exit. Mackenzie had never snapped at her even when Jenna was being sour for no reason. Nick looked like he wanted to say something, but wisely kept his lips sealed.

"We need to put pressure on the CSU to find muskrat fur," Mackenzie shot off at Peterson. She knew she was losing it as she watched Peterson scramble away. The thought of Sterling being tortured was like a machete to the gut. In moments of fury and betrayal, she had lain in bed wishing him pain. Justice, she used to think.

"Be careful what you wish for, Mackenzie," Melody whispered when they returned from burying the body in the woods. "You wanted him gone. Now he's gone."

But this wasn't what she wanted. It was like her body was filled with throbbing knots, contracting painfully every time she breathed. Her breaths turned shallow. She felt cool sweat pool in the crevices of her body. Even her vision began swimming. Before anyone could see her anxiety attack take over, she scampered away to the staircase in the fire escape. Nobody went there except Nick when he used to need places to smoke.

Shutting the door behind her, she rested against the wall

and tried not to choke. Her ragged breathing echoed in the staircase.

You're welcome, Mackenzie.

I will always protect you, Mackenzie.

My gift to you, Mack.

You're the reason.

Three women have been hurt in your name.

The words swirled in her head, threatening to explode her brain. When Austin appeared at the top of the stairs, she shivered. "What are you doing here?"

He climbed down a floor to stand level with her. "I heard. I'm sorry."

"Are you?" she said without thinking.

"Yes." He looked like he meant it. He rested an arm on the railing and bit his lip. "I also heard about the mass grave."

Mackenzie sighed. "Of course you did. So much for limiting case details to essential personnel."

"I had an idea. If you're willing to listen."

She raised an eyebrow, her gaze penetrating his tentative manner. Lately, he had either spewed accusations at her or thrown frustrated glances her way. "I'm listening."

"I heard that Hamilton refused to sign your warrant to look into that car rental company, so it seems like a dead end, and that it's all related to Hamilton's house."

"Who is slipping you information?"

"Nobody. I've been eavesdropping and snooping around your desks when no one's around."

She smirked dryly. "Well, at least you're honest. What are you getting at?"

"It's not legal..." he started hesitantly, mischief dancing in his blue eyes. "But since your official channels seem to be drying up, maybe it's okay to do something a little wrong for the greater good. You could sneak in."

"Sneak in?"

He nodded. "You want a list of people in that gentlemen's club to help you get closer to the client who rented the car that transported Courtney. Why don't you infiltrate one of their poker nights or whatever? See with your own eyes who's there."

Mackenzie was a stickler for the rules. But she was desperate. "We'll just have to make sure we aren't discovered. And we'll have to come up with an explanation as to how we stumbled upon a lead without admitting to anything illegal..." She groaned. "Fuck. This is how it begins. You do something wrong telling yourself it's the right thing to do, and the next thing you know it's corruption and conspiracy galore."

"You're being restrained by your own system," Austin reminded her.

"I don't believe in vigilante justice."

"But you're not dispensing justice. It's out-of-the-box thinking to find clues. Don't you think it's worth it at this point?"

Mackenzie was always unbending. She didn't yield. She was absolute and she liked it that way. All her life compensating for her participation in that night twenty years ago. But over the past year, something inside her had changed. She felt malleable, more pliant. At first, she thought she was losing her touch. But she eventually realized it was because she had finally learned how to care.

She nodded.

Austin released a breath. "You just have to figure out which night to go in. How will you do that?"

"I have an idea. I'll ask Senator Blackwood."

"No," Nick hissed in a low voice.

"He can make a few calls. Show interest in hanging out," Mackenzie repeated coolly. "Hamilton will never refuse a senator."

"I've never taken my father's help in my career, and I want to keep it that way." He picked up his coffee and crossed his legs.

"If I can learn to be more adaptable for the situation, then you can let go of your pride to save a life," she insisted. "We just need a solid lead. We've hit a wall with that club and the car company. Of course, your father won't attend. He'll cancel last minute."

Sully ambled into the conference room with a puzzle box tucked under one arm and a box of donuts under the other. "Is Becky on call?"

"I'm here." Becky's voice came on the line.

Sully pushed the box of donuts toward them. "Keep your sugar levels up. God knows how we'll survive this. I always liked Sterling. Stand-up guy."

"That he is," Nick agreed sardonically. Mackenzie elbowed him.

"All right, Dr. Weiss is a genius," Becky said. "She arrived with her team this morning and we already have a lot of information. Like I mentioned before, all nine sets of remains indicate female victims from the ages of approximately seventeen to early thirties. Bone analysis show that four victims were Caucasian, three were African American, and the remaining two were of South Asian origin."

Mackenzie took copious notes, even though the information would be available to her, just so that she remembered everything.

"Now what's interesting is the cause of death..." Becky's voice became unsure. "None of the victims were murdered."

"*What?*" Sully asked, crumbs of donut spraying out of his mouth.

"Out of the nine victims, six died from syphilis."

"You can tell that from just bones?" Nick raised his eyebrows.

"Yep. Dr. Weiss discovered lesions on the bones, star-like radial scars on the skulls and thickening of both bones and skulls. Also, there's evidence of surface pitting and localized enlargements, along with deposition of new bone on exterior surfaces. She and her team found no signs of assault or anything else that could be the cause of death."

"And the other three?" Mackenzie inquired.

"There were fractures of the spine in five of the victims, but Dr. Weiss estimated based on the patterns that the force wasn't consistent with assault or accident. She suggested that the fractures were caused by muscle spasms."

"Muscle spasms can do that?" Sully was floored.

"For two out of those three remaining victims, she was able to retrieve enough skeletal tissue to run tests and detect tetanus toxin. Extrapolating, we have concluded that the other victim probably died the same way."

"Tetanus?" Mackenzie asked, frowning. "But syphilis and tetanus are both treatable."

"That's what's so strange," Becky agreed. "But there is no evidence of anything else. No kerf marks. No bullet wounds. No broken hyoid bones. The tissue samples we were able to salvage contained no known poisons. Our conclusion is that it wasn't murder."

But they had been buried there. All nine women in one clearing. And it had something to do with whoever had been torturing and killing the people who had hurt Mackenzie.

She looked at her ring finger. The indentation from her wedding band had faded a long time ago. Now she had even forgotten what it felt like. That part of her life was long over. But why had someone decided to dig into her past?

"What about time of death?" Nick asked, bringing her back to the present. "You okay?" he whispered.

She nodded and focused on what Becky had to say.

"Times of death range from one year to forty years ago."

"Forty years?" Sully coughed.

"And it's random," she continued. "No regular pattern except for the cause of death. We are working on identifying the victims based on facial reconstruction and DNA analysis. Will take some time."

Mackenzie read through the bullet points she had jotted down. "So for the last forty years, young women who had died from STDs and tetanus were buried there? Tombstone has been a dumping ground this entire time?"

"No wonder that place gives everyone the creeps." Sully shivered slightly. "It's cursed."

After Becky hung up, the three of them sat in knee-deep silence. None of them knew what to say. The elephant in the room was the big secret that had just been revealed to them. A shame so horrific that it made Mackenzie question if there was any good in Lakemore at all, or if that was just wishful thinking. Every time she thought she had reached the town's rotten core, there was something worse hidden under another layer.

Maybe evil was like an uncontrolled infection. It was everywhere. Just some parts manifested more symptoms than others.

"That old lady, Mallory." Sully broke the silence. "She told me that the woman I was looking for was long gone." He stared into empty space. "How it wasn't the right time."

Mackenzie remembered what Mallory had said to her.

We've been waiting a long time. This land can't handle any more spilled blood.

It all made sense now. Her chest pinched as she realized that at the heart of all the fiction surrounding Tombstone lay something truly tragic. That the ghosts roaming those woods weren't looking for prey; they were lost souls waiting for justice.

THIRTY-FIVE

Following the chilling revelation of the truth behind that clearing at Tombstone, Mackenzie decided to try her luck again with Nick.

"I could go behind your back and ask your father for this favor myself. Hamilton will definitely tell him when they're meeting next, eager to get a senator in the fold." She wheeled into his cubicle after getting off another call regarding Sterling's disappearance. The caller had suggested that they'd seen him eating lobster at a restaurant. But Sterling was allergic to lobster. Still, Mackenzie had dispatched a deputy to ask around at the restaurant just in case.

"Whoever took those pictures of that clearing must have known the significance of it," Nick thought aloud, ignoring Mackenzie's threat. "Do you think it's possible that the memory stick belonged to Debbie herself? That it was on her when she was abducted and she swallowed it before she was killed so that the story she was trying to break made it out."

"We went through her hard drive, her phone, and her files. She wasn't working on anything remotely related to Tombstone." Mackenzie pulled out Lysol wipes from her desk and began cleaning the walls of Nick's cubicle to center herself. "And don't tell me you think it's another coincidence that the mass grave is in the same neighborhood as Hamilton's house, where Tag went and King of the Road drops off its clients."

He moved out of her way so that she could get to the back wall of the cubicle. "I'll call my dad if you stop with the cleaning. It's freaking me out."

Her shoulders sagged and she showed him the black goo on the wipe. "Sitting surrounded by *this* should freak you out."

"I'll be back." He grabbed his cell phone and left the office.

Mackenzie began formulating their plan for once they got in. They couldn't exactly just walk in the front door. They would definitely be denied entry. If Hamilton didn't want to bother his friends by having Mackenzie and Nick ask them questions, she doubted he'd let them crash their poker night.

Was it *just* poker night? Or did something else happen in that house, which was why Hamilton was being so cagey?

Mallory's voice rang in her ears.

They come here sometimes. They'll be here tonight after the sun goes down.

The old woman knew about them. She also knew about the bodies buried there.

Mackenzie twirled a pen between her fingers, her brain resisting the temptation to draw the most obvious conclusion. Her tumbling thoughts were disrupted by a piece of paper thrust into her face.

"Sorry to startle you," Andrew said. "But Robbie drew you this."

She took it from him. It was a drawing of a woman dressed like a cop. It was a stick figure, but she had red hair just like Mackenzie.

"I told him you've been having a rough time with this case, so he did this on his own," Andrew added.

Mackenzie traced the smooth texture of the color that

wasn't quite contained with the lines. "That's very sweet of him. I'll keep it."

"Thank you."

She pinned the drawing to her bulletin board, right in the center, making a mental note to get it framed later. Its innocence and heart instigated a hollow feeling inside her. Like a thousand knives had left holes all over her. "Maybe you should move back to Olympia and just commute," she suggested. "Lakemore isn't a good place for kids, especially sensitive ones like Robbie."

Andrew placed his elbow on the divider between Mackenzie and Troy's cubicles. "Have more faith in your town, Detective Price. I've studied many places and this one has a tendency to bounce back onto its feet."

"Yeah, but what happens when you cut off its feet? You were right about Sterling. But we were too late."

"Are you giving up on Lakemore?" He raised an eyebrow. "Did the indomitable Mad Mack finally reach her tipping point?"

"It's not like that." Her smile was watery. "I feel like we weed out one evil and two more grow in its place."

"This isn't just a town to you, is it?" he observed. "For someone who grew up in New York, you are fiercely loyal to it."

"It's never just a town. A community dictates what we allow and what we don't. It's a reflection of what we are and stand for. And Lakemore..." She trailed off.

"It's almost like you're trying to settle a score."

You have to help me bury him. Melody's voice whispered in her ear. She had done something so terrible when she was only twelve years old that she had dedicated her life to righting the wrongs of others. Because there was no way to fix her own wrong anymore.

She masked her surprise. Had her armor been slipping? Was she not as guarded as she used to be?

"Not a score. All of us have some motivation for being here, doing what we do."

Andrew nodded but didn't look convinced. "You know, before my wife was diagnosed with cancer, I was planning to leave her. We had been fighting and we got to a point where I would avoid interacting with her." He leaned against the edge of the desk, blinking rapidly. "I would just ignore her. And then when she was diagnosed, I felt like the biggest asshole in the world. Worst was, we knew she didn't have much time left."

"I'm sorry." Mackenzie had been there to help her grandmother when she was going through chemo. It was almost like a part of her was being torn away, slowly but inevitably. You'd think it would give you time to prepare, but that helplessness and desperation was all-consuming.

"So I dedicated myself to her. I did everything I could to take care of her and make sure her last months were smooth," he continued. "It stemmed from both love and guilt. And when she finally left us, I wondered if I had redeemed myself in her eyes. If she had forgiven me for all those times I didn't treat her as I should have."

"I'm sure she had. She loved you. She would have forgiven you."

Andrew nodded. "I know. But did I redeem myself in *my* eyes? I think that's a never-ending quest."

Mackenzie felt a kinship to him in that moment. She grazed Robert's watch on her wrist, knowing in her heart that he had forgiven her for being a coward and denying him his truth. There was peace inside her. That chaos that had perpetually fluttered in her chest all these years didn't have wings; it had claws. That beast was dead. But something was amiss.

"So what do you do?" she asked in a small voice.

"I decided to focus on the person I love—Robbie. And everything feels right; everything is worth it."

She snorted, despite feeling the tears stinging her eyes. "That's pretty cheesy. I thought you'd have some novel advice."

"It's what everything boils down to in the end."

Nick returned and gestured to Mackenzie to follow him.

"Excuse me." She left Andrew and went out.

"They're meeting tonight," Nick said quietly. "Eight o'clock."

"Then we'll get there at least an hour before and try to make our way inside."

He pursed his lips. "I don't like this. It's technically trespassing."

"What choice do we have?" She looked around to make sure nobody was eavesdropping. "Once we find a lead, and I'm certain we will, it will all be worth it."

It was what she was telling herself repeatedly. She just prayed that the gamble would pay off, that they wouldn't make things worse.

Mackenzie parked the car far enough from the house so as not to draw suspicion. For the first time, she was grateful there were no streetlights. This time the darkness would be their ally. She glanced at the house, where only one window had lights showing. There was a white van in the driveway, but she was too far away to make out any specific details or the license plate.

"Are you sure about going in alone?" he asked for the millionth time.

"I won't get murdered in a house full of judges, campaign managers, and other important people. Plus, you're here if that happens." She glanced out of the window.

The darkness had a bluish tinge to it. The woods were too still. Not a single leaf rustled. Not a single branch swayed. As if the place was waiting with bated breath for Mackenzie to stumble upon the truth.

Nick handed her an earpiece. "I need you to keep talking to me, Mack. If you don't, I'm going in and I don't care what happens to the case."

His hair was disheveled from constantly running his hand through it. The dashboard was littered with unused cigarettes he had chewed on on the drive over.

She put the earpiece in and they did a quick check to make sure it worked. "I also have my gun on me." She raised the hem of her jeans to show the Glock tucked in her sock. "We're good."

She got out of the car and marched toward the house. It was cordoned by a low wall, to keep animals away. She hoisted herself over and landed on her feet. Her heart sped up. Feeling like a thief, she tiptoed to the back of the house, constantly looking around.

"Mack?" Nick's voice sounded in her ear. "Are you in?"

"I'm round the back. I don't see anyone," she murmured.

She searched for a window she could crack open before realizing the back door was unlocked.

"Can you see the van?" Nick asked.

"There was no logo on it. I'll have to get to the front to get a plate number."

"Don't risk it!" he cried. "It's probably just catering."

Mackenzie opened the door carefully, just enough for her to slide through. Inside, the lighting was dim, like she was in the VIP area of a nightclub. "I'm in."

She tiptoed down a narrow hallway that pulsed to the beat of some music. "Sounds like a party."

"Maybe Hamilton was telling the truth," Nick said.

A woman walked by the end of the hallway. Goosebumps dotted Mackenzie's arms as she followed her. The music grew louder. There were no paintings or pictures on the walls. The contrast was jarring—how opulent the house was from the outside, and how sparse inside. It was obvious that there was zero focus on the aesthetics. As if nobody had bothered.

The feel of the Glock against her ankle was reassuring as she trod carefully. When she reached the door where the woman had disappeared, she pressed herself against the wall. The music blared more loudly now, the vibrations making her skin thrum. Mixed with the music she heard voices and laughter.

"Mack? What's going on?" Nick asked impatiently.

"It sounds like a party. Let me get a visual so that I can see who I recognize." With bated breath, she slowly arched her neck and peeked round the door to see what was on the other side.

It was a large room furnished with white couches. Some men were sitting, some were lying on them, and a few were standing around. They all had drinks in their hands.

They were surrounded by young women dressed in lacy white lingerie like it was a uniform. They were all shapes and colors. Scantily dressed and beautiful, they mingled with the men. Refilling their drinks. Laughing at their not-so-funny jokes. Stroking chests and hair. Whispering in ears. Kissing.

"Oh my God," Mackenzie whispered.

"What? What is it?"

"It's like a sex club. There's a group of women in lingerie serving the men."

"What the hell? Do you see Hamilton?"

Her gaze scanned the room and she finally spotted Hamilton sitting in an armchair. One woman sat on top of him, kissing his neck, while he kissed another. His eyes were glazed, his skin flushed pink. It was obvious that he was drunk. Grinning, he stood and led the two women up some stairs with a swing in his step.

"Oh yeah. He's gross."

There was nothing sensual about the interactions. It was apparent that old, powerful men were just on a quest to feel more powerful. And the women's brains were shut down, performing their tasks like robots. Anger bubbled hot in her veins. She was witnessing exploitation.

"Don't do anything, Mack," Nick said, like he could hear her thoughts. "Now's not the time. It won't help."

"Prostitution is illegal in Washington, Nick."

"But you're trespassing. And I'm pretty sure they can argue that it's not prostitution, because technically you haven't witnessed exchange of money for sex."

She hated that he was right. But when she watched Rathbone's chief of staff take a shot and then rest his head against a woman's chest as if she was nursing him, she wanted to punch him in the face. It was evident that the women weren't into it at all.

They were like mannequins.

"Who else do you see? I'm writing down the names."

"Rathbone's chief of staff, Judge Romano, Rafael Jennings, that lobbyist who was in the news last year, ADA Tonheim, Debbie's boss—I forgot his name—and others I don't recognize."

"Shit. Okay, get out of there."

"Yeah." She was turning to leave when she saw there was another staircase behind her. "Wait. I'll check out upstairs."

"Mack! Get out! That place is crawling with people who can ruin your life if they catch you."

"I'll be careful. Don't distract me."

She managed to pad her way up undetected. Reaching the landing, she was faced with a hallway with rows of doors on either side. Her palms were coated in sweat; she knew she was pushing her luck. The hallway was dark, though. If anyone came out of one of the rooms, they'd only see a silhouette and assume she was one of the women from downstairs. It gave her some relief.

Walking past the doors, she could hear men moaning and bedsprings squeaking. She'd almost reached the other end when she noticed that one of the doors wasn't entirely shut. Her heart thundered inside her chest. Licking her lips, she twisted slightly to get a glimpse inside.

Through the sliver, she saw a woman lying on the bed, straight as an arrow, staring at the ceiling. Hamilton was kneeling on the floor. He lifted the corner of the purple carpet to reveal a latch, then opened a secret compartment and placed a gun into it. Putting the carpet back, he proceeded to remove his jacket and unbutton his pants.

"Mack, you okay?" Nick checked again.

She made a humming sound, afraid someone might hear her.

With bile rising in her throat, she was about to leave when something caught her eye. The woman had raised her legs in the air as Hamilton settled between her thighs. Around her ankle was a barcode inked into her skin.

Mackenzie's brain turned off and restarted again like a faulty engine. She jogged back down the staircase and peeked into the room again. This time she paid attention to the women's ankles.

Every woman had that tattoo.

A barcode around their ankle.

Exactly like Jane Doe.

THIRTY-SIX

APRIL 21

Beams of light burned through Mackenzie's eyelids. As awareness slowly trickled in, she realized that her cheek was resting on leather. She rose with a jolt and registered her surroundings. The wood-paneled walls, the leather furniture, the dartboard, the perpetual whiff of wood and spice and whiskey.

"Ah!" she squeaked, seeing Nick standing over her holding a glass of green liquid.

"Good morning." He shoved the glass into her hands.

She wiped her eyes, still groggy. "What? Why am I here?"

Nick had just returned from the gym, with sweat matting his skin and his red T-shirt. He lifted the bottom of the shirt to wipe his forehead, and Mackenzie quickly averted her eyes.

"We came here to discuss the case in my lair." He jutted his thumb at the closed door: his office, where a bulletin board running the length of the room was covered in pictures and printouts of reports. "And then you fell asleep."

"Why didn't you wake me?"

"I tried. You didn't budge." He grinned. "I even tried moving you to the guest room, but you kicked me in the shin."

Mackenzie had no memory of kicking him, but she recalled sitting on the couch for a glass of wine before dozing off. "I thought you had protein shakes, not green smoothies." She swallowed it within seconds, relishing the freshness.

"I made it for you," he said. "I'm heading to the shower. I'll be out in a second."

"Have you seen my wallet?" She fished around her pockets.

"Oh, it's in there." Nick swung the door to his lair open and then froze, his back stiff.

"What happened?" Mackenzie came up next to him.

The window in his office was open. A cool breeze was swirling around, causing papers to ruffle and float. An uncapped bottle of bourbon sat on the desk, an empty glass next to it.

"Did you leave the window open?" she asked.

Nick was pale. "Nope. Neither did I open that bottle."

Mackenzie's blood turned to ice. "Nick, someone's after you..."

"What do they want?" he demanded. "Why would anyone climb through the window and open a bottle of bourbon?"

"To mess with your head! I don't know!" Her own head was beginning to throb. "You should make sure nothing was taken. I'll see you at the station."

As she stepped outside, panic beat in her chest. A voice whispered through her. Nick had a point—what was their endgame with him?

After a shower, Mackenzie felt a lot clearer. When Nick arrived, she was at her desk, scrubbing in between the keys on the keyboard, her mind jumping from the barcoded women to his office being broken into. He looked contemplative. She could tell he was preoccupied by the events of the morning.

"Was anything taken?" she asked softly, almost too scared to hear the answer. Perhaps that was what they were after. Some evidence. Since it wasn't possible to break into the Lakemore PD, this person was going after the detectives, hoping that they'd taken something home.

But if that were the case, why hadn't similar things happened to Mackenzie herself?

"Because of the squad car outside my house," she mumbled aloud.

"What?" Nick turned on his chair.

"Nothing. Um, maybe you should think about getting protection, Nick?"

He waved a hand dismissively. "Yeah, yeah. I ran the number plates of those cars we saw at the house, and a lot of them are registered to King of the Road."

"Well, Tag did boast about their clientele."

"We need to talk to Jane Doe." Nick checked his watch. "Or you need to. I heard she doesn't respond to anyone else."

"I saw what's happening to those women." The images filled her mouth with a bitter taste. "I understand why she's having trouble trusting male authority figures. Do you want to talk about it?"

"Talk about what?" he asked innocently, fiddling with a cigarette.

"Nick." She glared at him.

But they were interrupted by Andrew, who arrived with purpose in his stride and a glow on his face. He waved a file in his hands.

"I think I have something." He beamed and handed them sheets of paper.

"What are we looking at?" Mackenzie asked.

"These are blogs I pulled from the internet that discuss the documentary you were in," he explained excitedly. "I figured this killer must need some outlet for their obsession with you.

Just watching you from afar isn't enough. I scoured the net and there is one user who is active on all the blogs."

Mack1987 was highlighted with red circles on all the pages. Mackenzie was born in the year 1987. She glanced at Nick, who was already looking at her, having noticed the same thing.

"They've employed the same username on all the websites," Andrew said.

"That doesn't mean it's the same person," Nick pointed out.

"Which is why I analyzed the language—spelling, abbreviations, phrases, prepositions, punctuation. It's definitely the same person."

Denial slammed into Mackenzie. She tried poking holes in his theory. "But this doesn't mean that Mack1987 is our killer."

"It doesn't, but all they talk about is you." He drew their attention to the highlighted sections. "Look. Everyone else discusses other detectives and other aspects of the documentary. But Mack1987 is the only one whose focus is just you. Asking questions about your cases, your life, commenting on your answers, what you were wearing..."

As Mackenzie read the entries, her skin began to crawl. Mack1987 was curious about the moles on her skin, the shape of her collarbone, why she wore blue more than other colors, why her hair was always in a ponytail, where she went to school, how long she was in New York for, when she returned, whether she was dating anyone...

"I'll ask Austin to look into it." Nick broke the charged silence that had ensued. "He's been itching to contribute somehow."

Mackenzie nodded. Mack1987 was behaving unhinged online, but did it make them the killer they were after?

THIRTY-SEVEN

"Has Jane Doe said anything to you?" Mackenzie asked hopefully.

Andrew was by the water cooler, waiting in line and thumbing his phone. He clicked his tongue and shook his head, putting the phone back in his pocket. "Nothing useful. It's like she wants to completely sever herself from the past."

Mackenzie didn't blame her. But even though Jane Doe had been fortunate enough to escape, other women were still trapped. Still stuck in purgatory. She needed some help to rescue them—and lead her to Sterling.

"How about I chat with her?"

"You could, but she hasn't revealed anything in your presence either."

"Alone."

He flinched. "Alone? Why?"

"Maybe she'd be more comfortable that way."

"Okay." He rubbed the back of his neck, lines forming deep in his forehead. "I can take you to her and you can go for a walk. I'll stay in the car."

"Sounds good."

. . .

Jane Doe was one of them. That was what she had escaped from before she fell into Mackenzie's arms that night. That was what she was running away from. She was one of *them*.

Mackenzie looked at the woman walking next to her. She was wearing a long beige dress that brushed the ground. Her hair was even shorter now—a boy cut. It suited her, bringing out the heart shape of her face. Her skin had cleared up in the last few days. The scrapes and cuts had healed. She looked healthy.

Even though she still walked with shoulders drawn down by gravity, occasionally she watched her bare feet sink into the mud with wonderment. She would wiggle her toes and giggle.

"You might hurt yourself," Mackenzie said. "Are you sure you don't want to wear your shoes?"

Jane Doe shook her head. She frolicked ahead, carrying her shoes in her hands, a maiden in the woods, looking like someone who would pluck flowers to fill her handmade basket. A long way from the damaged puppet she had been. She was beginning to stitch herself back together. She still barely spoke, still hadn't told anyone what her name was or what had happened to her, but there was less fear in her eyes, fewer sudden bodily jerks, and more moments—albeit fleeting—when she wasn't haunted, but actually present. The filaments of her identity rearranging and fashioning themselves into a woman who wasn't scared.

Suddenly Mackenzie realized that they had reached their destination: the woods behind Hidden Lake. And Jane Doe had stopped to blow at a dandelion right where Mackenzie had buried a body with her mother twenty years ago.

It was a balmy morning. Not even a light jacket was required. The sunlight fell gently upon the scene. Much like the mass grave, this place for Mackenzie was forever marked.

And though closure and justice had been achieved, she was chained to it.

"Dr. Turner said you've been doing better." She leaned against a tree. "I can tell. Do you like him?"

Jane Doe nodded, distracted by the floating seeds.

"I needed to talk to you." Mackenzie took a deep breath. "About your tattoo."

Jane Doe's mood nosedived. The corners of her lips pulled down. Mackenzie hated reminding her of it, but there was no other option.

"You're not the only one with this tattoo, are you?" she ventured carefully. Jane Doe looked like a deer in headlights. "Please. You're not in any trouble. I just want to talk."

Silence stretched between them, then Jane Doe nodded glumly.

"I saw other women with the same tattoo. Last night."

"At the house?" she asked. "How are they?"

Mackenzie didn't know how to answer. "They're... working on autopilot, it seemed to me. What is going on?"

Jane Doe rested against a tree, scratching her arms and avoiding Mackenzie's eyes. "It's prison."

"You said this before. You were forced into it?"

She nodded.

"How many of you were there?"

"Too many. I never counted."

"And the tattoos?"

"To keep track of us. To call us by a number." She lifted the hem of her dress and twisted her ankle to show her barcode. "I'm number seven."

Cold shards of disgust and fear blasted into Mackenzie. The women were treated like cattle. Branded with numbers. Stripped of their identities. Dehumanized. Used and abused like they were just flesh and not living, breathing people.

"Tell me how this happened," she said. "I can help. We can save them."

Jane Doe's eyes rolled up and she shook her head over and over again like she had been electrocuted. "No. No. No."

"Okay, okay, I'm sorry." Mackenzie stepped forward, raising her hands. "You don't have to do anything you don't want to."

Slowly Jane Doe calmed down, and the flush that had spread up her neck began to recede.

"I get it. I saw the people in that house. Judges, lawyers, businessmen, lobbyists... They're all powerful. Too powerful. You don't know who to trust. And even if you find one honest person willing to help, you're afraid that it might go nowhere. That they'll get hurt too and your situation won't change. I understand. You're stuck. That's why you haven't said anything to us. Because the people who hurt you are among us." Mackenzie glanced at the spot where she'd sat watching her mother bury the body. "I brought you here for a reason. This place means something to me."

Jane Doe tilted her head. "Why?"

The only person in the world Mackenzie had shared her darkest secret with was Nick. She had lived her entire life locking it away, afraid of what the consequences could be, afraid of what everyone would think of her, afraid of how her life could unravel. But once the truth was spoken aloud, it lost some of its weight. Secrets found their power in silence.

"When I was twelve years old, my mother convinced me to help her bury someone right here." The words burned on her tongue. Jane Doe's breathing quickened, but she didn't say anything. "My mother lied to me. She manipulated me. But it didn't change the fact that I participated in something horrible."

"Why are you telling me this?" Jane Doe asked with tears swimming in her eyes, like she ached for Mackenzie.

"I'm giving you my trust, hoping that you could give me

some of yours. This last year, that's what I've learned. That I need to trust and there will be more to gain."

Jane Doe looked conflicted, squirming against the bark of the tree. "Are you scared because your ex-husband is missing?"

"Yes."

There had been no news of Sterling. This morning the CSU had confirmed muskrat fur deposits next to the door where they believed he had been abducted from. To make matters worse, the cameras covering the docking area had been damaged the day before. Something told Mackenzie that wasn't a coincidence.

Jane Doe put her hand into a pocket in her dress and withdrew a key. "I always keep this on me. I took it from Judge Hamilton." She was whispering, even though they were alone in the woods, as if even the trees were treacherous. "He kept it in a special box in his side drawer. In that house."

"You don't know what it opens?"

"No."

Mackenzie took the key from her. "But it must be important to him. Where were you and the girls held? Is Hamilton the lynchpin of this operation, or is it someone else?"

Jane Doe raised her chin and shook her head. "Don't ask more from me. You are surrounded by enemies."

Just like that, the moment between them vanished, like footprints being washed away on the shore. One step at a time, Mackenzie told herself. She held the key tightly in her palm, wondering what bone-shriveling revelations it would lead her to.

"We need to tell someone," Nick said at the station, primed by the coffee in his hands. "We can trust Sully."

Mackenzie looked around. Suspicion was firmly embedded

inside her head. Only Austin was in the office, talking on the phone. "I think we can."

"*Think?*" Nick was appalled. "Mack, it's Sully. He's one of us."

What did "one of us" even mean? She had faith in her sergeant. But still something was stopping her. Holding her back from divulging the truth to those around her without any evidence.

"Yeah, and who does Sully trust?" she challenged. "What if he trusts the wrong person? I didn't even see half the people there. Some of them were in the rooms upstairs. Can you imagine Captain Murphy being one of them?"

Nick raised his eyebrows. "That's a frightening image."

"We need hard evidence before we go to anyone." She showed him the key Jane Doe had given her. "Jane Doe swiped this from Hamilton's bedroom. He kept it inside a special box."

He took the key and inspected it closely. "It's our lucky day. There is a bitting code on it. Jenna can track down the lock from the manufacturer."

"And technically it's not a lie that we got this from Jane Doe, who has been doing better thanks to Dr. Turner. So we don't have to reveal yet how we found out about Jane Doe."

He smirked mirthlessly. "You've thought of every excuse, haven't you?"

"It's like we're getting shot at from everywhere." She felt a pressure building behind her eyes, trying not to think about what Sterling was going through right now. "And of course, any more warrants that we submit should go to a judge Hamilton *doesn't* like. That's the only judge I'll trust."

"Agreed. I'll give this to Jenna." The chair protested with a screech as he stood up.

As soon as he had left, upsetting thoughts swathed Mackenzie's mind. It was always those brief moments of silence and inactivity that would catch her off guard. An old memory resurfaced: she was in a pool, wearing floaters around her chubby arms.

"I'll drown!" she cried, hating the water that was lapping against her chin and into her mouth.

"Now, now, Mackenzie." Robert's gentle voice calmed her. His strong arms came around her, just hovering and not touching. "If you keep moving, you won't drown."

"Promise?"

"Yes. All you have to do is always keep moving."

She kept flailing her arms and legs, and though the water still splashed her face, she didn't drown.

"Clint got something for us." Nick gestured her to follow him. She snapped out of her daze and stood up.

"Is it the damaged part of the memory stick?" she asked hopefully.

"I think so."

When they reached Clint's stuffy office, he turned one of the many monitors to face them. His pale cheeks were pink, and his usually focused eyes were frantic. "Like I said before, there are some files that we just won't be able to salvage, but the recovery software was able to extract this file."

He played the grainy video.

Nick took a sharp intake of breath.

Mackenzie's legs almost buckled.

Women lay on a white floor. Someone wearing black boots and holding a camera walked around filming them, weaving their way through them. The women were clothed and moved weakly, either injured or drugged, Mackenzie couldn't tell. But whoever was filming them had no intention of helping them. They just recorded them like they were keeping an inventory. Like these women were soon going to be sacrificed in some way.

THIRTY-EIGHT

"It's been over twenty-four hours since Sterling Brooks was abducted from his apartment building." The new Debbie—Mackenzie had learned she was called Laura—spoke to the camera. "We are joined today by Sterling's partner, Ivy Pierce."

The camera panned to Ivy. Her wavy hair was tied in an untidy ponytail. Her nose was swollen; a handkerchief was balled in her fist. She wore a plain T-shirt in a muted color. She looked every inch a woman whose partner was missing.

"Thank you, Laura." She blinked tearfully.

"I'm very sorry for what you're going through. Do the police have any theories?"

"I wouldn't know, because the Lakemore PD hasn't been keeping in touch with me." Ivy paused. "I believe there is bias against me owing to the fact that one of the lead detectives on the case is Sterling's ex-wife."

Laura feigned shock, her jaw hanging open. "In your opinion, is it professional for his disappearance to be investigated by his ex-wife? Do you think she'll be able to be objective?"

Ivy shrugged and sniffed into the handkerchief. "I don't want to make any comments on her objectivity, but the Lakemore PD shouldn't allow her to be on this case or any of the ones that have been in the news."

"What do you mean?" Laura narrowed her eyes. She knew she was onto something.

"I heard from someone reliable that Sterling, Debbie, and that other woman, whose name I don't remember—I apologize—were all targeted because of Detective Mackenzie Price. They paid because of their personal connection to her."

"Damn it," Nick muttered and turned off the television. His eyes were ablaze as he marched to Rivera's office like a boulder rolling down a hill.

Mackenzie was on his heels, still reeling from the explosive interview. A thousand questions churned inside her, but they were all eclipsed by Nick's volatile reaction.

"Someone leaked confidential information to the media." He walked right into the office, not caring that he had disrupted a meeting between Rivera and Sully.

"What?" Rivera frowned.

Nick opened the clip on his phone and handed it to her.

Ice filled Mackenzie's chest. Needles stung her scalp. She watched as Rivera's face clouded with dread and Sully ripped open a bag of chips, stuffing a fistful into his mouth.

"This is unacceptable." Rivera removed her glasses and looked at Sully sharply. "How did this woman get the information? I thought we were very clear about leaks."

"I can vouch for our people," Sully assured her. "The leak could be from the medical examiner's office or the CSU, or even a witness."

"Don't take me off this case," Mackenzie begged, knowing where this was going. "I've been making progress. I don't think we should make any decisions based on optics."

"Oh, I have no intention of taking you off the case," Rivera said.

"You don't?"

"No. You're good, and I'm not an idiot. I'll deal with the fallout." Right on cue, the office phone trilled. She lifted the handset and slammed it back. "Do you have any updates?"

Mackenzie and Nick nodded at each other, on the same page about not confiding in their bosses about their reconnaissance mission. Instead, they told them about the video and the key from Jane Doe.

"I guess Dr. Turner is as good as his references said he was." Rivera sounded satisfied. "How did Jane Doe know Judge Hamilton well enough to end up in his house?"

"She provided him with... services," Mackenzie replied.

Rivera held her head in her hands.

"Judge Hamilton?" Sully frowned. "Who would have guessed?"

"And that video with those women?" Rivera questioned. "Could you get any other information out of it? When was it taken? Who are the victims? *Where* was it taken?"

"The quality is really bad, but Clint will try to clean it up so that we can get a clue as to where they were," Nick said. "But whatever operation this is, it is related to the mass grave, as it was on the same memory stick..."

"Which is connected to our murders and disappearances." Rivera finished his sentence.

"But we haven't been able to link Hamilton and that house with the mass grave or the memory stick, have we?" Sully asked.

"No." Mackenzie sighed. "But we will find something."

"If they're related," Sully pressed.

"Of course." She looked at Nick. She refused to believe that Hamilton and his club full of barcoded women had nothing to do with the mass grave.

The chances of two horrible crimes in close vicinity to each other not having a connection were minuscule, and the conspiracy that was unravelling in front of her was monumental and sickening. But if Lakemore had taught her anything, it was that evil didn't have any limits.

When they left Rivera's office, Austin was waiting for them outside, sitting on a chair and bouncing his knee. He stood up abruptly, eager to spit out his discovery. "That Mack1987 in the blogs?"

"Do you know who they are?" Nick asked.

He pressed his lips in a thin line. "No. We can't get anything from the websites. But I contacted the producers of the documentary, and they said they received many fan letters and emails. One of the emails was signed *Mack1987*." He showed them a copy. Even the email address was *Mack1987* and a combination of numbers and digits.

Did Detective Mackenzie Price talk at length off camera about her romantic life with Valerie Cohen? If so, what did she say?

"What the hell is this?" Mackenzie said, crumpling the paper in her hand, her voice strident. Valerie Cohen had interviewed her, and other detectives, for the documentary. She remembered how she had talked about almost every topic under the sun. Never had she thought someone would pay this close attention.

"Can we track the email address?" Nick asked.

Austin shook his head. "It's not in use anymore. This was over two months ago. But I spoke with Valerie Cohen out of curiosity to see if anyone tried contacting her directly, and she said her home office was broken into."

Just like Nick's home office was broken into.

Mackenzie's entire body tightened.

"Was there an investigation?" Nick asked, seemingly unruffled. Perhaps he hadn't made the connection.

"Yeah, but it was a dead end. Nothing was taken. There were no cameras around." Austin lifted a shoulder. "I'm pulling out the incident report to make sure."

"We have no leads," Mackenzie said in deep dismay.

"Turner has suggested keeping an eye on the blogs," Austin said. "Mack1987 is still sporadically active. Maybe some comment will give us information on their identity." His phone rang and he excused himself.

Mackenzie turned to Nick. "Is that why your office was broken into? To look for clues about my life?"

"Why wouldn't they just break into your place?" Nick countered. "They're more likely to find evidence there."

It was a good point. Except after what had happened last year, she had installed cameras and extra locks. If this person had been watching, they might have noticed the security. Unless they had assumed...

"They could have drawn the conclusion that something's going on between us," she said, feeling squeamish at the cruel invasion of her life.

"Maybe." To her surprise, he didn't deny that that was a possibility. But she couldn't think too much about it, because her phone buzzed with a message.

"Dr. Weiss has identified one of the victims from the mass grave." She read aloud from her phone. "Phoebe Townsend. She was reported missing three years ago by her cousin."

THIRTY-NINE

The car lurched forward as Mackenzie struggled to read the information she had found on her phone. Her motion sickness was at the cusp of being triggered. Usually Nick would moan about her reading in the car, but this time he didn't say anything. The clock was ticking. They couldn't afford to have another dead victim on their hands.

Phoebe Townsend was a twenty-year-old female who had enrolled in nursing school but then later quit to pursue her life-long dream of becoming an actress. She had a pretty face, big cat-like eyes, and layered black hair. Something about her was very Old Hollywood. She was last seen in Seattle three years ago.

"The Seattle PD opened an investigation," Mackenzie read from the HITS file she had downloaded on her phone. "But there were no witnesses, no evidence. It's a cold case."

"She was a wannabe actress last seen in Seattle but ended up in a mass grave in Lakemore dead from syphilis?" Nick wondered aloud. "How the hell does that happen?"

"Maybe her cousin can give us some answers."

Nick rolled the car into downtown. The streets were

choked with traffic. A loud, bustling gridlock. The contrast between sleepy Lakemore and a vibrant city like Seattle was jolting. Even the colors shone brighter, like light reflected better on surfaces here. Seattle was more familiar and comforting to Mackenzie when she'd initially moved to Lakemore. It was the closest thing she could find to New York—even though the two cities were nothing alike. She looked out the window, catching an old memory of walking holding Sterling's hand. They'd often come here together to their favorite oyster bar.

Nick found parking, and they headed to a condo building that looked like a tall glass tower. Getting off on the top floor, they knocked on the door, and a young, well-built man wearing a gray hoodie and hair buzzed down to the scalp answered the door.

"We're with the Lakemore PD." Nick did the introductions. "You're Luke Townsend?"

Luke's face fell as he let them in. "Oh my God. It's Phoebe, isn't it? You found her?"

Seeing Mackenzie and Nick's solemn expressions, he broke down in tears. "Dammit. Dammit. Dammit." He fell onto a chair, his shoulders quaking.

Mackenzie took a moment to make a quick appraisal of the apartment, which looked like it was straight out of the IKEA catalogue. On the wall was a picture of Luke and Phoebe, taken many years ago.

"I'm sorry for your loss, Mr. Townsend," she said after a few minutes. "But we have some questions."

Luke nodded and wiped his nose with his sleeve. "Of course. I knew something terrible must have happened. Phoebe wasn't the type to just disappear. She was never a rebel."

"You're her cousin, but you're listed as next of kin?" Nick asked.

"Her parents passed away when she was only sixteen. My parents adopted her. Our fathers were brothers."

"When was the last time you spoke with her?" Mackenzie asked.

"Gosh, it was in August, three years ago. I was in Denmark for a few months on contract for some work." He sniffed. "I can't believe it. We talked once a week over the phone..." Pain marred his face. "I had no idea that phone call would be our last one. What happened to her?"

Nick hesitated before answering. "She died from syphilis."

"*What?*"

"But there was foul play," Mackenzie added. "We don't have the full picture yet."

"But syphilis is treatable. I don't get it." He shook his head. "And she was a nurse."

It made no sense for Phoebe not to seek treatment, which only left one option. She had been held captive against her will. Someone had taken away her freedom.

"Did she ever mention Lakemore to you?" Nick pressed.

Luke thought about it. "No. It's that town the Sharks are from, right?"

"Yes, that's where she was found," Mackenzie said.

"I'm sorry, I have no idea why she'd be there. We didn't have any friends or family living there."

She bit her lip, thinking hard about how someone who'd wanted to be an actress ended up in Lakemore. Had she been held against her will?

"Did you think it was odd?" Nick asked. "That she suddenly decided to quit nursing and become an actress?"

"I know it sounds strange, but we grew up together and Phoebe was meant for the silver screen," Luke said fondly, a wistful smile on his lips. "She had that charisma. And she was in drama club at school and college."

"During your last conversation, did she sound upset or stressed?" Mackenzie asked.

"Not at all. She was hopeful. She said she was looking into potential leads all over the country."

"Did she mention any specific leads?"

Luke shook his head. "It was all very new. She'd quit nursing only two weeks before our last conversation. So she was in a good mood. She was yet to face the rejections that come with that line of work. But I had faith in her. She is a very positive person... was a positive person."

Disappointment crashed into Mackenzie. She had been hoping for something. Maybe Dr. Weiss would identify more victims with time...

"Did anything strange happen before or after she disappeared?" Nick asked desperately. "Anything at all?"

Luke was about to shake his head again, but something crossed his face. His eyes widened and his mouth fell open. "Oh, yes! There was that man."

"What man?" Mackenzie pushed.

"This middle-aged guy. A year after Phoebe went missing, he visited me quite a few times asking for information about her." He scratched his head. "His name was Cameron... Fletcher! Cameron Fletcher."

Mackenzie internally sifted through all the details she had retained about this case. From Sophie to Courtney to Debbie to Sterling and the mass graves and Jane Doe. But the name was unfamiliar.

"Did he say who he was?" Nick asked.

"A retired FBI agent."

Phoebe's disappearance case belonged to the Seattle PD. The FBI hadn't touched it. Why had a retired FBI agent decided to take an interest in it a whole year after she was last seen?

FORTY

Nick placed a glass of wine in front of Mackenzie at her desk.

"What's the occasion?" She closed the CSU's report on Sterling's abduction site. Her eyes had started to ache from trying to look for something new. But once again the only thing their perpetrator had left was muskrat fur from the coat they couldn't identify.

"The occasion is that I don't want to waste this bottle, which will happen if we don't finish it today." He took a sip from his mug and made a face. "It's basically vinegar."

Mackenzie tasted it. "Jesus, Nick. When did you open it?"

"A few days ago." He straightened, all business. "Anyway, I looked up Cameron Fletcher and called my friend at the Bureau. Fletcher retired eighteen months ago and has no connection with Phoebe Townsend."

"If he had no connection with the victim, why was he so interested?" Mackenzie wondered, chugging the wine like it was medicine. Fortunately, it was late at night, and they were the only ones left in the office.

Mackenzie liked the station at night. There were a few uniforms around on the graveyard shift, and the cleaning crew, but activity had collapsed. It felt like time had slowed down and she could savor being in the belly of it all. Sometimes it was easy to forget how grim and violent her world was, how every day she was confronted with the mind-boggling actions people could be driven to. At night, when she heard the janitor pass by the office humming "Killing Me Softly", she would be reminded.

"I got an address for Fletcher. He lives in Tacoma now," Nick said disrupting her train of thought. "We'll go there first thing tomorrow."

She nodded. "I mean, he must have contacts. Maybe there was something about this case that got him interested."

"One can only hope." He topped up his mug with more wine and offered her some, which she refused. "Sterling is a tall, healthy man. It would be no easy feat to abduct him."

"Tox screen for Courtney and Debbie showed chloroform in their systems. That's what must have been used on Sterling." She waited for the wine to make her feel light-headed and shrink her anxiety. "It's interesting how there's no other evidence. This person abducted four people, killed three in different ways, left their bodies at different locations... I didn't expect such a clean job."

"Why not?"

"Because of their motivation. According to Dr. Turner, this is someone with a deranged side triggered by that documentary and latching on to me. It's not some hardened criminal. And still the crimes have some standard of professionalism to them."

"Maybe it's someone from the CSU or medical examiner's office," Nick joked.

"They would certainly have enough knowledge to do a clean job and make things harder for us."

He stared at her like she was speaking a different language. "Mack, I was kidding."

"I'm not!" Maybe the wine was getting to her. "I saw the

men in that house engaging in illegal activities. Why is it ridiculous to assume that the person we're looking for is someone we're working with? Perhaps all those years of cutting open bodies or cleaning up after crime scenes damaged something inside them."

"We are trying to track whoever sent those questions to the production house and broke into Valerie Cohen's office," Nick pointed out. "Austin is very keen to follow up on that report. I bet he'll dig up something."

Mackenzie's heartbeat was tied in a strangling knot in her throat. No matter which way she turned, she was always under a looming shadow. How many enemies did she have?

"I'm not denying that it's impossible." He cracked his knuckles. "But we can't get that paranoid without any evidence." He leaned forward, elbows on his knees. "We can't fight this alone, Mack."

"Then why does it feel like we are?"

He didn't reply, and they shared a silence. A silence pregnant with fear and suspicion.

"Your lips are purple," he said after a while.

She touched them on reflex and took out a tissue to wipe them.

Why was he looking at my lips?

Mackenzie heard it first. The sound of heels clicking against the floor. Jenna waltzed in, wearing her classic boots.

"What are you still doing here?" Nick asked.

She waved a paper in her hand. "Tracking down the key you gave me."

"And did you?" he asked hopefully.

"I sure did." Jenna smiled and handed him the information. "I got the manufacturer from the bitting code and talked to him. This key opens a unit in a self-storage facility right here in Lakemore."

"Did the manufacturer tell you who he sold it to?" Mackenzie asked.

"Someone by the name of Kai. It was an online order."

Nick was up, wearing his jacket. "Let's go."

The self-storage facility was located in the industrial part of town, where now only one factory operated. There was a time when four factories were fully operational. A time when Lakemore had more prospects. The first one shut down over twenty years ago. Ten years ago, the second one. And just one year ago, the third. It looked like a ghost town, with structures covered in graffiti, spare tires and cold cars sitting around, holes in the barbed wire intended for security.

"There it is." Nick pointed ahead at the building. "I'm scared to leave my car here."

"I'd be more scared to be *in* it. Carjacking is highly likely here." Mackenzie glanced at the run-down area, not finding much solace in the fact that she had a gun.

Nick parked the car as close as he could to the facility. Getting out, Mackenzie shivered as a stinging wind slapped her face.

"What number did Jenna say it was?"

Nick checked the paper. "B-31."

The facility was cold and unwelcoming. There was obviously no temperature control. Rows of units extended down the dimly lit hallways. They headed to row B and sprinted along, looking for unit 31.

"Who do you think Kai is?" Mackenzie asked. "I would definitely remember coming across that name. It's not very common."

"It's a fake one." He shrugged. "Hamilton probably needed to give a name and didn't want his actual name out there."

They reached number 31. Nick produced the key from his

pocket and inserted it into the lock at the bottom of the door. It turned without resistance, followed by a clicking sound.

"Moment of truth." He grunted as he and Mackenzie lifted the door. It slid up, making a screeching sound.

Mackenzie fumbled for a switch on the wall, and with one flip, light flooded the unit.

"What the hell?" Nick frowned.

The unit was empty, except for one thing. A black duffel bag was sitting in the center of the room. Under the flickering white light, it looked ominous, like this ordinary bag contained something special.

"Renting a whole unit just for a bag?" Nick wondered incredulously. "Why wouldn't Hamilton just keep it locked away in his house?"

"Maybe because he doesn't want anyone finding it and is being extra cautious." Mackenzie walked up to it. "You know, technically we're not allowed to open this. We need a warrant."

They both stood over the duffel bag, which was zipped closed. Mackenzie felt the anticipation tickle her. There was something inside that was worth hiding in a storage unit. Something Hamilton valued and didn't want in his house for anyone to accidentally find.

"Fuck it." Nick kneeled on the floor.

"Nick! Seriously?"

He was the one who had been a stickler for the rules lately. But he looked up at her with a pensive expression. "Mack, we can't afford to lose any leads. What if Hamilton realizes that his key is gone?"

Mackenzie nodded and crouched next to him. He at least had the sense to put on gloves before he opened the bag. Then he dipped his hand inside and extracted a DVD case.

"Who even uses these anymore?" he asked.

"Is that all there is?" She peered into the open bag, which contained piles of DVD cases.

"Look, they have dates on them," Nick pointed out.

"We have a DVD player back at the station."

They looked at each other. Mackenzie's nerves sizzled. In all their years together, they had never stepped so boldly out of line. The worst Mackenzie had done was work on a lead when she was supposed to be on leave. But this was drastic and something they couldn't come back from.

There were many reasons not to do this. But the fear of having another dead body on her hands, sacrificed in her name, was a burden too heavy to carry.

She picked up the bag. "There's no going back now. Let's see this through to the end."

Mackenzie and Nick moved the DVD player and the screen out of the conference room and into their office, away from the prying eyes of those working the graveyard shift. Nick fanned out the tapes on his desk, arranging them in chronological order. Mackenzie kept an eye on the door, realizing that closing it would draw more suspicion. Plus, the screen was angled away from it.

She didn't like this feeling of being a rebel. It was like she was being shocked with currents every few seconds. She was jittery and resisting the urge to bite her nails.

"The oldest one is from 1998." Nick plugged the player in. "A year after DVDs first came out."

The recording was old. The screen was frequently interrupted by static. The camera faced a faded blue couch with rips against a white wall. A few seconds in, an attractive woman dressed in a white blouse and denim skirt came in from the side and sat on the couch, smiling shyly. A man stood in front of her, only his lower half visible. They were talking, but there was no sound.

"It's probably because the tape is so old..." Nick said, but then his voice faded and his face went pink. The woman was now performing oral sex on the man. "Okay, we're done watching this."

"It's a porn film? Why would anyone go to such lengths to hide that?"

"Let's play a more recent one." He selected a random DVD. "This is from a year ago."

It was the same routine. The same blue couch against the wall. Another pretty girl, in a dress this time. And an anonymous man standing in front of her. Except this time, there was audio.

"Look, I got contacts in this industry. It's a hard one to break into. It's just something everyone does, you know?"

"Do you recognize the voice?" Mackenzie asked.

Nick shook his head. "The quality isn't the best. But it doesn't sound like Hamilton."

The girl swallowed hard and hugged her chest. "I don't know... I'm not... It just feels weird."

"It's your choice," the man said coolly. "I don't want to force you. I'm not a bad guy. I just find you really beautiful and would like to be with you."

The girl squirmed, biting her lips and rubbing her palms together.

"If you want me to help you, I would need something in return, right?" he continued silkily. "But there's no pressure. If you don't want to, then I wish you all the best." He made a show of turning around, but the girl stopped him.

"Wait! Wait!" she cried with glassy eyes. "Okay. Okay. I'll do it. Just once, right?"

"Yes."

"And will you be..." she paused, "gentle?"

He cupped her chin. "Of course. I'm not a monster."

They proceeded to have sex. The man's face was never visible on the camera.

"So Hamilton is a porn addict?" Nick said, bemused. "Can't you find this kind of stuff on the internet now?"

Mackenzie watched the video with a clinical eye. Nick had a point. It made no sense for Hamilton to collect porn DVDs from the last twenty years and hide them in a storage unit. But then it hit her like a punch to the gut.

The girl didn't look at the camera even once.

"This is not porn," she said, blood draining from her face. "This is real. These girls were lured into having sex and recorded secretly."

FORTY-ONE

APRIL 22

Mackenzie stood in front of her weeping willow. It was her favorite thing in the garden. Over the last two years, she had neglected everything else but this tree. The grass was overgrown and uneven. Weeds had taken over the frayed flower beds. But the willow stood strong and absolute. Dramatic, with its long branches falling into an arch just touching the ground. She stepped under the canopy, relishing the light green leaves with silver undersides. As the sun began to climb up the sky, light leaked through the falling branches. She was shielded from the outside world. Inside a bubble where she could think more clearly.

Last night, they had watched a few more DVDs and discovered that they all shared the same pattern. A man convinced a young woman to engage in sexual activities in exchange for industry contacts. None of the women seemed to have any idea they were being recorded. Once they were done, the man promised to be in touch and dismissed them.

Were those women anything to do with the ones Mackenzie had seen in that house? Or were they the ones in the mass grave? All she knew was that the events unfolding were making her insides hurt. She closed her eyes, thinking about all those women dead from treatable infections. Buried there so callously, like animals that were no longer of any use.

"Detective Price?" Andrew's voice came from the driveway.

Mackenzie exited the weeping willow. "Hey, thanks for coming."

"No problem." He looked at the house behind her. "That's a nice place you got here." He made that face again, like he was trying to piece her together. Despite her improving relationship with him, that was something she still hadn't warmed to. "Did your parents plant that tree?"

"Excuse me?"

"You looked like you were trying to find refuge in there." He raised his eyebrows at the weeping willow. "When people feel unsafe, they return to childhood memories associated with their parents, who used to make them feel safe."

Mackenzie blinked, and the sound of Melody shrieking as her head smashed against the mirror rang in her ears. But then she recalled that memory—one of her earliest—of Robert planting seeds in the soil from which a Douglas fir later grew.

"My parents didn't spend a lot of time making me feel safe." She held back a bitter bark of laughter.

"Huh. Your grandmother, then?" When Mackenzie fidgeted, he relented. "You don't have to answer me. I don't mean to intrude. Besides, it's a perfectly healthy habit."

"You think so?" She snorted. For some reason, she felt like nothing she did was healthy. She had focused on perfecting her exterior and somewhere deep down had let her mind run amok.

"It's the familiar things we hold on to in times of uncertainty." He looked around at her quiet neighborhood, brimming with morning activities. "Familiar things or people. When my wife passed away, it was Robbie that kept me going. I held on to him like a life raft."

"You're lucky to have him." She wrapped her arms around

herself and glanced at the house, which suddenly seemed far too big for one person.

"From what I can tell, you have someone too." Andrew's smile was almost teasing. Mackenzie's heart skidded, but he didn't linger on the topic. "I just visited our Jane Doe today."

"How is she? Has she told you anything?"

"No." He looked disappointed. "In fact, I was going to talk to the lieutenant about letting some agency or organization take over."

"Why?" she demanded, disturbed. "I mean, is it okay to just let her go?"

"She's much better now. She talks, but nothing about her past or who she is." He flattened his mouth. "It's clear she is healing, but she continues to dissociate from her past. I believe she should be rehabilitated, set up with a place of her own, a job."

"But what about the case?" Mackenzie crossed her arms. Only she and Nick knew of Jane Doe's connection to Hamilton and their investigation.

"It will remain open with no active line of inquiries." He shrugged. "I know you took her out yesterday. Did she tell you anything?"

Mackenzie shook her head. It felt too heavy on her shoulders. Like her body was weighed down by the lies and secrets. But she wanted to keep things close to her chest for now.

"Well, then we can't do anything."

She nodded. "I needed a favor from you."

He blinked. "Okay, sure."

She handed him a USB stick. "This contains some videos from the last ten years. Can you show them to Jane Doe and ask her if she recognizes anyone?"

Andrew's eyes narrowed. "Why? I didn't know you were on her case too. Did you find something?"

"No. Not really. I'm not allowed to discuss details, since

you're technically a consultant, but I'm just following a hunch." She lied through her teeth.

Andrew clearly wasn't convinced, but he didn't protest further.

Cameron Fletcher lived in a rustic house atop a hill in Tacoma. Mackenzie envied the view he had. White-tipped crests whipped by the wind lapping against the sharp outline of the coast. A knot of trees not too far from the shoreline. This place was remote. It was exactly what she needed after this case was over.

Except when she stepped inside the house, she realized that this wasn't a house built for escape, but one to hide in. The dusty, stale air and the dilapidated state of the building spelled defeat.

"Would you like some coffee or water?" Cameron asked. He was sitting on a chair, resting a bandaged leg. He was a stocky man, with a double chin and a large forehead, and even larger elvish ears.

"We're good," Mackenzie answered, watching him light a cigarette with palpable disinterest. The former FBI agent had showed no reaction when they arrived.

"How come the Lakemore PD is knocking on my door?" he asked in a scratchy voice damaged over the years by the same habit that had turned his teeth yellow.

"We want to talk about Phoebe Townsend," Nick said.

An array of emotions flitted across Cameron's face before only regret remained. "That one. Did you find her?"

"We did," Nick replied.

Cameron took a long, shaky drag. The smoke spiraled out of his nostrils and dissolved in the stuffy air. "Dead?" He tried to keep his hand steady, but Mackenzie caught the slight falter.

Nick nodded.

The spark in Cameron's eyes diminished.

"Murdered?"

"Not exactly." Mackenzie shoved her hands in her pockets. "Why were you interested in her disappearance? That case wasn't with the FBI."

Cameron stared at the pair of them as if he was contemplating something. Like he was applying years of training to dissect their characters and intentions. "Maybe I was just curious and bored."

"She died from syphilis," Nick shared. Cameron's face registered surprise. "She and several others."

"Who told you about me?" Cameron's gaze turned paranoid.

"Phoebe's cousin," Mackenzie said, looking him in the eye. "Nobody else. We know something big is going on."

Cameron stood up and pushed the cigarette into the ashtray. He limped to the window and opened it, breathing in the salty air. "My name stays out of this. Are we clear?"

Mackenzie and Nick nodded at each other and then at him.

Cameron hesitated before spilling the words. "Around fifteen years ago, a young girl went missing in Colorado. Aria Fields."

Mackenzie felt electrified. One sentence had crushed all her other thoughts into oblivion. The last name she was expecting to come out of Cameron's mouth was Aria's. Nick took a sharp intake of breath.

Cameron didn't seem to notice their shock and continued speaking while looking out the window at the choppy sea. "It wasn't my case, but I was helping out on it. It led me to the discovery of a prostitution ring in Washington. It was why I transferred to the office here. And it wasn't just me. Some fellow agents working on missing persons cases noticed discrepancies, doors being shut, things just not making sense. Their investigations kept hitting a wall. And so we decided to work together unofficially to bring down this ring. It was just the four of us."

It all sounded too familiar.

"Unfortunately, over a year ago, our efforts must have been spotted. Because conveniently enough, two of us were transferred to the East Coast, one of us was suspended, and I was encouraged to retire early. All within a span of six months."

"Who was responsible for this? Your boss?" Mackenzie asked.

Cameron shrugged. "These decisions came from different channels. I always knew someone powerful was behind this ring. But I underestimated their reach. Or maybe there's more than one of them."

Those men in the house. Hamilton and his friends—from judges and lawyers to businessmen and lobbyists. They had infiltrated all layers of society and positioned themselves to wield a lot of power. Especially together.

"What did you discover about this prostitution ring?" Nick asked.

"Just that young women were tricked into sex acts and secretly recorded. Then the tapes were used to blackmail them into becoming escorts to service rich and powerful people."

"Did you ever find out what happened to Aria?" Mackenzie asked. She didn't know what she was hoping his answer would be.

"Two years ago, Aria's twin found me."

Mackenzie blanched. Sophie.

"She remembered me from my time in Colorado. Nice girl." He gave a wan smile that soon faded. "She told me she'd come across Aria in a porn film."

That was why Sophie was murdered. Because after all those years, she'd discovered her sister in a film linked to a prostitution ring run by powerful people. Someone must have found out that she was sniffing around and had her silenced.

"Did you suspect who was behind this operation?" Nick asked.

Cameron paled, visibly uncomfortable. "There were a few names. The former mayor of Riverview. A few people in the governor's office in the executive branch. The state auditor at the time, I think. But we weren't able to find any hard evidence that could actually land them in jail."

Together they were invincible. Each of them like part of a wave. Rising and bringing destruction, taking in more and more victims, growing and thriving. But the wave had to crash sometime.

"Were you never able to rescue anyone from this ring?" Mackenzie asked, fighting to keep her determination strong. But if four FBI agents didn't have a shot, then what were two detectives from Lakemore PD going to do?

Cameron's face was drawn tight, like he was trying not to cry, like the memories he was recalling had sharp edges. "These girls were terrified. The men who trapped them by blackmailing them with sex tapes and the men they were forced to sleep with were the people who were supposed to protect them. In all those years, there was only one girl I was able to get to talk to me. Her name was Salma. She gave me some details. How Judge Romano had a doctor who would give them birth control shots and perform abortions if needed—"

"Judge Romano is a conservative. He's known for his pro-life views," Mackenzie blurted in disbelief.

Cameron snorted. "Yeah. Sure. That's how it works."

Nick shrugged off his jacket and sat on a stool without a word. Mackenzie knew that when he reached his tipping point, he didn't show his anger or disappointment. His body always reacted—the cords jutting out on his arms, that tight clench of his jaw, and his measured breaths.

Mackenzie felt surreal. Her brain was slowly absorbing the information—a defense mechanism.

"Where is Salma now?" she asked.

"I don't know." Cameron's face fell. "We lost touch and I was never able to find her again. Though she did tell me something else."

"What was that?"

"Since their medical care was all under the table, it was very limited. If anyone got sick, they weren't provided with treatment. She said she knew two girls who died from some STD, and that another girl told her that it wasn't uncommon. Whatever happened to their bodies was anyone's guess."

That was how they'd ended up in the mass grave. First they were manipulated into having sex, then blackmailed into becoming escorts, and those who had the further misfortune of catching an STD or tetanus were left to die and buried in that clearing.

"Did you know that Sophie's fiancé is a detective?" Mackenzie asked. "Did she mention him? Why didn't she ask him for help?"

"She was scared!" Cameron limped back to the chair. "She wanted to, but I told her to keep this to herself. Anyone who has tried to get to the truth has suffered consequences. From transfers to suspensions, you name it. We were all silenced. I advised her to keep her fiancé out of this to protect him. Did she?"

Mackenzie nodded. "Did you keep any evidence you'd uncovered? Anything related to your unofficial investigation?"

"Stay away from this, Detective Price." He shrugged, but Mackenzie knew it was a facade. "Before you lose everything. We learned it the hard way."

"We will keep your name out of it," Nick assured him. "But we are a part of this now and we can't walk away."

Cameron was wound up tight. "Anyone who gets involved in this is hunted down! The fact that I'm talking to you right now means I'm putting myself in danger as well as the two of you." He reached across to a side table and poured himself a glass of bourbon. That was when Mackenzie noticed the row of empty bottles on the windowsill behind him. He had been drowning himself in alcohol and cigarettes.

"So no one's looking out for them," she whispered.

"My buddy went missing," Cameron admitted. "He was a reporter." A lone tear cascaded down his rough cheek. "Knew him for over twenty years. We started talking about the case. Weeks later, he vanished. A missing person case was filed, but nothing came of it." His hand clenched and unclenched around the glass. "They took my friend away from me."

"I'm sorry." Mackenzie shook her head. "But they will keep taking women from their families, their futures."

Cameron's chin trembled as he took a sip and belched. "We're not superheroes, Detective Price. The sooner you realize that, the less disappointed you will be with yourself."

Mackenzie wasn't naïve enough to believe that she could change the world or that she would be the one to save everyone. But she feared Cameron's fate. She didn't know if she could live like that, constantly haunted by failure.

"So did you keep any evidence or not?" Nick asked.

Cameron nodded reluctantly. He stood and walked slowly into the next room, returning with a wooden box. "Nothing is electronic. Computer files can be hacked. I didn't want to take any risks. This is all I could collect, and it wasn't enough." He hung his head low. "I'm sorry."

Heading back to the car, Mackenzie held the box in her hands like it was treasure.

"That was depressing." Nick unlocked the car and climbed in. "That's what a man looks like when a dream dies."

"Dream?"

"The dream that you'll always do the right thing."

A storm was brewing, and the sound of waves crashing

below was growing louder. Even inside the car, Mackenzie was rattled by the wind whistling atop the hill. She opened the box, revealing a stash of folded papers. She sifted through them. Newspaper clippings. Surveillance pictures. Statements.

Together they assessed everything, looking for a concrete clue that could tie their investigation with Cameron's.

"Wait a minute." Nick's eyebrows knotted. "Kai."

"What about it?" she asked.

"Looks like that's what Cameron and his buddies called this operation. Like a code name." He compared two sheets of paper. "That reporter friend he mentioned who went missing? He wrote Cameron this letter."

Mackenzie took it from him, quickly reading and absorbing the information. "It says here that he was asking around and heard that it was someone called Kai who recruited the girls and made sure they behaved. One of the girls he spoke with said they all feared Kai."

Her nerves crackled. Kai. It was the name Hamilton used to order the key for the storage unit.

FORTY-TWO

"We're in deep shit." Nick ran his hands through his hair, then desperately patted his pockets for cigarettes. "Maybe we need to wait to gather more evidence."

"What evidence?" Mackenzie demanded, spreading her arms. "We need to get those tapes to Clint and have him tell us where they were being recorded. We stepped out of line to get a solid lead, and now we have one."

They were standing outside the back of the station under a covering. Angry rain lashed around them, rattling on the sidewalks and tops of cars with a loud ferociousness. Bolts of lightning gouged the velvet black sky. Thunder growled so deeply that Mackenzie could feel the vibrations under her feet. It wasn't supposed to rain. A storm especially. But she felt like this was something more. Like they were being told not to turn back now.

Nick's face was ashen. "I just can't believe it. This is beyond Lakemore. This might go beyond Washington."

"Look, I have no naïve expectations that we'll resolve everything—"

"We might," he said suddenly.

"Why do you say that?"

"Whoever killed Sophie, Courtney, and Debbie is a part of this. Sophie was abducted by these people for looking into Aria again, and our killer had access to her. And Debbie was held, but she managed to find that damning memory stick and swallow it. Someone amongst them has risked exposure by becoming fixated on you. Think about it. If they hadn't developed this obsession with you, we would never have discovered any of this."

"Yeah. I guess those three didn't die in vain." Sarcasm dripped from Mackenzie's voice.

Nick rolled his eyes. "That's not what I meant. I'm sorry it had to happen this way. But maybe we have an opportunity that Cameron and his friends didn't have. *You*."

Her heart careened from beat to beat. She hadn't asked to find herself in the middle of something so big. But she also knew she couldn't walk away. It wasn't just Sterling whose life was hanging in the balance. The images of those women lying drugged somewhere was still burning in her head.

Her thoughts were punctured by the sharp, keening sound of an alarm ringing.

"What's that?" she cried, plugging her ears.

On instinct, and not caring about the rain, they jogged toward the blaring alarm in the parking lot. It came from a black car. The front door was open and the headlights blinked and flashed.

It was Nick's car.

A prickling sensation tickled down Mackenzie's spine. She looked around the parking lot as Nick closed the door and turned off the alarm, her view distorted from the rain beating down on her eyelashes. There was nobody around. But someone had clearly tried to break into Nick's car. When they'd forced the door open, the alarm had gone off and they'd run.

"Now will you for fuck's sake take this seriously?" she

yelled. Nick breathed hard and turned around, and a blood-curdling thought crossed her mind.

What if this was the killer's process to select their next victim? What if they stalked and studied the target in excruciating detail before snatching them?

They were met with stony silence in the conference room. Sully's thoughts had carried him far. He was visibly dissociating, while his hands played with slime. Peterson's fretful eyes glanced around as he rocked back and forth on a chair. Jenna didn't show any expression—she rarely did, other than that of scorn. Austin's chest heaved in choppy breaths. Andrew was thoughtful.

But it was Rivera who looked downright frightening. She drummed her fingers on the table, her sharp eyes drilling into Mackenzie and Nick. "Do you know how many times you broke protocol? Not to mention the *law* when you trespassed on Judge Hamilton's property."

Austin opened his mouth, but Mackenzie talked over him, knowing he was about to come clean to Rivera. "If we had gone through the regular channels, we wouldn't have discovered any of this."

"Sophie's twin is still out there? She's alive?" Austin asked, worry creasing his face.

She nodded. "Sophie didn't tell you because she wanted to protect you."

"I'm extremely disappointed in both of you, for the record." Rivera was on her own tangent. "This is not the way to do things. I ought to suspend you!"

"Is this Cameron Fletcher willing to go on record?" Sully asked out of nowhere.

Rivera glared at him. "Sergeant."

"We can suspend them once the case is closed." Sully

displayed a rare firmness. "Once we rescue Brooks and those women."

"This entire investigation is now compromised," she argued, a muscle in her forehead throbbing. "People will get off scot-free."

"Maybe. But if it means we end up saving lives, I think it's worth it," Sully insisted.

Rivera risked a glance around the room. Mackenzie held her breath, hoping that everyone would be on board. She saw fierceness in their faces. No hint of reluctance or fear. Rivera must have seen the same, because she nodded curtly. "All right. Dr. Turner, did you show Jane Doe the videos Detective Price gave you?"

"I did." He shuffled in his seat. "She recognized three women. To her knowledge, they are still alive."

"Has she confided in you about where she was kept?" Austin asked. "I think that's where Sophie must have been held captive too."

"Unfortunately not. I asked, but she still shuts down."

"Well, she has shown some improvement, so maybe you should continue trying," Rivera advised. "I can't even imagine how traumatized that girl must be. Being barcoded like that and forced into prostitution. Have Dr. Weiss and Dr. Sullivan finished identifying the bodies from the mass grave?"

"They were only able to identify six out of nine," Nick replied. "The rest either didn't have enough DNA on them or enough tissue on their skulls for facial reconstruction."

"And you mentioned that Clint was working on some facial recognition software to identify the women from the tapes?" Rivera continued.

"Yes, but he just shot us an email telling us that even after cleaning up the videos, they still aren't clear enough for that," Mackenzie said. "We don't have access to state-of-the-art software."

Rivera turned to Peterson, who straightened like an arrow upon being addressed. "Officer Peterson, I want you to personally watch the videos and compare the women in them to missing persons listed by Washington State Patrol, NamUs, and the FBI. We need to identify as many as we can."

"Yes, Lieutenant."

"Jenna, get the details of the victims identified in the mass graves and contact their next of kin. They have been waiting for answers for a long time. Then work with Peterson to see how many of them were reported missing and were in those videos."

"You got it." Jenna nodded.

"I think I need to have a crack at Fletcher," Austin said with purpose. "He might reveal something to me."

"You think so?" Sully raised an eyebrow. "The guy seemed pretty cagey. And rightly so."

"It sounds like he had a soft corner for Sophie. Probably because she was Aria's twin. Just let me give it a shot. Please."

It was evident that Austin didn't want to sit idle and was itching to do something. Sully gave him a nod.

"You two will bring in Judge Hamilton for questioning." Rivera interlinked her fingers.

"What?" Mackenzie blurted.

"I think you have enough on him to confront him," Sully said with a conspiratorial smile. "At least we can add some pressure on that fucker and hope he makes a blunder."

"There's something else," Mackenzie said, making everyone pause as they began to disperse. Nick shot her a warning look. But this time it was her turn to look out for him. She relayed everything that had happened to him. "Maybe he needs some protection. Or just off the case."

"Off the case?" he said in disbelief. "Are you for real?"

"No one close to me is safe." Her voice cracked. "What if they escalate things?"

"There's a pattern to these abductions and killings," he protested. "I don't fall into that."

"Which is why not a hair on your head has been hurt," Andrew said darkly. "But you are significant to Mackenzie. Surely the killer has noticed that."

Mackenzie folded her arms, feeling awkward, and avoided Nick's probing gaze.

"Perhaps it's because he's a trained police officer," Rivera suggested. "And a senator's son. The killer must have realized that going after him won't be easy, so they're taking their time."

"But what's their endgame?" Austin questioned. "How is lurking around Nick's house and trying to get into his car going to help them?"

"What do you think?" Mackenzie turned to Andrew. Even he was slightly taken aback. She had never asked for his opinion directly. But the thought of Nick in danger was like someone was trying to carve her heart right out of her chest.

"I believe the killer is conflicted," he replied. "Their intention has been to eliminate those who have wronged you, but your relationship with Nick is making them jealous. I think they're... making up their mind. Trying to decipher how they feel about Nick."

"And they may decide to hurt him?" she asked.

He nodded. "Their possessiveness toward you increases with the body count."

"Where are we with tracking that Mack1987 user?" A grimace pulled on Sully's lips.

"Clint said tracking them electronically isn't possible," Peterson informed him. "But we are going through their online activity to see if it can give us any clue about their identity."

"Redouble your efforts," Sully instructed. "The last thing I want is to worry about Nick too."

FORTY-THREE

Mackenzie dusted the cuffs of her shirt and rearranged her ponytail. It was late, but still she had sent uniformed cops over to Judge Hamilton's house, asking him to meet her at the station urgently.

"Wow. You almost look like your old self." Nick walked in the room and blinked.

"Old self?"

"Scary." He smiled.

She rolled her eyes and then frowned. "I'm not scary anymore? I'm losing my touch."

"Definitely not. It's more of a switch now as opposed to your perpetual state of being." He sat next her, pushing coffee in her direction. "I know you've started experimenting with it."

She smirked and took a sip, gagging at the bitter taste.

"Ugh. How do you drink this? It tastes like expired urine." Mackenzie handed Sterling back his latte.

Sterling chuckled, shaking his head. "Like a child."

The memory dissolved behind her eyes. She felt nothing for him. Not a pinch of love. But she *knew* him. He wasn't a stranger in peril.

"Mack, we'll find him in time." Nick snapped her out of her thoughts.

She nodded, not sure if she believed him entirely. All she knew for sure was that thinking about Sterling and how he was probably being tortured made sobs bubble in the base of her throat.

Judge Hamilton appeared at the door, dressed casually and escorted by a deputy, who let him into the conference room before standing guard outside.

"Detectives." Hamilton nodded courteously. "What's the matter? This is most unusual."

Mackenzie's face remained hard and unyielding. She had witnessed with her own eyes how debauched Hamilton truly was behind his friendly facade. Nick sat back, and she knew he wanted her to take the lead. She was always better at playing the bad cop.

She placed her elbows on the table. "Do you know that prostitution is illegal in the state of Washington?"

Hamilton's innocent expression changed. It was fraught with discomfort. "I... Of course I know." He scratched his ear. "What's going on?"

"What is going on is that you and your friends get escorts on your poker nights," Mackenzie said sharply. "Your *gentlemen's* club."

Brick by brick his composure shattered, but still he denied the charge. "Detective Price, that's absurd! I'm sure someone started a nasty rumor about—"

"Barcodes on their ankles. Really?" Hamilton's face was ashen. He fumbled for words, but Mackenzie continued, "You have a wife. You have three granddaughters. How would you feel if someone numbered them like cattle and passed them around at parties?"

"On what basis are you making such unbelievable accusations?"

"The fact that I saw it with my own eyes."

"How dare you enter my home without my permission?" he seethed.

"I didn't. I showed up hoping to talk to you. The front door was open and I walked right in. Everyone was too preoccupied to notice me for the two minutes I was there," she lied breezily. "I saw you take two of them upstairs."

He wagged his finger. "This is slander. I'm a well-respected—"

"You're scum, Judge." She spoke calmly. "We also have some damning videos in a storage unit that we can link to you."

Hamilton looked at Nick. "Are you going to sit back and let her speak to me like this?"

Nick gave him a Cheshire Cat grin and raised his mug. "I'm enjoying this."

"Let's see how your evidence holds up in court." Hamilton gritted his teeth, his face contorting with anger. "I'm sure you have obtained all this *bogus* evidence through questionable means."

"I'm good with that. Your career is effectively over regardless. How do you think your wife and family will react when they find out?" Mackenzie tilted her head, feigning curiosity.

Hamilton slammed the table with his fist. "You're messing with the wrong person!" he roared.

"Is that a threat?" She blinked, leaning forward.

Then everything happened quickly.

The sound of glass cracking and air whooshing for a millisecond. Something grazed the back of Mackenzie's head, and suddenly she found herself on the floor, toppled over. Something was happening to her. Her vision kept cutting to black. Her heart had jumped into a gallop. Everything was burning.

"Mack!" Nick's face loomed above hers. She had seen him

like this only once before, when Luna had been in danger. "Mack!"

She was slipping away. Falling into an abyss. She was trying to hold on, but something was pulling her under. It was almost like sleep. Except this was far worse.

"Mack. Don't leave me." They were the last words she heard before everything was obliterated.

FORTY-FOUR

When Mackenzie woke up, she was in her old house. The one where she'd grown up until the age of twelve, after which she'd been shipped off to New York. The one that had always been eerie and uninviting. But it didn't feel the same. The air tasted different. The light curved around objects more brightly.

She was in the kitchen.

The same kitchen where she had found a dead body.

It hadn't changed at all in the last twenty or so years. The walls were lime green. The floor tiles a dirty yellow. The cabinets were painted a darker shade of green, with pictures of fruits and vegetables on a white strip stuck across them. A bare bulb dangled above the dining table. It looked like it was right out of the eighties.

She must be dreaming. But then something changed inside her. She wasn't dreaming. This was real... except it couldn't be. Her heart rate skyrocketed. Blood roared into her ears.

It was like all your life you were supposed to exist within certain boundaries, within a system defined by the established laws of science. But there was a tear in that reality. By some accident, she had stepped into a different place, got a glimpse of what lay beyond.

"Mackenzie."

A voice came from behind her. A woman's voice. Mackenzie recognized it before she turned around. When she did, she saw her mother sitting at the table. A thick mane of curly black hair crowned her head. Her gray eyes were like saucers. Her lips puffy.

She looked exactly like Mackenzie had always remembered her.

"I'm so proud of you, sweetheart."

"Mom?" She felt her heart slow down. It was too slow now. Barely beating at all. "What's going on?"

"You've come a long way. I used to worry I'd ruined you for good," Melody said softly. She didn't look happy, but neither was she sad. She looked neutral, with an air of tranquility surrounding her.

"Do you regret it? All the lies you told?" Mackenzie asked.

Melody nodded. "I didn't realize my weakness would destroy so many lives. I've watched you overcome so much gracefully. But I still see myself in you."

"I'm not like you." Mackenzie looked around, trying to make sense of what was going on. She remembered a few tricks she'd read to wake up from a dream. She caught her reflection in a mirror and slapped herself. "Wake up. Wake up."

She spotted the clock on the wall. It said 9:15. She counted to a minute in her head and looked at it again. 9:16. But time was supposed to be warped in dreams. She tried to control the elements around her. Tried to make something happen, but nothing did. She had zero control.

"Are you done?" Melody smiled.

Mackenzie pressed her hand into her chest. *Thud.* And then thirty seconds later. *Thud.*

"Honey, there was a time in my life when there was happiness right in front of me, but I didn't reach for it."

"Robert?"

Melody nodded. "I loved him, Mackenzie. I know you won't believe me, because my actions were so deplorable. But I did."

"What happened?"

"I was weak. I had bad habits. They cost me my chance. You and I could have had it all."

Everything Mackenzie felt was severely diluted. Both positive and negative emotions barely brushed her by. Even her confusion at being in this place was tempered. Like she was detached from it all and herself.

"Don't do what I did, Mackenzie. You've been doing so well. But it will all be for nothing if you don't realize the final prize at the end of it."

"What's that?"

Melody smiled. "I think you know. Don't let your habit of not wanting to be vulnerable cost you *your* chance. Life is supposed to be lived. But you can't live if you don't love."

Then everything collapsed.

Mackenzie's eyes opened with a jolt. Her heart was racing again. Racing too fast. She was panting, like she had just run a marathon. It took her a few moments to take in her surroundings. She was in a hospital room. And someone was holding her hand.

Her neck ached as she craned to see who it was. Nick was sitting on a chair, but his head was on the bed by her waist, resting on his forearm. His other hand was atop hers.

Mackenzie's chest felt like it was disintegrating. Suddenly the machine started making a beeping sound. Apparently her heart rate had jumped too high.

Nick woke up suddenly. "Huh? What? Mack! Are you okay?"

"Yes," she croaked. "How long have I been out for?"

"It's been a few hours since your surgery." He clicked a button to call the nurse.

"What happened?" It was all hazy. Her neck felt stiff. The back of her head was sore. But her body felt fine other than a general weakness.

"You were shot."

"Shot?" she shrieked. Then it all came back to her. How they were with Judge Hamilton in the conference room when she heard the glass crack.

Before they could continue talking, a doctor and a nurse filtered inside the room and began asking Mackenzie a million questions and performing routine examinations.

"You have a fracture in your skull, but it will heal," the doctor informed her. "Your vitals look good. You're very lucky. The bullet grazed the back of your head."

"How long do I have to be here for?"

"I'm ready to discharge you in a few hours. I just want to monitor you for delayed symptoms. Your blood work came back normal. We did a CT scan when you were brought in, but I want to do an MRI too to check for any hemorrhage. You'll need to rest at home for the next few days."

"Thanks, Doctor." Mackenzie had no intention of resting once she was out of here.

Before the doctor left, she glanced at Nick, who was sitting in a corner, scrolling through his phone. "He's a keeper, that one. Hasn't left for a moment since you came in."

Mackenzie gave her a tight smile.

"That had to be a sniper, right?" she said once the doctor and nurse had left the room. "This was a hit man."

"Yeah, we're still investigating." He sighed. "Guess Fletcher was right. We are getting too close, and look what happened."

Mackenzie clutched the blanket tightly. "Do you think Hamilton was in on it? Or was it one of his friends?"

"He panicked. Either he's a great actor, or he didn't know that was going to happen."

"He *is* a great actor," she muttered petulantly. "Who would have thought that saintly Judge Hamilton would be involved in this shit?"

"Or maybe Hamilton was the target." Nick frowned like the thought had just come to him. "Maybe someone else involved in this prostitution ring got spooked that he might spill the beans to us. So he tried to take him out."

"Hamilton was sitting across from us," Mackenzie recalled. The memories were hazier than the strange dream she'd had. "A sniper's aim can't be that bad. But you were sitting right next to me..." Perhaps Nick was the target.

"Why would anyone hire a hit man to kill me?" Nick asked.

"Why would anyone hire a hit man to kill *me*?" she countered. "The killer doesn't want to hurt me. If it's someone from the ring we're investigating, I guess they wanted to hurt either one of us."

"Somehow I doubt our killer is a sniper. Fletcher was right. We're way out of our depth with this, Mack." He shook his head.

There was a knock on the door and Andrew poked his head in. "Am I disturbing you?"

"No, no." Mackenzie sat up, her head still a bit woozy. "Thank you for visiting."

"Robbie was here earlier, but you were asleep. He left those flowers for you."

She noticed the fresh sunflowers in a vase. "Thank you. These are my favorites. How did he know?"

"I told him. I'll bring him over later."

When Nick's phone started to ring, he excused himself and slipped out of the room.

"Is there chatter at work? That I should be off the case because someone tried to kill me?"

"Not that I know of." Andrew hesitated. "But I think there should be."

"What are you talking about?"

He stepped forward, tilting his head and watching her closely. "I'm worried for you, Detective Price."

"I'm not the only one working this case. Maybe Nick was the target. Maybe others are in danger too." The back of her head began to throb, and she winced.

"May I?" Andrew asked, his hand hovering over the PCA pump. When she nodded, he pressed a button that pushed morphine into her system. "I've been thinking more about the killer." His voice lowered as he leaned closer. "About what their endgame is."

"Their endgame?" Her head was starting to swim.

"Their ultimate goal is you," he whispered. "They're doing all this for you. If you don't reciprocate, they'll become a danger to you."

"Reciprocate? How?" She was trying to stay conscious, but the painkiller was taking over.

"If you don't express your gratitude or show interest, then they'll turn against you and come after you."

Mackenzie's eyes shut of their own accord. The last thing she saw was Andrew's face hovering above hers with a concerned look. The edges of his face began to swirl like he was underwater. And then everything went black once again.

FORTY-FIVE

APRIL 25

When Mackenzie stepped into the station, she was greeted by almost everyone who passed her by. Troy, who was speaking to someone in the waiting area, gave her a salute. "O Captain! My Captain!"

She flipped him off with a sweet smile. She had been discharged earlier that morning, after having to spend one more night at the hospital "just in case". Fortunately, all her results had come back normal, and after taking a shower, she'd headed right back to work.

In the conference room, everyone was standing around the table in clusters, with drawn eyebrows, shaking heads, deep sighs, and tense shoulders. Mackenzie paused for a second. She barely remembered anything that had transpired in the hospital after she'd woken up from her strange dream. Spotting Nick frowning at Jenna and loosening his tie, she squared her shoulders and headed inside.

"Are there any updates? Any leads on Sterling?"

They all stopped talking and looked at her. Rivera's eyes blared disapproval. Austin looked too drained to care. Sully was visibly uncomfortable at the sight of her. And that was when

Mackenzie remembered Andrew telling her in the hospital how he believed she needed to stay away from the case. But he was nowhere to be seen.

"It's pointless," Nick explained to the rest of them.

Sully had already given up. "There were forty-three DVDs. Peterson was able to identify twenty-eight of them with missing persons reports filed in Washington and other states. And Jenna found an overlap of six women from the mass graves with the videos."

"So we have confirmation that they're all connected." Mackenzie nodded encouragingly.

"Yeah, but we've still no idea how to track down where the videos were shot." Nick sighed.

"I'll look through them," she offered. "Fresh pair of eyes."

"Well, at least it will keep you away from the field." Rivera gave her the green light.

Two hours later, Mackenzie had found a corner of the station where she could view the videos privately. She had reduced the speed and was watching every single frame from start to finish, focusing on details other than the two people in them.

Nick sat down next to her. "Which year are you at?"

"October 2010." She glanced at him, noticing that he was growing a beard. "I hate it."

"You saw me like a few hours ago. You only just realized?" He stroked his chin.

"I've been a bit out of it." She grazed the bandage taped to the back of her head and turned back to the video. "Oh!"

"What?"

"He dropped the camera." She played the frame again, slowing it down. The camera was on the floor, facing a window that looked out. She paused it and zoomed in on the view out the window. "That's the clock tower!" She pointed at the pixelated snapshot. "So the building is northeast of the tower."

Nick pulled up a map of Lakemore on his phone and zoomed in around the tower. "How far away do you think the building is?"

"My spatial awareness isn't the best."

"I know. It's a wonder that you're such a good shot," he teased. He peered at the screen. "That's definitely less than a mile, but I think more than half a mile."

"If you're right, it makes it one of these buildings." She pointed at a cluster surrounded by trees.

"That's a residential complex." He looked at the paused video again. "I can't pinpoint which building, but it looks like one of the higher floors."

Mackenzie agreed. "Let me finish watching the rest. Maybe there'll be some other clue."

"Sounds like a plan." He sat back and crossed his legs, sipping his coffee. When she glared at him, he shrugged innocently. "What?"

"Are you going to sit here while I watch sex videos?"

He turned crimson and cleared his throat, standing up. "Of course not. I'll... I'll check the county property records to see if Hamilton owns a unit in one of those buildings."

"Good idea."

Once he'd gone, Mackenzie turned her attention to the video again, pressing the play button and hoping that she'd catch a glimpse of the man. But as he picked up the camera and placed it back in position, mumbling an apology, all that was visible was the gray tiled floor and his generic black shoes.

She moved on to the next video. Her skin crawled at how icky it all was. There was no consent. It was surrender. It was evident from the faces of these women that they weren't into it, but it didn't matter to the man.

The next video was January 2011. Everything played out like it always did. The room looked exactly the same. Then something happened that caught her eye. The man's movements on the couch became aggressive, and the couch slid back, revealing that the floor was hardwood.

Her eyebrows dipped low. She double-checked the previous video: the floor was tiled. She saw Peterson walking by and called him over.

"We believe that this unit is in a building in this residential complex," she explained, showing him the area on the map. "We are looking for a unit where the flooring was changed from tile to hardwood between October 2010 and January 2011. I think that will narrow it down. Maybe the residential office will have a record; if not, then check with flooring companies in town."

He scribbled down the details on a notepad. "Did you know that wet wood, unlike dry wood, can conduct electricity? I'm so sorry."

"It's okay, Peterson."

"I'll be right on it." He nodded eagerly and hastened away.

Nick came around the corner and gestured to Mackenzie to follow him to the interrogation room.

"What's happened now?" she asked gingerly, noting the deep frown marring his face.

"Ballistics came back on the bullet." He stopped in front of the two steel doors. One led to the interrogation room and the other to the observation room.

"And?" She held her breath.

"It was a Remington Model 700. A sniper rifle. My dad uses one for hunting."

She twisted her lips. "Does that help us?"

His eyes searched hers. "It's also used by the military. So I followed a hunch." He paused before ushering her into the observation room.

Mackenzie gasped. Courtney's husband, Brett, was in the interrogation room, sitting across from Austin.

"I saw the news." His lips quivered, hot tears rolling down

his face. "That missing man's girlfriend said how this was all happening because of that detective!" He was shaking, his eyes bloodshot, only a fragment of the man Mackenzie remembered meeting. "Why should innocent people get pulled into whatever she is a part of? Why did my wife have to die? Why did I have to tell my kids that they'll never see their mother again?"

Mackenzie wanted to press her hands against her ears. His wails were like shards of glass piercing her eardrums. But she couldn't look away. The least she could do was witness the carnage left behind in her name.

"You really fucked up," Austin said in a measured tone.

"You don't understand!" Brett shouted, his lips tugging downward. His voice was angry, but his face was tragic. "How would you feel if someone you loved was murdered because of her? What would you have done?"

"Austin should not be on this." Nick was about to leave, but Mackenzie grabbed his arm.

"Don't. Let him."

She felt like she was observing an intimate moment. But she wanted to know what Austin thought. He had stopped downright despising her, but she wondered if he still had something against her.

"I would have hated her for a long time," he confessed. "Even though I would have known that I was just misdirecting all that rage. But I would have thought of what I had to lose, and what was the right thing to do."

"Yeah, and what's that?" Brett challenged.

"Being there for your kids, you asshole," Austin retorted.

Brett's face crumpled, and he started howling into his hands, droning on about how he didn't know how to move forward anymore.

"This is what we've come to." Nick clicked his tongue. "Now we have to worry about the victims' families retaliating."

"Have charges been filed?" Mackenzie asked.

"Hell, yes." Nick's eyes were aflame.

"What if I don't want to press charges?"

"Are you out of your mind?" He grimaced. "He doesn't even regret it. He'll do it again."

"He has kids! He's all they have now."

"That's exactly why I think he should go to prison. Remember the case of that guy who couldn't handle his wife dying in a car crash? He poisoned his son and then hanged himself."

Mackenzie remembered it all too well. The memory of it always left something foul in its wake.

They were interrupted by Peterson, who was breathing like he had just run a mile. "I got something. Luckily the residential office keeps records of all the units that have had any major renovations. They gave me the unit number and the name of the owner." He bit his lip, his eyes twinkling. "It's Rafael Jennings."

"That NFL team's co-owner?" Nick was aghast. "Wait a minute. You saw him at the house, didn't you, Mack?"

"I did. Let's go get him."

FORTY-SIX

Rafael Jennings had bought a house in Forrest Hill, the plush cul-de-sac housing local politicians, athletes, and influential industrialists. It was not only a safe haven, being a gated community, but was also pleasing to the eye, with iron gates, high-end cars, and Italian-style mansions. Mackenzie always thought of escapism whenever she was in this neighborhood.

She waited in the lavish foyer adorned with large paintings and antiquities. She was staring at a painting of a watering can with flowers on, wondering how much money Jennings had dished out for something so simple.

"Has to be money laundering," Nick commented from her side. "Can't imagine anyone spending more than a hundred dollars on something like that."

They heard footsteps clacking against the marble before two men appeared on the sweeping staircase leading into the foyer. One of them was tall, slender, with eyelashes so thick it looked like he wore eyeliner. His hair was a shiny black, obviously dyed. With one hand in his pocket, he had a lopsided, amused grin on his face.

"Detectives." He shook their hands. "How can I help you?"

The lawyer, Tom Cromwell, was behind him and gave Mackenzie and Nick a sly wave.

"We need to talk. Can we go somewhere private?" Nick looked pointedly at the staff working in the living room.

Jennings gave him a tight smile before directing them to a study. He poured himself a Scotch and offered the bottle to Mackenzie and Nick, who refused.

"You must have heard that there is an investigation opening into Judge Hamilton," Nick said.

Jennings and Cromwell exchanged a loaded look.

"There have been rumors." Jennings sat in a leather chair behind the elaborate oak table. "I don't know much. We don't talk regularly."

Cromwell nodded approvingly, standing behind Jennings. Mackenzie knew this was all rehearsed.

"Mr. Jennings, do you own an apartment at the Livmore?" Mackenzie asked. "It's a residential complex in Lakemore. About a mile from the town square."

His grip around the sculpted glass tightened, whitening his knuckles. "I'd have to check. I own a lot of properties."

"You do, actually." She took a piece of paper from her jacket pocket, showing proof that the unit was registered to him.

"I see." He scratched his head. "Well, then I must."

Cromwell's eyes darted between the paper and his flustered client. "What is this regarding?"

"You see, we found some DVDs," Nick said, like he was talking about the weather. "Filmed in your apartment. Women being coerced into having sex in exchange for contacts in the media industry."

A nervous laugh bubbled out of Jennings as he took out a handkerchief and wiped his forehead. "That's rich."

Cromwell was clearly bewildered, but being the savvy lawyer he was, he was quick on his feet. "Like my client said, he owns several properties. He doesn't live at that address. What others do at his property isn't his responsibility!"

"We thought you'd say that." Mackenzie nodded. "We came prepared. You see, that building has a very good security system. They keep backups of their security logs from the last three years."

"We have you going to the building on the same dates those videos were filmed," Nick added.

Jennings gulped the Scotch in one go and looked away, letting his mouthpiece handle the situation.

"Do you see my client's face in the videos?" Cromwell narrowed his eyes.

"No," Mackenzie said. "But—"

"Well then. I'm sure if he searches his memory, he'll remember entertaining some friends in that apartment, and of course he can't have knowledge of what happens in every room." He shrugged. Mackenzie knew that he had concocted this explanation on the spot. The way he kept licking his lips and shifting his weight from one foot to the other gave away how unprepared he was for this line of questioning.

"We have audio from those tapes," Nick said. "I'm sure Mr. Jennings won't mind volunteering a voice sample that our IT guy can analyze for comparison."

Jennings opened his mouth to protest, but Cromwell placed a hand on his shoulder. "My client has to head out of state for an important matter. So if you don't have a warrant, then—"

"Oh, actually we do have a warrant," Mackenzie said. "A judge just signed it, and another detective will be here any minute to execute it."

They had come prepared, after making sure to submit their affidavit to a judge who was known to lock horns with Hamilton and hence couldn't be a part of his inner circle.

"This is a coup!" Cromwell yelled angrily. "This is harassment. I shouldn't be surprised, considering your—"

"We also have an eyewitness placing Mr. Jennings at Judge Hamilton's house late at night." Mackenzie kept her eyes glued to Jennings. "With a prostitute."

Jennings slammed his glass on the table and pressed a closed fist to his mouth.

"Of course, if you're ready to give details, I'm sure the DA will cut you a deal," Nick said to Cromwell.

"What kind of details?" Cromwell snapped.

"About this whole operation. In particular, where the girls are kept," Mackenzie said.

When Jennings and Cromwell maintained a stoic silence, she tried to hide her growing frustration. They were impenetrable. And someone in their circle had Sterling. *If he was still alive.* But at least they had ruptured this bubble. She would hunt them all down one by one if she had to.

There was a sharp knock on the door. Jennings and Cromwell barreled out of the study and opened the door with Mackenzie and Nick on their tails. Austin stood there with a team of cops behind him. He read out the search warrant as the rest of the cops filtered inside the house. As soon as he was done reading, Cromwell snatched the warrant and read it with a keen eye.

"We're confiscating all the electronics, anything that can store photos or videos, and any hard copies of photos," Austin summarized to Mackenzie and Nick. "Basically, we can search every corner of this house, because you can hide a USB stick in the smallest of spaces." He waggled his eyebrows insinuatingly.

Mackenzie pulled on latex gloves, ready to join the search. "Hopefully that will give us access to places he's visited. I bet that's where Sterling is being kept too—wherever they keep those girls."

"I think that's where Sophie was held captive too," Austin said quietly. "Was Clint able to track where that video was filmed? The one with the women lying on the floor?"

Nick shook his head. "There were no identifying markers."

They dispersed in different directions. Cromwell and Jennings seethed in a corner, watching Austin bag Jennings' laptop and computer. There were cops opening drawers and kitchen cabinets, flipping mattresses in the bedrooms, going through his golfing equipment. Mackenzie went to his study, where there were people flipping through all the books on the shelves. She sat down at his expensive table and skimmed through the drawers and the paperwork, hoping to find something.

But Jennings' empire was vast, which meant that whatever clue they were looking for could be a needle in a haystack.

Trailing her fingers over the dips and ridges of the carved wood, she recalled how Sterling had wanted a table like this when they were furnishing their house together.

"That's a bit much, isn't it?" She kissed him on the cheek. "You're a lawyer, not some evil lord."

"If I were an evil lord, I could have a secret compartment." He tapped the table at the furniture store with his knuckles. "A table like this can have one."

Out of curiosity, Mackenzie knocked the table in different spots. Jennings appeared in the doorway, making his displeasure known as the cops tore through his study and one of them bagged a video camera. When he saw Mackenzie fiddling with the table, he stiffened.

Mackenzie noticed. Without tearing her eyes away from him, she resumed her examination, feeling for any hollow spaces other than the drawers she had been through. There was something here. Panic was rising like a wave behind his eyes.

She knocked on a section at the bottom. It was hollow. He started breathing hard, stepping forward but then stopping himself. Mackenzie bent down. Upon closer inspection, she noticed light grooves in a square. Except there was no knob or lever. She was about to ask for a hammer to break the table if she had to when she noticed a button on the underside. She pressed it and the compartment door slid open.

"Bingo."

She pulled two things out of it as Jennings watched. One was a plastic folder containing some documents. That made him sweat and turn white as a ghost.

Second was a gun.

"That's not mine!" he cried, puzzled. "Cromwell! Cromwell!"

Mackenzie turned the gun in her hands.

Cromwell came into the room, volleying some excuses. But her brain was firing in all directions. When Nick arrived, she addressed only him, tuning the others out. "Looks like a .38."

Nick nodded. "The same caliber that killed Debbie."

"Murder!" Jennings was taken aback. "I didn't kill anyone. This is a setup. This whole thing is a fucking setup."

"There are a lot of .38 guns out there. This doesn't mean that my client killed Ms. Arnold. He never even met her!"

Mackenzie eyed Jennings, who was breaking apart in front of her. Was he their elusive killer? The one who was obsessed with her?

"You make a fair point, Mr. Cromwell," she said, sounding way calmer than she felt. "But the serial number on this weapon has been shaved off. Under the gun control act of 1968, it is unlawful for any person to possess or receive any firearm which has had the serial number removed, obliterated, or altered." She recited the law verbatim.

"Rafael Jennings, you're under arrest." Nick asked for handcuffs and recited his Miranda rights.

FORTY-SEVEN

The drive from Jennings' house was shrouded with skepticism. Jennings was being processed at the station, but he had a cunning lawyer by his side, along with partners in crime in high places. Mackenzie's faith was fractured. All she could do was play her part. But an arrest didn't imply justice. It was a long and thorny road to that.

"Are you thinking what I'm thinking?" Nick asked.

"What *are* you thinking?"

"That Rafael Jennings doesn't look like someone who is obsessed with you. But then again, it is someone in their circle. I can imagine they're all... sophisticated."

"According to Andrew's profile, it's someone highly intelligent and resourceful—and not new to killing. But then I never believed it was some junkie living in a basement."

"We didn't find anything at his place that would indicate an obsession with you."

"He has many houses." She crossed her arms. "We just need to get him to tell us where Sterling is." She rubbed her chest, feeling as if a block of ice was sitting on it.

"You look like you're sick. Should I turn on the AC?" Nick asked.

She shook her head. "I'm just... I just want it all to be over."

"The case, you mean?"

She looked at him, thinking about the dream she'd had about Melody and all the thoughts that had been creeping into her mind. Thoughts she didn't want to dwell on too much. Thoughts that scared her. It was too monumental.

Finally she knew why people could be terrified of something that could be so good.

"You're staring. Again." He tried not to smile.

"I was thinking." She looked away.

"About?"

She scrambled for an excuse. "How maybe we can play Jennings and Hamilton against each other. To collect more evidence to bring the whole thing down. Right now, Hamilton is at home strategizing with his team of lawyers while we open an investigation. Nothing is official yet. But do you think Jennings has been stalking you too? It's just hard to imagine a successful and busy man like him taking the time to do something like that." She took out her phone. "I'll call Andrew."

"Looks like someone's coming around to the psychologist," Nick quipped.

"He's been insightful. And helpful to me."

"How?"

Awareness ran through her. "I don't know how to put it, but he puts things into perspective. Like with everything that's happening... sometimes he'll say something that will make it all converge. Anyway..."

When Andrew picked up, she updated him on their discovery.

"I see." He sighed. "If Rafael is behind this, then he must have hired someone to do his dirty work. A man like him wouldn't get involved personally. I would request a warrant to check off everyone on his payroll."

"We have him under arrest, so we have a pretty good case to get that."

"That's good news. I'm at the station right now, and Peterson just told me that they tracked down some information on that user Mack1987."

"I'm listening." Mackenzie straightened and put him on speakerphone for Nick.

"In one of the blogs, Mack1987 discussed your hair, and mentioned a salon called Black Sheep Hair—"

"That's the salon I go to," she blurted. It hadn't been mentioned in the documentary. The revelation shouldn't have been so sickening, considering she knew that someone obsessed with her had been watching her. But still fear twisted inside her violently.

"They said they intended to check it out—and it seems they have an appointment there in thirty minutes. Shall I meet you there?"

When Mackenzie went quiet, it was Nick who answered, then disconnected the call.

"This is good news, Mack," he assured her, clamping the wheel harder. "Meanwhile, I'll ask Jenna to get Jennings' financial records. We've got two solid leads. One of them should pan out, right?"

Mackenzie nodded, trying not to be too hopeful.

By the time they reached the salon, the soft breeze had transformed into a hungry wind trying to rip away leaves from the branches. When Mackenzie stepped out of the car, she had to struggle to close the door behind her. Her hair spilled out of its elastic band, falling on her face. Nick's tie whipped around, trying to escape his neck. His dark hair played in the wind. The sun was cloaked behind a thick, unmoving layer of clouds, but she still wore her sunglasses, to keep the dirt from peppering into her eyes.

They were ten minutes early. Black Sheep Hair Salon stood in front of them, wedged between an ice-cream store and a print shop. Despite it being the end of the working day, there were only a few vehicles around.

Mackenzie didn't like it. Everything was gray and gloomy. The air felt brittle. It didn't feel like Lakemore. Lakemore was usually rainy and stormy; it was turbulent but never hollow. Today, the weather felt soulless.

"Jenna's on those bank records," Nick informed her, checking his phone. "She should have something for us in a few hours. I think she's warming to you. She didn't ignore you the last time you talked to her."

Mackenzie leaned against the side of the car. "I think she's scared of my guardian killer. After Sterling, who's left?"

Andrew crossed the parking lot, carrying a coffee tray.

"Bless that guy," Nick muttered. "Thanks."

"No problem." Andrew smiled and offered the last cup to Mackenzie. "I noticed you've been experimenting."

She took it graciously. "How do you think we'll recognize Mack1987? We have nothing to go on."

"Did Peterson pick up anything from the blogs that might help us identify them?" Nick asked.

Andrew shook his head. "He told me that none of the posts offered any personal information."

"Let's try our luck." Mackenzie took a sip of coffee and regretted it.

"You'll grow to love it." Nick chuckled, seeing her expression.

It was almost time for the appointment. They remained out of view, in case Mack1987 spotted them and bailed. The clouds drifted away, revealing a peachy sky. But the gusting wind roared loudly. It almost looked apocalyptic. Streaks of fiery yellow populated the sky, making the light fall sharply on the ground.

They were chatting about Sully's new hobby, tattoo tracing, when Mackenzie drew their attention. Two people were approaching. A middle-aged man and a woman. They were too far away to make out their faces. The man went into the print shop, but the woman carried on to the salon.

"Could be a walk-in," Mackenzie suggested.

"Let's find out," Nick said.

The three of them entered the salon. There was only one customer. She wore a pink coat and stood at the reception desk with her back to the door.

"I'm here for my appointment," she told the receptionist.

Mackenzie recognized the voice. But she couldn't place it.

"Oh yes, you wanted to color your hair?" the receptionist replied. "Red?"

"That's right."

Mackenzie's heart rose to her throat. Her vision tapered around the edges until only the woman in the pink coat was visible. She was just a few feet away from her, requesting that her dark hair be dyed red, just like Mackenzie's.

Mackenzie inched forward, raising a hand to touch the shadow that had been looming in her life.

The woman turned around.

"You?" Mackenzie whispered.

Ivy Pierce gasped, drawing in a sharp breath.

FORTY-EIGHT

Ivy Pierce sat in the interrogation room, squirming like a cornered animal.

"Sterling's girlfriend?" Sully asked, watching her from the observation room.

After Mackenzie, Nick, and Andrew had confronted her, Ivy had stonewalled them with silence. But the slight twist of her lips and her flickering nostrils gave away her frustration. She was a defiant little thing. Both scared and angry at the same time.

"Trust your ex-husband to find a psychopath," Nick mumbled, reading up on Ivy's background information brought to him by Peterson.

"He found me too. Just saying." Mackenzie frowned.

"Oh, you're the biggest psychopath of all, Mad Mack," he said dryly, making Mackenzie snort despite the circumstances. "Ivy grew up in several foster homes. Not a stable family life. Peterson is fetching her computer for Clint to confirm that she's Mack1987."

"But why?" Mackenzie asked. "Let's talk to her."

"No, no," Sully said, his jaw snapping as he chewed gum. "Turner is taking this one."

"Why?" Nick quizzed.

Sully shrugged. "He said something about how there's a higher chance of her opening up if you're not there."

Mackenzie and Nick exchanged a displeased look. It was their case; they had never let a consultant take over the questioning.

Andrew entered the interrogation room, his steel-colored suit blending in nicely with the white-gray tone of the room. Ivy straightened, surprise flickering in her eyes, as if she had been expecting Mackenzie.

"Ms. Pierce." He smiled, sitting across from her so that Mackenzie and Nick could only see the back of his head. "I'm Dr. Andrew Turner."

"Doctor?" She frowned.

"I'm a forensic psychologist consulting with the Lakemore PD."

Ivy nodded curtly, crossing her arms and looking away.

"Ms. Pierce, are you Mack1987?" When she opened her mouth to deny it, he interjected. "Your computer is in the process of being confiscated right now, so it's better if you don't lie."

She sighed, frustrated tears misting in her eyes. "I... I should get a lawyer."

"Let's not talk about that." Andrew sat back. "You're not under arrest. We're looking into the disappearance of your boyfriend, Sterling Brooks. How about you help us with that?"

"Why would she hurt Sterling?" Mackenzie voiced the thought, reading Ivy's softening expression. "She loves him, right?"

"Do you know where he is?" Ivy asked. Snot dribbled from her nose. "Why hasn't he come back? Why did he leave?"

"Uh-oh," Nick muttered. It dawned on Mackenzie that Ivy

was perhaps even more unstable than she'd assumed. Darkness spilled out of her like tendrils. Gone was the concerned girlfriend Mackenzie had encountered. Through the mirror, she saw someone who looked like a child abandoned by her parents.

"Ivy, why would Sterling leave you?" Andrew asked gently. "Weren't you happy together?"

She scowled. "He spoke about her all the time."

"Mackenzie?"

"Yeah..." She drank some water and wiped her mouth with her sleeve. "Maybe I wasn't enough for him."

"I can imagine you being curious about her."

Ivy held her face in her hands. "I just wanted to understand at first. Why was Sterling so in love with her? Why did his eyes light up when he mentioned her? He talked about her in his sleep... One time he even called me by her name while we were getting intimate."

Mackenzie wanted to melt. She was standing with her boss, who was now aware of some intimate details of her life. Fortunately, Sully had a habit of deleting most of the information from his brain. Nick, on the other hand, rolled his eyes at Ivy's revelations.

"It was clear he wasn't completely over her," Ivy continued. "So I thought... I thought if I..."

"Dyed your hair?" Andrew prompted.

She nodded. "Maybe he liked redheads."

"Hmm..." He traced his lips with the tip of his finger. "It must be hurtful to fall for a man who still has feelings for his ex-wife."

"He thinks she could have hurt him?" Mackenzie couldn't hide the doubt in her voice.

"It is." Ivy grimaced. "Especially when that ex-wife is *everywhere*. That documentary came out and everyone was singing her praises. He was so proud of her."

Hollowness bloomed inside Mackenzie. Sterling's support

and compassion tugged at her. But why was Ivy talking about him in the past tense? Where was he?

"I get it," Andrew conceded. "You just wanted to get to know Mackenzie better. And obviously you couldn't do that conventionally, so you turned to blogs. How do you feel about her now?"

Ivy's hand tightened around the glass of water. Her tendons bulged beneath her skin. "She is the woman my boyfriend still has a very large soft corner for. What do you think?"

"You're right, you're right. You are clearly an attractive and successful woman, Ivy," Andrew said. "I believe Sterling should appreciate you more."

"Exactly." She ground her teeth. "I'm actually here for him. Unlike Mackenzie Price, who was always too busy working and is too selfish to be a mother."

Mackenzie staggered back. Ivy's words were like a whiplash. She saw Nick's clenched fist rising to knock on the glass, his face tight with fury. But Sully beat her to the punch.

"Nick, take a walk," he ordered.

"But she's—"

"Take a walk," Sully repeated with warning eyes.

Nick let out a sharp hiss of breath and marched out of the room.

"And now Sterling is missing because of her!" Ivy screeched, terror gripping her face. "It's all her fault. He admires her so much and now his life is in danger for that very reason."

"I bet when we find him alive and well, he'll realize that you're the one who deserves his attention and admiration," Andrew assured her.

"I hope so. The lengths I'm going to..."

"What lengths?" he asked casually.

She pursed her lips and shook her head, looking away.

After a few more minutes of trying to get her to talk, Andrew left the room to join Mackenzie and Sully. Nick returned too. Mackenzie stood next to him, looking at him questioningly.

"I didn't smoke," he groaned.

"Just making sure."

"What do you think, Doc?" Sully asked. "I doubt she'll hurt him."

Andrew wore a mask of grave concern, folding the file in his hands. "On the contrary, I think she is very much capable of inflicting harm on him. Hell hath no fury like a woman scorned."

"That makes no sense." Mackenzie shook her head. "People have been targeted for hurting me in some capacity. And those messages about protecting me..."

"She hates you. There's no doubt about that," Andrew replied. "But there is one other profile we didn't consider. This could be the work of someone who's obsessed with causing you harm."

"I don't follow," Sully confessed.

"Think about it. People getting killed in Mackenzie's name has not only caused her emotional distress but literally endangered her life. Ivy could have easily guessed that those messages would eventually become public, with everyone from uniform to forensics having access to the evidence. And that interview she gave. It was because of that that Brett flipped out and almost killed Detective Price."

"But why would she want to harm Sterling?" Nick asked. "Surely her entire purpose is to have him for herself."

"I don't think she has any intention of killing him. In fact, it explains why he was easily abducted, considering he's a strong guy. He trusts her. In her head, Sterling would blame Mackenzie for his ordeal after being rescued and then finally see Ivy the way she wants him to. Unless..." Andrew bit his lip, hesitating. "If she starts believing that Sterling's feelings for you won't change, then she might snap and kill him."

"Too bad we can't hold her," Sully complained. "She's free to go."

"I believe you will find that Ivy Pierce is linked to the prostitution ring. She did time in juvie and bounced around foster homes. She fits the profile. I suggest you find the connection, because there is no guarantee that she won't kill Sterling out of spite."

FORTY-NINE

APRIL 26

"How do you think Sterling will react after he finds out that his girlfriend is crazy?" Nick spoke around the cigarette. "How many bank accounts does Jennings have? Jesus."

Mackenzie and Nick were in the conference room with piles of papers—Rafael Jennings' financial statements. However, people like Jennings didn't have transparent finances.

"We won't find anything here," Mackenzie growled, pushing away another pile. "There's no record of him paying King of the Road, even though we know he used one of their cars to drive to Hamilton's property."

"Must be from one of his offshore accounts." Nick pressed the heels of his palms into his eyes. "Did Peterson find any connection between Ivy and Jennings?"

She shook her head. "Their educations, careers, social groups don't intersect. Unless they met randomly somewhere..."

He dipped his thick eyebrows low, deep in thought.

"You have nice eyebrows," Mackenzie said.

His expression didn't change as he took out the case she had gifted him years ago and put the cigarette back inside it. "You have nice nostrils."

"Nostrils?"

"I was just matching your poor flirting skills," he teased dryly.

"I wasn't flirting!" She hid her face behind a piece of paper while he chuckled. But her eyes darted outside the conference room and her breath hitched.

Tag was being brought in by the police, his hands behind his back.

"Nick! It's Tag. From King of the Road."

They shot from their seats.

"Is he embroiled in some other case?" Nick wondered.

Tara Hopkins, a short, stout detective with the Special Investigations Unit, directed two uniforms to escort Tag to be processed. As he reached the top of the stairs, he turned around and winked at Mackenzie.

"What's going on?" Nick asked Tara. "He's a person of interest in our serial killings."

"That boy was behind the shutdown that took our servers and backup systems out." She was engrossed in a file. "He said he was just messing with us. Either way, we got enough to charge him."

When Tara left, Mackenzie shook her head. "I thought it was a random glitch from the storm, but it was intentional."

Nick's forehead bunched. "They must have found some evidence of a hack and followed it up."

"The hack that deleted a crucial video?"

"He did boast about doing a lot of jobs." He scratched his head. "I think we should take that gun found at Jennings' house to the crime lab ourselves and wait for it to be tested. The last thing we need is for that to go missing."

Soon the bright lights of Seattle came into view. Weaving through the traffic, they reached the crime lab and headed straight for the lab. They found Anthony peering into a microscope and then shouting at a tech who didn't look a day older than twenty. Mackenzie tapped on the glass, drawing his attention.

"He's always in a good mood, isn't he?" Nick said, amused.

Anthony's lab coat swished in the air as he strode toward them with purpose. "Do you have it?"

Mackenzie handed him the evidence bag containing the gun. "Thanks for squeezing this in. The sooner we prove this is definitely Jennings' and was used to kill Debbie, the sooner we can charge him with murder."

"It will only take me a few minutes. We got a firearms serial number restoration kit. When a serial number is stamped on a gun, it compresses the underlying metal grains. They react differently to chemical etching and can be restored even after someone files them off. Once I'm done, I'll send it over to ballistics. Just wait here."

They stood in the hallway as Anthony took the bag into the lab.

Mackenzie chewed the pad of her thumb and then realized what she was doing and stopped. "Are you worried?"

"Yeah." Nick leaned against the wall, crossing his ankles. "Jennings and Hamilton will have alerted one of their associates, who is probably covering up evidence or moving the girls as we speak."

She nodded. She caught her own reflection in the window. There'd been a change in her. Some of that hardness had softened. Less like a statue carved out of marble and more like one molded out of clay—pliable and supple.

When Anthony came out, he gave them the serial number. Nick immediately called Jenna, asking her to check it. He stayed on the line, waiting.

Mackenzie spoke a silent prayer that they'd get confirmation about Jennings.

"*What?* Say that again?" Nick said in disbelief. "Are you sure? Okay. Yeah. Thanks." When he disconnected, he looked dazed.

"What is it?" Her insides were held captive by a tight wrench of unease. Something was wrong.

"The gun is registered to Dr. Andrew Turner."

FIFTY

A state of panic and shock had taken hold in Sully's office. His cross-stitch kit lay abandoned on his desk. The silence was heavy and oppressive. Mackenzie had never seen him look so disappointed. It was like he was re-evaluating everything. Nick's fingers twirled an unlit cigarette, his eyes twitchy.

Rivera returned to the room, her phone in her hand and distress on her face. "Dr. Turner is not answering his phone. I called his sister and she said she hasn't heard from him since this morning."

"Where's Robbie?" Mackenzie asked.

"He's with her. She picked him up from school. She sounded very worried." Rivera took a shuddering breath. "I'm sorry. This is my fault. I brought him in. No wonder we were always one step behind. He's been part of the team and even supplying information to the rest."

Nothing gnawed on the soul with sharper teeth than betrayal. And Mackenzie held a grim view of the world. The older she got, the more experiences she garnered, the more she realized that there were only going to be a handful people who would never betray her. Whenever she thought of Andrew, red spots dotted her vision.

"When you two went to Hamilton's house, did Andrew know?" Sully asked.

Nick shook his head. "That's why he wasn't able to warn them off."

"No wonder he was so keen on coming to Lakemore," Mackenzie said. "And he's been at Jane Doe's side the entire time."

"When Jane Doe handed you that key, was Dr. Turner around?" Rivera asked.

"No."

"The one time you were together without him." Nick ran a hand through his hair. "So that's why he was so invested in her treatment."

Sully picked up the cross-stitch and tossed it, frustrated. "He was keeping an eye on her so that she didn't reveal anything."

"And he conveniently wanted to hand her over to another organization after she gave me that key. Maybe he suspected something and was looking for the opportunity to send her back into the prostitution ring," Nick said.

"It was Andrew who brought in the Ivy Pierce lead. After we found out about Jennings and arrested him, he changed the direction of the case and scrambled for an explanation, randomly suggesting that Jennings and Ivy could be related," Mackenzie spat.

"We already had Jennings." Nick nodded. "So he tried to save his own ass."

"He played us like a fiddle." Rivera clicked her tongue. "Go to his house. Maybe you'll find some clues there. We'll get Clint to try and track down his location. And we'll issue an APB."

Mackenzie and Nick went back to their desks and collected their jackets and Glocks.

"Fucker," Nick mumbled, checking the bullets. "I'm going to make him pay."

Mackenzie's hopes threatened to plummet. If Andrew was aware they were onto him, it might be too late to save Sterling.

Mackenzie's boots squelched in a puddle as she got out the car. Sheets of rain were blasting across the town that night. It wasn't the kind of rain that made leaves glossy; it tried to strip trees bare. The cold droplets traced patterns on her skin. There was no thunder. There was no lightning. There was no pitter-patter. Only white noise blaring. Water was already collecting in the roads. There were flood warnings.

"It's that way!" Nick yelled over the racket.

Mackenzie winced under the slapping stings of the rain falling on her back. It was a struggle to keep her eyes open. There was no point in using umbrellas. They wore raincoats instead.

Andrew Turner's cabin was located at the end of a hunting trail. In this thick darkness, Mackenzie couldn't make out any geographical markers that might give her a sense of where she was headed. She relied on Nick for navigation. They both had to wear flashlights around their wrists to see the path ahead and to spot each other. As they walked, Mackenzie's feet caught in creepers and her face was brushed by branches and thickets.

At last she saw the shadowy outline of a cabin ahead of her. There were no lights on. The place looked abandoned. They headed for the front door. Reaching the porch, they found some respite from the rain.

"What the hell is wrong with this weather?" Nick groaned, ruffling his hair to get some water out.

Mackenzie's clothes weighed a ton. Her red hair had fallen out of its ponytail and was plastered to her face.

It was too loud for anyone to hear if they knocked or rang the bell.

Together they slammed their shoulders into the front door. It ripped from its hinges and hung loosely. They stepped inside, waving their flashlights around the open-plan living room and kitchen. Mackenzie found a light switch, but it didn't work. The storm must have messed up the wiring. But at least inside they were shielded from the rain and the noise.

"What are we looking for?" she asked.

"Anything that might give us a clue about where Sterling and those women are being held, or where Turner could be," Nick said. "I'll check upstairs."

"Okay." She wasn't comfortable alone in the pitch blackness, but she didn't protest as he headed up the spiral staircase.

They were on a clock.

All she could see was whatever the beam from the flashlight was illuminating. A part of her kept expecting something to jump out at her from the darkness. She could hear Nick's footsteps above. It made her breathe easier. Her light fell on a wall that held a framed picture of Andrew and Robbie as a baby.

Sadness washed over, thinking about what the boy's fate would be now. Would his aunt take care of him? Was she good to him?

She moved ahead and noticed there was another door. A chill crept up her spine. Getting closer, she opened it to find a small room. When she arced the light around it, her heart thumped painfully against her ribcage. The wall was covered with surveillance photos of her.

On her morning jog.

Standing in her front yard.

Grabbing takeout from the Chinese place across from the station.

Walking with Nick back to the car.

There were old pictures too. From her yearbook when she

graduated primary school in Lakemore. When she graduated the police academy. When she got married. Snippets of her life were mapped out. Captured for posterity and displayed on a bulletin board. Multiple copies of the same pictures.

"Oh my God." She felt like snakes were crawling on her. She had an inkling she was being watched. This was vile. Like her life wasn't just hers. There was an invader taking up space without her permission.

She was sifting through the room, looking for any clue to Andrew's whereabouts, when she noticed a cupboard. The door was slightly ajar. When she opened it all the way, a scream clawed out of her mouth.

A body dropped on top of her. She fell back, sandwiched between the floor and the heavy weight. She screamed until her voice grew hoarse and her throat was dry.

"Mack..." There was a strained whisper in her ear.

It was Sterling lying on top of her. He was alive. Why wasn't he moving away?

"Mack!" Nick's voice boomed in the darkness. And suddenly he was there, removing Sterling from on top of her. "Jesus Christ. What the hell happened?"

Mackenzie gasped when she saw Sterling's face. It was covered in lacerations. One eye was swollen to the size of a golf ball. His hands had been tied behind his back with zip ties.

"He needs medical attention. Stat," she said frantically.

Sterling's head lolled. He muttered something under his breath. Some of the blood plastered on his face had dried, but some of it was fresh. It was evident he had been beaten up. But at least he was alive. She tried to focus on that. Sterling was alive. They just needed to get out of here and back to the car.

Outside, they were met with ferocious rain again and darkness wasn't their ally. But their flashlights still worked. Mackenzie and Nick held Sterling up, but the path back to the car was too narrow and winding. They kept tripping and bumping.

"It's fine. I'll carry him," Nick yelled.

"Are you sure?" she shouted back.

"Yes!"

Mackenzie trailed them, occasionally offering help when Sterling seemed to slip from Nick's grip. After what seemed like an eternity of being hammered by the rain, she could see the car a few feet ahead. As she took a step forward to help Nick in this last stretch, a hand suddenly came from behind her and wrapped around her arm. Before she could make a sound, something heavy smashed into her head. Her vision cracked. She swayed. And then she was out.

FIFTY-ONE

"You will bleed, Mackenzie," the voice said.

A cold shiver erupted through her. Before she could muster the strength to reply, the lights turned on. Rods of white flickered overhead. She was in a basement, as she'd suspected. But she knew this basement. The strong gray rock walls. The boiler in a corner along with the electricity distribution system. The fuse box with that dent she remembered well. To her right was a brick wall. And a staircase in front of it that had been remodeled.

When Mackenzie used to live here, one of the steps was missing.

A click.

A dark corner of the basement in front of her was lit up. Mackenzie drew a ragged breath. Strapped to a chair with a cloth stuffed into his mouth was Andrew. There was a bloody gash on his forehead. His eyes were closed. But he was still breathing.

"Why?" she whispered.

Jane Doe emerged from behind her, wearing a muskrat fur coat.

Mackenzie almost didn't recognize the woman. Gone was the timidity. Gone was the mousy girl who stared at everyone with paranoia and winced at sudden sounds. Everything about her was different. Her walk, her posture, the glint in her eyes.

She wasn't a victim. She was the huntress.

There was boldness in her step. A certain pride in the way her chest swelled. A laser-sharp focus with a touch of madness in her dark eyes.

She teetered on the edge of insanity. One foot in lunacy and the other in ingenuity.

"I believe you recognize your old house, Mackenzie?" She looked around, waving a knife in the air. "The latest owners made some changes. It's been in foreclosure for the last three months. Which works out for us."

"I don't understand." Mackenzie grimaced at the pain shooting up her arms. "Why? You got away... you escaped..."

"I didn't escape," Jane Doe confessed, and Mackenzie realized how even her voice had changed. It was deeper, stronger. "I made sure you found me."

That didn't make any sense. Mackenzie remembered that night clearly. She had been lingering outside the carnival, by the edge of the woods, simmering in her thoughts, when she noticed the disturbance in the trees and an injured Jane Doe had stumbled right into her arms.

"Who are you?" she demanded, her voice dripping in accusation.

"I'm Kai."

Kai. It was the codename of Fletcher's operation. The name that had popped up in his inquiries. How the girls feared Kai.

Except it wasn't Judge Hamilton's alias. It was this woman.

Kai strutted around Mackenzie, watching her like she was a prize. Like she was her muse. Her inspiration. But behind her adulation, there were glimpses of something else. A burning hatred. Intangible wickedness.

Like she was that child who expressed love for a doll by picking it apart.

"That can't be true," Mackenzie breathed. "You are one of them."

"I *was*." Kai's eyes were faraway. "I was taken a very long time ago. I don't even remember my old life."

"And then what happened?" Mackenzie's brain was a sponge, absorbing everything. She needed to understand.

"I had a mother. Whenever I cried, she would sing this lullaby..."

Kai sang like a nightingale, her voice filling the basement. She sang like she was all alone, and not with a woman she had chained to the pipes and a half-unconscious man she had tied to a chair. It was a beautiful song, bursting with love at the seams, a jarring contrast to the blood and violence around her.

When she had finished, she slithered down the wall and hugged her knees. "You have no idea what it was like. How it felt to have to let men touch you and do things to you. First they blackmail you to make you sleep with just one friend of theirs. And then there's more and more and more. The next thing you know, you aren't a person anymore. I forgot what I was like." Her forehead wrinkled. "I forgot the voice of my mother. It's easier that way. When you stop thinking of yourself as a person, it doesn't hurt as much."

Mackenzie had stopped struggling, too captivated by Kai's tale.

"I was just flesh and bones. My only purpose was to let them run their hands and lips and... other things all over my body." Bitterness leached into her voice, and she began scratching her arm aggressively. Mackenzie watched in horror as she drew blood. "But I'm a survivor, Mackenzie. Soon I realized I wasn't like the rest. I wasn't stupid. I had a spirit they wouldn't crush that easily." She tipped her chin high. "So I helped them."

"You helped them?"

"Hamilton, Jennings, and all the other men I'm sure you'll find the names of soon."

Andrew made a gurgling sound. He was coming around. When his eyes found Mackenzie, he started shouting, but his words were muffled behind the cloth. Kai stood up, pissed off at being interrupted. She marched over to him and made to strike him with the hilt of the knife.

"Please don't," Mackenzie begged. "I think he needs to listen too."

Kai lowered the knife and turned to face her. "I became more than just flesh and bones. They needed someone to control the girls. Someone to find new ones. Someone who could easily gain their trust..."

"You helped them recruit new girls?" Mackenzie gasped. "After everything you went through, why would you—"

"I chose *me*." Kai spoke with a fierce determination. "I couldn't escape. Who would I have gone to? The police? I knew the men I was being forced to sleep with and how far their reach was."

"So you helped them inflict that same pain on others?"

Kai got in her face. "I have a mantra. *Better you than me*. You see, when no one in this world protects you or stands up for you, you have to choose yourself. Even if it means hurting others. Eventually I was allowed more freedom and control. I wasn't a victim anymore. They didn't break me. I joined them. I was so angry at my damn luck, at those men who thought they had the fucking right to touch me without my permission. This life had decided that my existence was going to be empty, pointless, and only for the pleasure of the scum of this earth. It was so *unfair*." Her jaw trembled violently and she had to take deep breaths. "There is no reward for good and no penalty for evil. That's life. Those men continued living in their mansions with their perfect families and careers, safe and protected. Meanwhile, I and other girls like me, who were *good*, who were *innocent*, spent our time being passed around at parties. So yeah, I made a call. I saved myself once I accepted that morality is just fiction. At least I wasn't hurting anymore."

Mackenzie saw it play out in her head. Once Kai's humanity had been painfully decimated, the only way to survive was to let go of it completely, to stop trying to protect it so that it would stop hurting every time it was chipped away.

"Then *you* happened." Kai tilted her head, smiling at her lovingly.

Mackenzie had never felt terror like this. Not even when she was facing the barrel of a gun. Her insides knotted. Her blood was ice cold. Her soul shivered, trying to unhook itself from her body and float away.

"I saw you in that documentary and I saw everything that was right in this world." Kai dropped the knife, cupping Mackenzie's face in her hands. "Your honesty, your integrity, your innate goodness... it awakened something that was long dead inside me. I remembered. I remembered my mother's voice. Maybe this world wasn't as bad as I thought it was."

Mackenzie was afraid to talk, afraid to even look away.

"You reminded me that there was something good left in life. And I... I just wanted to help you. I wanted to make you happy. Because you deserve it." Tears welled in her eyes as she ran her hands gently over Mackenzie's face like she was a child. "I decided to take care of you. To make your life easier."

Mackenzie wanted to argue. But she saw Andrew shaking his head and warning her with his eyes. Kai was unhinged and dangerous.

"Why were you stalking Nick?"

"I saw your connection with him and got curious. What was it about him that you trusted him so much? That you loved so much? I didn't hurt him, Mackenzie. I would never do that to you. I looked into your past and you'd been through so much."

Kai tutted softly. "A drunkard father who beat his wife. Shipped off to New York right after your father disappeared. I couldn't do anything about that. But I found out about Courtney. How she made your life hell at school. She paid. Then there was Debbie. Talking shit about you in public out of jealousy." Her nostrils flared. "She should have revered you. For what you are. For what you do. I still remember her screams." She closed her eyes and swayed, relishing the memory, a look of delirious pleasure crossing her face. "It really scared the other girls.

"Then I discovered that cheating husband of yours." Spit sprayed out of her mouth in anger. "It was easy to capture him. All I had to do was pretend to be a damsel in distress. Of course, he dropped his guard, and the minute he was close enough, I knocked him out with chloroform. How dare he hurt you like that. How dare he not realize how wonderful you are. He deserved to die too... and I almost did kill him, but I saw how sad it would make you." She played with Mackenzie's hair. "I love how red your hair is. I didn't kill Sterling. I couldn't. I spared his life."

"What about Sophie? She'd done nothing to me."

"That wasn't me. That was Hamilton." Saying the name snapped Kai out of her gentle state. She was detached and cruel again, swinging from one extreme emotion to another. "Sophie showed up demanding to see her sister. Some FBI agent let it slip that he suspected Hamilton was behind it all. You should have seen how much Hamilton panicked." Her laugh was a dry rattle in Mackenzie's ear. "We kept her with the girls, but she was being problematic. Too feisty. Wouldn't bend like the rest." She clicked her tongue. "He lost it. Decided she was better off dead. Took him so long to strangle her. He has essential tremor. His hands shake."

The hesitation marks.

"He stored her body in one of the freezers usually reserved

for fish. But you see, it was kismet, Mackenzie. I was meant to help you, to find you."

"But you gave me that key you swiped from Hamilton. Why would you do that? And why did you find me?"

She looked conflicted. "I needed to be closer to you, Mackenzie. And Hamilton sent me to keep an eye on the investigation after he discovered that Sophie's body had been found by the police. Of course, he had no idea that I put her body there. And he didn't know that I didn't really intend to hide his dirty secret."

"Why not?"

"Because you could put an end to this." Kai began massaging Mackenzie's shoulders. "I'm sorry, you must be in pain, but I know you'll run away from me."

"Why do you want to put an end to it? You're a part of it."

"I was just making the best of a bad situation, Mackenzie. I couldn't bring it all down without risking my life. But you could. You could do anything. And you did. With Hamilton and Jennings caught, the dominoes will fall one by one."

"Why didn't you just tell me?" Mackenzie choked out. "Instead of slipping me a clue, you could have come clean to me about everything. You could have trusted me."

"I trusted you, but I didn't trust anyone around you. You have no idea how easily people have disappeared who have gone up against them. Just a snap of their fingers and evidence was manipulated, files were deleted, investigations were stalled... Sometimes people even went missing."

Mackenzie remembered Fletcher's haunted eyes when he spoke of his friend, and how that video evidence had been mysteriously wiped from their servers.

"So I had to be careful," Kai continued. "Hamilton had given me some freedom, but I was still on a tight leash. Giving you that key was a huge risk. I was terrified he'd figure out that it was missing. Fortunately, it paid off."

"Then why are we here, Kai? Why all this?"

Mackenzie had seen plenty in her career. She had seen first-hand what the human mind was capable of when stretched and bent and distorted by circumstances. From entitlement and misunderstanding to vigilantism and revenge. But this was something else. Kai was born out of tragedy. Her actions were born out of her twisted definition of love.

"You and I are destined to be together." Kai spoke calmly. "Andrew is here to take the fall for it all. That's why I left Sterling and those photos in his cabin. And I purchased the gun in his name. Once the police find our bodies, they'll assume that Andrew killed both of us."

Andrew started crying and protesting, rattling in his chair, making it scrape against the floor.

"I don't want to die, Kai," Mackenzie stated firmly, yanking fruitlessly on the ropes. "*Please*. I'm sure we can figure something out."

Kai was forlorn but resolute. She shook her head. "I'm sorry, Mackenzie. This is how it ends. The only way I can be with you is in death. This world wouldn't allow me otherwise. That's why I chose your old house. It's poetic. I'm going to go and make some arrangements now. It will be all over in a few minutes." She trailed a cold finger across Mackenzie's cheek. "Thank you."

FIFTY-TWO

Mackenzie had been faced with her mortality often. It came with the job. And still she had never thought much about how she would die. Whether it would be from a bullet in a shootout, or being stabbed by a psychopath, or in a car crash while chasing a suspect—or maybe as an old woman warm in bed. She should have thought about it more. Especially when death had brushed her only recently.

But perhaps it was its looming presence that meant she hadn't dissected the topic as much as she might have. Now, as she watched Kai glide away from her, humming her mother's lullaby, it began to dawn on her.

No one knew where she was. No one would think to check her old house of all places.

As Kai shut the door to the basement behind her, Mackenzie's survival instincts kicked in.

No. Not today. Not like this.

She saw the knife Kai had dropped on the floor. Still hanging from sore arms, she stretched her leg as far as it would go and tried to get a grip on it with her toes. Andrew stared at her helplessly and tried to wrench free from his restraints.

It took her a few attempts, but at last she got hold of the knife and lifted her leg up. "Ah!" She grunted, feeling a muscle pull in her inner thigh. She mustered all her strength to lift herself higher, grateful now that she did hanging sit-ups from time to time. Once she had the knife in her hand, she began cutting through her ropes blindly. The blade slashed into her skin, but the adrenaline flowing through her dulled some of the pain.

Eventually the ropes were severed and she fell to the floor with a thud. She sprang to her feet and pulled the cloth away from Andrew's mouth.

"This is my fault!" he cried as Mackenzie worked to untie the ropes binding him. "I should have known. She fooled me."

"She fooled all of us."

"But I'm the professional. She grabbed me when I was at home... I'm so sorry. How's Robbie?"

"He's with your sister. He's fine." She freed him, her mind working at full speed on the next steps.

"Andrew, we need to get out of here. I have no idea what she's planned. You can move, right?"

He nodded.

"Come on then."

Her head was still heavy as she climbed the stairs and tried the handle of the door leading out of the basement. "It's locked."

"Can we break it open?" he asked.

"It's heavy. Iron." She searched around like a rabid animal for anything to use. But there was nothing here that could break down an iron door. She felt Andrew's eyes on her. And suddenly the basement became very quiet and cold.

"Do you smell it?" He sniffed the air around the door. "I think it's propane."

"There has to be a way!" She paced around, her bones trembling as reality started to set in. "I don't get it. Why does she want to die? Does she have a split personality disorder?"

"She doesn't want to die, Detective Price." Andrew slumped down on the floor, clutching his bleeding head. "Neither does she have two distinct personalities."

"Then what the fuck is wrong with her?" she hissed angrily. She didn't even have her gun. What were they going to do?

"She sees you as the only link to her humanity." He breathed hard, holding back his tears. "She wants to be reunited with it after having suppressed it as a way to adapt to her trauma."

"She tortured and killed two women..."

"It was misdirected rage. She couldn't hurt the people who'd hurt *her*; they're too powerful. So she found those guilty of hurting you."

Mackenzie didn't care. The myriad of emotions slamming into her were enough to knock her out. She was overwhelmed to the point of being dysfunctional.

"There is some stationery over here." Andrew got back on his feet and limped to a table where some old papers and pens had been left behind by the last owners.

They looked at each other. He didn't have to say anything. The silence they shared made Mackenzie's heart sink and wither.

This can't be happening.

"It won't survive if this place goes up in flames," she said in a small voice, refusing to accept what was going to happen.

"There's a breaker box behind you." He tipped his chin. "It's our best shot. Just in case..."

A feeling of doom came over Mackenzie. She grabbed a pen and paper. Andrew sat away from her, turning his back as he scribbled ardently.

She was at a loss. She couldn't breathe. Her throat was closing.

Her breaths were sporadic. She shut her eyes and thought about what she'd want to do on her last day. What she would have wanted if she was given one day. It came to her with blinding clarity.

When she opened her eyes again, there were fresh tears. Despair filled her to the brim. It was too late now. For the first time in her life, she poured her heart out.

Dear Nick...

When they were done, Mackenzie placed the letters inside the box. Closing the door, she pressed her head into the cold metal. It was surreal, but it made sense, if she thought about it, for her to have had that strange dream about Melody speaking in riddles she understood only now, for her to end up at this house again where it had all started, and for her last case to be what it was.

A chance to relive her life. A chance to revisit old memories. To be an observer rather than a participant.

Andrew sobbed into his shirt behind her. She touched Robert's watch on her wrist—her talisman—and a memory materialized before her eyes.

"Come on, Mackenzie!" Robert hovered in front of her encouragingly. "You can do this."

It was a hot, sunny day. Her skin was sticky. She was an adamant four-year-old on a tiny bike trying to maintain her balance.

As soon as Robert let go of the handles, she fell down. Again.

"I can't! I can't!" she cried.

But he picked her up and readjusted her helmet. He wiped her tears, his lips pulling into a smile.

"Never give up, Mackenzie. If you can promise me anything, promise me that."

A fire surged through her veins, hot and heavy. "We're not giving up."

"There's no way out of here!" Andrew cried.

"But there must be a way to lure her back," she whispered.

"What would do that?" She searched his eyes desperately. "Think, Andrew. Think. You know her. You were mistaken before, but now you know her."

Andrew's gaze bounced around, his face crimson under the pressure. "She won't respond to cries of help. She won't be fooled by you wanting to negotiate with her or pretending to understand her..." Then his eyes enlarged like he had an idea. "She'll protect you."

"She's trying to kill all of us! Including me."

"Yeah, but only *she* is allowed to kill you. If anyone else tries, she won't take it. To her, she's setting both of you free. But if I'm killing you, I'm doing it to hurt you."

Mackenzie nodded understanding.

They set the stage. She prayed that this would work. There was a rusty pipe heavy enough to knock someone out. She grabbed it and placed it next to the bottom of the staircase, out of sight of anyone coming down the stairs. Then she lay next to it, so that her hand could easily reach it.

"Ready?" she asked. "Make it look convincing."

Andrew licked his lips and nodded. He straddled her and wrapped his hands around her neck, and she began to scream until she thought her lungs would tear. Seconds later, they heard footsteps approaching.

Andrew took the cue to growl angrily, "This is all your fault! Your fucking fault!" He squeezed her neck hard to make it look more authentic.

The door opened an inch. Then Kai whipped it wide and hurried down the stairs. "Get away from her!"

In her panic, she lost her footing and fell on top of Andrew, almost crushing Mackenzie. She pushed Andrew away, baring her teeth like an animal protecting its child. Mackenzie wormed her hand to grab the pipe, but at the last minute, Kai spotted it.

For a brief second, her eyes flashed with betrayal. Then Mackenzie swung the pipe. Kai ducked just in time. The pipe grazed her, and she stumbled back from the impact. But it wasn't enough to injure her. They were both on their feet now, circling each other.

"Why would you do that, Mackenzie?" A tear slipped down from her eye.

"The thing is, I don't want to die. Especially not on your terms." Mackenzie tightened her grip on the pipe, holding it in front of her. "Andrew, get out of here."

"But you..."

She kept her eyes on Kai. "For fuck's sake, Andrew, get out of here and get help."

He faltered, then started for the stairs. But before Mackenzie could react, Kai grabbed him, spun him around and pressed a knife that she had slipped out of her pocket against his neck.

Shit.

"Drop the pipe, Mackenzie. Please." For someone intent on killing everyone, her tone was serene and polite.

But Andrew was a tall man and Kai was a tiny woman. He tried to break free and shove his elbow into her gut. She twisted his arm at an unnatural angle until there was a crack. Then she kicked him in the back of the knee and he fell to the floor, wincing and groaning in pain, incapacitated.

A sick smile curled up her lips. "Drop the pipe."

Mackenzie growled in frustration and released it. But complete psychosis had clouded Kai's face. With one quick movement, she sank the blade into the side of Andrew's neck.

Blood spurted out in arcs, splattering Mackenzie, who was frozen in shock. His face lost color. His body began to sag. The blood wouldn't stop pouring. And then just like that, he went still.

Lifeless.

A throttled sound came out of the back of Mackenzie's

throat as Andrew's blood slowly trickled and pooled around her feet, soaking them in stickiness.

Then another spike of adrenaline injected into her body, jolting her into action. She ran up the stairs with Kai right behind her. Reaching the top, she banged the door shut in Kai's face. There was no latch. It could only be locked by a key, and she couldn't see one.

No time.

Her heart thundering and brain frazzled, she ran like a madwoman through the house she had grown up in. The last time she was here was over twenty years ago, but she knew the way. The basement led to the back of the house. To get to the main door or the backyard, she had to go through the kitchen.

As she reached it, she registered the smell of gas. Then she heard something coming at her from behind. She ducked out of the way and Kai's momentum caused her to collide with the dining table. She held the pipe in her hands now.

"You're ruining everything, Mackenzie!" she howled, like a child throwing a tantrum.

She whipped the pipe in arcs. Mackenzie stooped and ducked to evade it, backing away as Kai kept coming at her. They were circling around the kitchen. That same darn kitchen. But this time things would be different.

This time she wasn't scared. She had let go of fear.

She grabbed a chair, hoisted it up and threw it at Kai. Kai yelped, tripping back and letting the pipe slip from her grip. Mackenzie channelled all her rage. She threw a punch across Kai's jaw and then another into her stomach.

But Kai knew some tricks too. She kicked Mackenzie in the soft portion above the knee, making her fall. As Mackenzie grabbed the edge of the kitchen counter to pull herself up, Kai twisted her around and looped her arm around her neck, trying to cut off the circulation.

Blood pooled in Mackenzie's face, making it bloat and puff.

She writhed in Kai's grip, flapping her arms helplessly. Then, summoning all her strength, she lifted Kai over her back, hurling her onto the dining table.

Kai's neck landed on the edge of the table. There was a loud crack, and the table buckled. Her still body slid down it and landed on the floor, lying face down.

Exactly where Mackenzie had found a body on that fateful night over twenty years ago.

FIFTY-THREE

The adrenaline began to recede. The sudden stillness was grating to the soul. Mackenzie looked around the kitchen and then at Kai's body. With her own body tender and aching, she managed to limp to the basement.

Seeing Andrew lying motionless made her throat close. She was exhausted. She kneeled next to him and pressed her fingers into his neck, with the tiny hope of finding a thready pulse. But he was gone.

A boy had a lost a father. She had lost a friend. The price of resolution was too high and unfair. It was mind-boggling. She should have gotten used to it now. Used to the soul-shredding losses. Used to lives changing shape for the worse. Used to the scrapes and bruises that were inflicted every day.

The world told her to be strong. Being strong would make everything more bearable. But when she stared at her friend's paling face and hollow eyes, she realized she didn't fully understand the meaning of that word.

She closed his eyes and took out their letters from the box. She didn't open Andrew's. There was only one person who had a right to his last words.

She didn't have a cell phone and neither did he. There was no landline. She had to call for help. As she plodded back upstairs, her surroundings morphed. The walls and cupboards and furniture all slowly melted and blended into what it had looked like when she lived here.

She took a shaky breath. She felt like she was floating as she roamed around the house, reliving the fading memories—the corners she used to hide in, that chair where she always sat to eat, the top of the stairs from where she would watch Melody get beaten up.

She left bloody footprints all over the house. But being in the belly of this dreadful place, the epicenter of everything that had gone wrong with her life, didn't spark any response. She waited. Waited for her heart to pound. Waited for her skin to tingle. Waited for her breathing to get ragged. Waited for her cells to feel like they were going to burst.

Most of all, she waited for her mother's voice.

But it never came. Nothing happened. The voice was silenced for good. Those ugly memories had lost their sheen.

They had disintegrated into oblivion.

Venturing into the sticky night, she touched Robert's watch on her wrist and the letters in her pocket. They made her feel something. And they always would. Because Andrew was right. He'd come into her life for a reason. He'd made her realize just how strong love could be. And then he'd gone, leaving a gaping hole.

A couple walking their dog came into view.

Mackenzie limped across the driveway into the street. They saw her and jumped, horrified at the state of her. Her shirt was soaked in blood. Her body was covered in bruises.

"I'm Detective Price from the Lakemore PD. Can I borrow your phone?"

EPILOGUE

APRIL 29

Mackenzie had spent the last two days recovering in the hospital, trying to convince Nick that she wasn't scarred for life, and giving her official statements. Her first day out, she went to the playground.

She watched Robbie play with a golden retriever. His aunt kept a watchful eye on him from a distance. When he spotted Mackenzie, he sent the dog to fetch a frisbee and came over to her.

She bent down level with him, her heart bursting at the seams with the affection she felt for the little boy. He hadn't stopped crying since his aunt broke the news to him. It was only yesterday that they got him the dog to help.

He smiled up at Mackenzie. But his eyes were pained. And Mackenzie felt shame, shame that Robbie was displaying so much strength and she had been so weak for so much of her life.

"I have something for you." She touched his cheek and fished out the letter Andrew had written in the basement. She hadn't read it. "It's from your dad."

Robbie took it with moist eyes. She grabbed his tiny face in her hands and planted a kiss on his forehead.

"I miss him," he admitted.

"I know. The ones who love us never really leave us. They always stick around, just in a different way."

Robbie gave her a small smile and went to sit on a bench to read the letter.

"Thank you." His aunt joined her. "Andrew told me how you connected with him."

"I did. I'm glad he has you in his life."

She nodded. "I hope you'll visit us sometimes. If that's not asking for too—"

"Of course not. I definitely will."

May 1

"Hawkins." Mackenzie nodded, moving to stand next to Vincent Hawkins at the sports bar.

"Aha, Detective Price," he exclaimed in his rich baritone. "To what do I owe this pleasure?"

She always locked horns with reporters. They were too sensationalist for her taste, especially in a town like Lakemore. And after the unwanted attention she had received, the last thing she wanted was to interact with anyone in the media.

But Hawkins was one of the good guys. She admired both his integrity and his tenacity.

"Tomorrow the FBI is going to open an investigation into a prostitution ring spearheaded by Judge Hamilton, Rafael Jennings, and around ten other extremely influential names."

Hawkins set his beer down slowly, his eyes widening.

"There's a retired FBI agent. Cameron Fletcher." She slid a folded piece of paper toward him. "That's his address. He has information. And you want to figure out why that neighborhood in Lakemore is called Tombstone."

He narrowed his eyes at her. "Pardon me, Detective Price, but you're the last person I expected to share anything with me."

"You're right. But I don't know how deep corruption runs in this case, and there should be someone on the outside to shed light on it." She clinked her beer bottle with his and chugged it in one go.

Hawkins watched her in awe. "Thank you. I appreciate it. Maybe sometime in the future..."

"No." She smiled. "Don't get used to this. The first and last time I'm being a source."

He grinned. "I wouldn't have it any other way. See you again, Detective Price."

May 2

"We have breaking news!" Laura declared, a delirious look on her face. "The Lakemore PD has arrested Judge Hamilton after discovering twenty-seven women being held on his yacht at the Olympia Boat Club. Our sources tell us that the women have given statements that they were forced into prostitution by blackmail and intimidation."

The women had been rescued and were being evaluated at the hospital. Their next of kin were being notified. The police had also found evidence of Debbie and Sterling being tortured on that yacht—and the freezer where Sophie's body had been stored. There were enough eyewitness accounts to corroborate the same.

Visuals of Hamilton being escorted to the squad car played on screen. He was surrounded by police, with Mackenzie and Nick leading. His cuffed hands were hidden under the blazer draped over his arms. People showered him with questions and thrust cameras in his face. He scowled and dodged them all before Mackenzie gratefully pushed him inside the squad car, knowing that at least Hamilton was gone for good.

May 3

Mackenzie watched Austin pace the conference room and toy with his watch. She stood outside, leaning against the wall with her arms crossed.

"How's the head?" Nick joined her.

"Floaty. I might have a permanent bump in the back. Like in cartoons."

He raised an eyebrow, and she grinned at him, which made him even more suspicious. "Oh, now I'm concerned."

"Why?"

"You're smiling way too much."

Her smile dropped when she saw a young woman reach the top of the stairs, escorted by Rivera. Her breath hitched in her throat.

Aria Fields was almost identical to Sophie, though her hair was straighter and her body curvier. She wore a timid, reserved expression. When Austin set eyes on her, he looked like he had seen a ghost. The last time he had seen his fiancée was two years ago. He had searched tirelessly for her. And now someone who looked exactly like her had showed up in front of him like an apparition.

Once he had composed himself, he shook her hand politely.

"Can't imagine what he must be feeling," Nick commented.

"He told me he's going to help her get into college and cover her tuition," Mackenzie informed him.

"That's a good man right there. Sophie would have wanted someone to look after her sister. She died trying to save her."

Together they watched Austin and Aria converse in the conference room. They were strangers, meeting for the first time. But something deeper bonded them. Sophie had loved them both. Mackenzie found some solace that perhaps Sophie was at peace now.

May 5

It was a soft night. The wind was pleasant. The moon was full. The stars were like snowflakes, peppering the dark sky. The spring air was fragrant. It had been a good day. Finally things were going back to normal, with the loose ends of the case wrapping up, the handover to the FBI nearing completion, and Mackenzie feeling much better physically.

When she reached Nick's door, she waited for a moment. A moment to hesitate. A moment for fear and anxiety to creep in and chew up her insides. A moment for her heart to race. But none of that happened.

All she felt was peace and certainty. She rang the bell. Nick opened the door dressed in a black T-shirt and track pants, holding a glass of whiskey.

"I only have white wine," he said.

"It will do."

They hung out in the living room, drinking and playing darts like they usually did.

Mackenzie laughed until she snorted wine out of her nose. "Oh look, wine is coming out of my nice nostrils."

"Best ones I've seen." He managed a straight face, but she kept laughing. "I don't know why you're not taking me seriously. By the way, did you get a chance to talk to Sterling?"

"Yeah, he broke up with Ivy. I hope he finds someone else."

She put her empty glass down and dug out a letter from her pocket. "This is for you."

He frowned. "What is it?"

"A letter."

He was curious and set his glass on a coaster. Even though he didn't believe in coasters; it was just so that Mackenzie didn't get bothered.

"I wrote it in the basement. When Andrew and I thought we wouldn't get out of there alive." The thought of Andrew still brought tears to her eyes. She'd made it out and he hadn't.

Nick opened the letter and began reading.

Dear Nick,

The world is a cruel place. The universe is designed to keep you unhappy. Being negative is easy. It doesn't require any work. Anger, hopelessness, grief, aloofness, anxiety—they come swiftly without facing any barriers. But to acquire hope, happiness, and love, many obstacles must be overcome. It isn't fair, but it is what it is.

Happiness is a constant struggle. The only way to thrive has been to scratch and claw for every second. It can be laborious and draining. Life isn't like a story where there is a happily ever after. The prizes are the small victories along the way, catching those few moments of contentment when everything aligns perfectly, before entropy strikes and chaos throws it all off. Again. And we struggle to put things back into place. Again. It's a cycle that we are all trapped in, unfortunately.

I write this with the knowledge that I might not get out of here alive. But I'll be escaping this cycle with regrets. I've lived almost all my life in the past. I believed that confronting my past and gaining closure would absolve me and set everything right. But I was wrong.

Distancing myself from the bad wasn't enough when I never learned to embrace the good. I just ended up being stuck in limbo. I regret that I didn't cherish the good times enough. I regret that I resisted happiness initially because I thought I didn't deserve it, and then later because I was scared I'd lose it.

You see, it takes bravery to love and have hope, and believe in happiness. Because belief requires us to abandon something very powerful—fear. But fear exists for one reason alone—to be conquered.

If I could have a do-over, I would not be scared anymore. I wouldn't fear the bad and I wouldn't fear the good. I would tell you that every good I've had has involved you. I would tell you that you were the person I thought of when I was staring death in the face. And I wish I had known that the motivation I'd been searching for to keep going had always been in the cubicle behind mine. So thank you. Better late than never. You taught me to be fearless.

M

When he was done reading, he looked up at her, his black eyes somewhere between surprised and beaming.

She realized that it didn't scare her that she had laid herself open. Expressed herself in the rawest fashion she could. "If you joke about how cheesy it was, I will literally murder you," she warned him seriously.

He folded the letter and put it in his pocket. Grinning ear to ear, he put an arm around her and kissed her on the head. She curled up on the couch, snuggling into him, feeling content and safe as he looked for a movie to stream.

"Oh! There's *The Birds*!" she said.

"Don't you think *Casablanca* is more appropriate?" he asked. "You know, with the current mood."

"The mood is for *The Birds*."

"Wow. I really misunderstood that letter." But he made no attempt to move his arm.

"You're just scared of it; that's why you're looking for excuses not to watch it, aren't you?"

When both their phones trilled with a notification, Mackenzie teased him. "Saved by the bell."

"I guess we'll never know, will we?" He feigned innocence, but then his expression turned serious as he looked at the screen. "Dammit."

Mackenzie sighed, her mood plummeting. "Three bodies at the cemetery."

And just like that, she was back on the road, driving through the dark and dreary streets of Lakemore, doing what she did best—locking away one criminal at a time.

A LETTER FROM RUHI

Dear reader,

I want to say a huge thank you for choosing to read *The Lost Bones*. If you did enjoy it, and want to keep up to date with all my latest releases, just sign up at the following link. Your email address will never be shared and you can unsubscribe at any time.

www.bookouture.com/ruhi-choudhary

It has been a joy to write about Mackenzie's adventures in Lakemore. I would be very grateful if you could write a review. I'd love to hear what you think, and it makes such a difference helping new readers to discover one of my books for the first time.

I love hearing from my readers—you can get in touch through Twitter or Goodreads.

Thanks,

Ruhi

ACKNOWLEDGMENTS

Writing is a lonely job, but publishing is all about teamwork. I'm extremely grateful to my editor Laura Deacon for her hard work and commitment that shaped and strengthened this story.

Thanks to Lucy Dauman for her continued support.

Big thanks to editors Jane Selley and Shirley Khan, cover designer Chris Shamwana, voice actor Kate Handford, and my publicist Noelle Holten for their commitment and brilliance. The entire team at Bookouture has been very kind and accommodating.

My parents for their love. My sister and friend, Dhriti, for always being in our hearts and looking after us. Akanksha Nair for being my rock and always encouraging me. All my friends especially Rachel Drisdelle, Dafni Giannari, Scott Proulx, Kaushik Raj, and Sheida Stephens for their excitement.

Most of all, I'm grateful to the readers. Thank you so much for taking the time! I appreciate each and every one of you and would love to hear what you thought of the book.

CPSIA information can be obtained
at www.ICGtesting.com
Printed in the USA
BVHW081002030522
635992BV00007B/128